The Sinking Admiral

BY CERTAIN MEMBERS OF THE DETECTION CLUB

SIMON BRETT
KATE CHARLES
NATASHA COOPER
STELLA DUFFY
MARTIN EDWARDS
RUTH DUDLEY EDWARDS
TIM HEALD
MICHAEL JECKS
JANET LAURENCE
PETER LOVESEY
MICHAEL RIDPATH
DAVID ROBERTS
L.C. TYLER
LAURA WILSON

Edited by Simon Brett

COLLINS
CRIME
CLUB

COLLINS CRIME CLUB

An imprint of HarperCollins*Publishers*
1 London Bridge Street
London SE1 9GF
www.harpercollins.co.uk

Published by HarperCollins*Publishers* 2016

1

A catalogue record for this book
is available from the British Library

HB ISBN: 978-0-00-810043-8

Set in Sabon by Palimpsest Book Production Ltd,
Falkirk, Stirlingshire

Printed and bound in Great Britain by
Clays Ltd, St Ives plc

MIX
Paper from
responsible sources
FSC™ C007454

To the memory of P.D. James,
a loyal member of The Detection Club,
who had promised to
write an introduction to this book –
but was sadly prevented from doing so

INTRODUCTION

The Floating Admiral 'by Certain Members of the Detection Club' was published in 1931, fairly early into the association's existence. The 'Certain Members' who produced that original collaborative novel were, in alphabetical order: Anthony Berkeley, G. K. Chesterton, Agatha Christie, G. D. H. and M. Cole, Freeman Wills Crofts, Clemence Dane, Edgar Jepson, Milward Kennedy, Ronald A. Knox, John Rhode, Dorothy L. Sayers, Henry Wade and Canon Victor L. Whitechurch. Since that time the novel has appeared in many foreign editions and been republished twice, by Macmillan in 1981 and by HarperCollins in 2011. The royalties deriving from the book have done much to defray the expenses of the events for which the Detection Club exists, three congenial dinners a year.

Since I took over the Presidency in 2001 I have nurtured the desire to produce another volume 'by Certain Members of the Detection Club', partly again to help the association's finances, but also because I thought it would be fun. The fact that you are reading this book now means that I have succeeded in my ambition.

Of course I owe that achievement to the goodwill, good humour, and literary skills of the other writers who agreed to collaborate on the novel. *The Floating Admiral* had fourteen contributors (if you count G. D. H. and M. Cole, a married couple who wrote together, as two), and *The Sinking Admiral* boasts exactly the same number.

There, though, the similarities between the two endeavours cease. In her introduction to the original volume, Dorothy L. Sayers wrote: 'Now, a word about the conditions under which *The Floating Admiral* was written. Here, the problem was made to approach as closely as possible to a problem of real detection... Each contributor tackled the mystery presented to him in the preceding chapters without having the slightest idea what solution or solutions the previous authors had in mind. Two rules only were imposed. Each writer must construct his instalment with a definite solution in view – that is, he must not introduce new complications merely "to make it more difficult". He must be ready, if called upon, to explain his own clues coherently and plausibly; and to make sure that he was playing fair in this respect, each writer was bound to deliver, together with the manuscript of his own chapter, his own proposed solution of the mystery. These solutions are printed at the end of the book for the benefit of the curious reader.'

Now there are a lot of reasons crime writers in the early twenty-first century could not write a collaborative novel by the same method as they could in the early 1930s, and one of the most important is the way in which the genre has changed in the intervening years. Though Dorothy L. Sayers and her band of collaborators had individual styles, they were all basically writing the same kind of book, the classic whodunit. So it was entirely possible to write a chapter, setting up a variety of clues that could be followed and elaborated, and pass on the literary baton to the next writer.

Nowadays that just won't work because very few authors are actually writing traditional whodunits. Also, crime fiction is now a very broad church. The genre has divided up into a large number of subgenres. There are police procedurals, psychological thrillers, legal thrillers, forensic thrillers, financial thrillers, historical mysteries, and many more. All of these have skilful exponents and enthusiastic fans, but a book that continually jumped from one subgenre to the next would be unlikely to make a lot of sense.

So, early on in the planning for *The Sinking Admiral*, the decision was made to home in on the individual specialities of the contributing authors. If one of them was an expert in the world of high finance, then he or she should write the chapter about the shifty City financier. The same approach should be followed into the worlds of politics, publishing, journalism, the law, cookery, and so on. Some of the story threads – for instance, the ongoing police investigation – should be followed through by the same writer and interwoven into the rest of the text.

The resulting book, by comparison with *The Floating Admiral*, turned out therefore to be not so much a sequential game of dominoes as a jigsaw puzzle. And something of an editorial nightmare – enjoyable but complicated.

When everyone had made their main contribution and the book was complete but for its last two chapters, we held a Whodunit Dinner at the Groucho Club. For the contributors able to attend, two questions had to be answered that evening. One, who committed the appalling crimes outlined in the narrative? And two, who was going to write the chapters of the denouement? I am glad to say that both questions were answered with the collaborative ingenuity and geniality that has characterised the entire process of creating *The Sinking Admiral*.

The way the book was assembled of course offers its readers a second level of whodunitry. Not only will they be trying to identify the perpetrators of any crimes that might occur, they will also be faced with the puzzle of who wrote which bit of the book.

I hope they enjoy this double challenge. And I hope that some of the more acute mystery buffs among them will recognise a few moments of *homage* to *The Floating Admiral* and the history of the Detection Club.

In bringing *The Sinking Admiral* on the arduous journey to publication, I would like to thank David Brawn and Julia Wisdom of HarperCollins for their enthusiasm for the project, the Detection Club's agent Georgia Glover of David Higham for her support, and particularly Corinne Hitching, the Club's Assistant Secretary, for managing to take coherent notes from the complicated and frequently hilarious planning meetings between the contributors.

Now it's over to you, the reader. Hope you enjoy it.

Simon Brett – President of the
Detection Club 2001–2015

CHAPTER ONE

It's amazing the attraction television has for ordinary people. Not watching the wretched box, but appearing on it. People seem prepared to undergo any kinds of humiliation for one brief moment of having their faces seen in the nation's sitting rooms. And that situation's got worse since the unrestricted spread of so-called 'reality' shows.

A demonstration of this syndrome was being acted out at the Admiral Byng pub in the Suffolk seaside village of Crabwell. It was a March Monday, one of those biting cold ones when it seemed that winter would never release its icy hold. The much-quoted view that in that part of Suffolk there was no protection from the cold winds off the Ural Mountains was wheeled out once again in many huddles around village fireplaces. It was a time of year when business at the Admiral Byng would normally have been even worse than usual, but on this particular March day the pub was heaving. And that was because word had got around Crabwell that a television documentary was being made there.

The programme was being fronted and produced by Ben Milne, a journalist in his early thirties, highly skilled in the business of turning cameras on people long enough for them to make fools of themselves. And then working on the footage in the editing suite to make them look even more stupid.

He had cut his teeth on an ITV series called *Skeletons in the Cupboard*, which tapped into the growing online enthusiasm for genealogy. But, unlike the previous, more benign BBC version of the show, whose high spot was always making the celebrity subject cry, Ben Milne's programme basically tried to dig the dirt on the celebrity's antecedents. Illegitimate births were gloated over, appearances in the Newgate Calendar, and transportations to Australia were welcomed with open arms. And involvement in the Slave Trade or a murder enquiry proved to be pure televisual gold. As with many ITV programmes, *Skeletons in the Cupboard* was a red-top interpretation of the BBC's more sedate original.

Of course, when discussed by Ben Milne, he was keen to emphasise the series' serious agenda, and he spoke in just the same way about the documentary he was making in Crabwell. At a time when across the country up to twenty pubs were closing every week, it was, as he would state in his sober-faced introduction, 'important to focus on the realities of the licensed victuallers' business, which is why I have brought my cameras to a typical, traditional English pub, the Admiral Byng in Crabwell'. He was a good-looking young man with very short hair and brown eyes, which he knew how to make look caring and empathetic. He switched on their full charm as he told each member of the Admiral Byng's staff and the regulars how much he hoped his documentary would help save their village pub from the fate of so many others.

Amy Walpole, the bar manager, was not taken in by him. She was red-haired, freckled, tall, thin as a rake, with the kind of supple body that men drool over. And from her position behind the counter she had witnessed much drooling as evenings lengthened and her customers got more drunk. But Amy wasn't taken in by any of it. Experiences from her varied emotional history had rendered her, now in her late thirties, immune to the manipulations of men. She no longer nurtured hopes – or at least she would never admit to anyone that she nurtured hopes – that somewhere out there was the perfect partner for her. So, while recognising that Ben Milne was attractive, she also recognised that he was not the kind of man to be trusted further than she could throw him. In fact, she thought he was probably a bit of a prick.

Nor was she taken in by his assurances that his television programme would turn around the fortunes of the Admiral Byng. Her job as bar manager made Amy Walpole all too aware of the dwindling profits of the business. Winters were always bad, but none had been as bad as the one that was currently extending its stay into March. All the factors gloomily detailed by the newspapers – general belt-tightening, ever more expensive fuel, the availability of cheap beer and spirits in supermarkets – were having their effects on the Admiral Byng. The rest of the staff weren't aware of how close to the wind they were sailing, but Amy was kept up to date with bad news by the pub's owner.

Geoffrey Horatio Fitzsimmons, landlord of the Admiral Byng, must have been well into his seventies. He was never referred to, incidentally, by his full name. The closest anyone got to that was calling him 'Fitz'. But more often – and perhaps inevitably – he was known as 'the Admiral'. Certainly that was how all the pub staff referred to him. His bluff manner and drawling vowels, together with his silver hair and moustache, his uniform of gold-buttoned blazer and cravat, gave the impression of a patrician public-school background, but nobody in Crabwell actually knew much about his past. There was also a common assumption, from the way he talked, that at one stage of his life he had been extremely rich. Some of the staff, gossiping in the kitchen, believed he still was.

Well, if that were the case, Amy Walpole knew his wealth didn't come from the Admiral Byng. She was too close to the account books to believe that. And from conversations with the Admiral she recognised how genuinely anxious he was about the future of his business. The idea that Geoffrey Horatio Fitzsimmons had a vast fortune stashed away somewhere and wasn't using it to bail the pub out just didn't make sense. Apart from anything else, although the kitchen and casual bar staff had received their regular stipend, Amy Walpole herself had not been paid for three weeks. The Admiral kept saying he would regularise the situation 'soon', but she knew that the money just wasn't there.

Amy liked her boss. He could be infuriating, though. He

was one of those alcoholics who never appears to be drunk, but is just permanently topping himself up. His constant tipple was red wine – preferably something robust and French, he didn't believe in all this new-fangled New World rubbish – but in the evenings he could also get a long way down a bottle of malt whisky. Laphroaig was his favourite. What effect his lifetime's drinking had had on his health Amy didn't like to speculate. The Admiral himself always said that if he gave up the booze his body would drop dead from sheer shock.

He was also, by her standards, something of a Luddite. He didn't even use a mobile phone. 'When I'm home people can ring me on the pub number,' he always said. 'And when I'm not home they can leave me a message. No telephone call is so important that it can't wait a couple of hours.'

Fitz's dinosaur attitudes applied to other technology as well. Amy had had to argue for a long time to persuade him to upgrade his old bar-room till to a more user-friendly electronic model. And her strongest powers of persuasion were also required to get him to buy a laptop and printer for the pub's tiny office. But the idea of touching either of the devices was anathema to him. Fitz, Amy often thought, would have been happiest living in the 1950s, before any of this troubling technology had become available to the general public.

Whether he'd ever been married or in any kind of permanent relationship no one knew. Certainly there had been no romantic skirmishes since he'd moved to Crabwell. Amy knew she was an attractive woman, and long experience in the pub trade had inured her to the advances of land-lords, but the Admiral had never so much as touched her on the shoulder. She was certain he wasn't gay, but his emotional history – like many other areas of his life – remained unknown to the people of the village.

In spite of the more annoying aspects of his personality, Amy still had a fierce loyalty to the Admiral, remembering the generosity with which he had welcomed her when she first arrived in Crabwell.

She had been quite surprised, though, when he'd agreed to the intrusion into his pub of Ben Milne and the camera crew. She didn't think he would buy into the theory of the publicity bestowed by the documentary turning around the Admiral Byng's fortunes, and it seemed out of character for him deliberately to threaten his protective secrecy. But there was no doubt that the television people were there with the Admiral's consent.

They didn't see much of him, though, on that first day of filming. Running the whole width of the Admiral Byng's first floor there was a long, low gallery. In a previous incarnation it had acted as the pub's function room, but fewer and fewer people in the Crabwell area seemed to be having functions these days. Or maybe for weddings, birthdays, and post-funeral wakes they now booked venues slightly less shabby than the village pub.

Besides, Geoffrey Horatio Fitzsimmons had rather colonised the space for himself. Though his bedroom was on the floor above, this gallery, which he referred to ironic-ally as 'the Bridge', was where he spent most of the time when he was not downstairs in the bar. And the clutter of his files and documents had spread over time until there was no surface in the room uncovered. It was from the Bridge, with its broad view across the steely expanse of the North Sea, that the Admiral conducted his business. But none of his employees was bold enough ever to ask him what that business was.

On the first day of Ben Milne's filming at the Admiral Byng the landlord spent most of his time up in the Bridge. Amy Walpole had been kept so busy at the bar dealing with the uncharacteristic flood of custom that she hadn't checked them out in detail, but she'd been aware throughout the day of a procession of visitors going up the side stairs to visit the Admiral. Presumably he'd made some private arrangement with Ben Milne to be interviewed another day. There was no way the journalist was going to make his film without talking to the Admiral Byng's landlord.

Amy Walpole's unenthusiastic attitude to the invasion of documentary-makers was not typical of the Admiral Byng's staff and regulars. Most of them responded with the customary reaction of ordinary people to the prospect of being 'on the telly'. They all wanted their fifteen seconds of fame.

Of no one was this truer than Meriel Dane, the queen of the pub's kitchen. Honey blonde since anyone could remember, and always dressed a good ten years younger than her real age; she was a woman of unbridled aspiration. Nobody who didn't dwell inside Meriel Dane's head could be aware of the glorious futures she constantly created for herself (despite some less than successful experiences in her past). Frequently these fantasies involved impossibly glamorous men who would succumb to her substantial charms, but she had career ambitions too. Meriel Dane was convinced that she was about to become the next big thing in television chefs, so she regarded her participation in Ben Milne's documentary as a kind of audition.

'You see, Ben,' she confided as she rolled out the pastry for the day's pies, 'I always add a couple of *special* ingredients when I'm doing steak and kidney. They impart a subtlety to the taste, which is commented on by many of the Admiral Byng's customers. *Satisfied* customers, I should say. People who order my steak and kidney pie never regret their choice. They are always *satisfied*. One of my secret ingredients,' she went on slyly, almost winking at the camera, 'is Worcester sauce – just a little shake of the bottle into the mixture. I'm never one for measuring things too exactly. I have an *instinct* for the right amount. Most of my cooking is *instinctive*. I am rather a creature of *impulse*, you know.'

She leaned forward to the camera, fully aware of the amount of ample cleavage that the movement revealed. It was Meriel Dane's view that there was a lack of glamour in the current stock of television chefs. Most of them were men, for a start – and not very attractive men at that. What British television needed was a series by someone who put the sex back into cookery. Someone remarkably like Meriel Dane, in fact.

'And my other secret ingredient, Ben, no one *suspects*. But being here by the sea in Crabwell – and me being the kind of person who is really *drawn* to the sea, I do add a little maritime flavour to my steak and kidney. Oysters. Not a lot of them – it's not a steak and oyster pie – but just enough to provide that little salty tang. And nobody – but *nobody* – can identify what gives the pie that oh so *distinctive* flavour.'

Meriel Dane smiled. A warm smile, promising who knew what delights ahead. She reckoned the little piece she'd just done to camera, confiding the secrets of her steak and kidney pie, would edit neatly into a show reel to engage the enthusiasm of even the most jaded television executive.

She looked at her watch and felt a little *frisson*, knowing the delights that lay ahead for her that evening... if she played her cards right... and Meriel Dane was always confident in her ability to play her cards right. In the meantime, flirting with Ben Milne was a reasonably pleasant way of passing the time. He was quite attractive in an angular way, and Meriel Dane always rather fancied herself in the role of cougar.

And then Ben went and spoiled it all by asking her about the budgetary restrictions on the Admiral Byng's food operation.

Because they had driven up from London that morning, Ben Milne's cameraman Stan, according to some abstruse ruling known only to his union, had to stop work at five for a three-hour break. He left then, and went to the B & B in a nearby village, which he'd booked in preference to one of the Admiral Byng's bedrooms. Ben, though, was staying in the pub. Unable to shoot any further footage for the time being, he bought himself a large glass of Chilean Merlot and sat in a corner of the bar, drinking as though he'd earned it. Amy Walpole still didn't trust him. Though without his cameraman he couldn't actually record anything that happened, she still sensed that he was vigilant, listening out for those telling details that might contribute something to his eventual hatchet job.

But the absence of the camera had an immediate effect on the day's business. All of those locals who kept away from the Admiral Byng most of the year but had 'just happened to drop in' that day suddenly vanished when there was no further chance of them being immortalised on video. Though Amy was in no doubt that a lot of them would be back the following morning.

The stresses of the day were catching up on her. She'd been so busy that she hadn't had a chance to get any lunch and she felt headachey. What she needed was a brisk walk along the Crabwell front to blow away the cobwebs. And Ben Milne was now the only customer in the bar.

Grabbing from its hook the beaten-up Barbour jacket that Fitz had given her, Amy Walpole told him she had to go out for a while. If he needed a refill or anything else before she was back, he should call through to Meriel in the kitchen. She'd help him out.

The wind from the Urals was predictably invigorating once she got outside, but Amy was used to it. All the Crabwell locals instinctively adopted a particular stance, leaning into the wind as they walked. Amy comforted herself with the thought that at least it wasn't raining. But the weather was dull and miserable, almost impossible to see where the slate grey of the sky met the slate grey of the sea. It was one of those Suffolk afternoons when there wouldn't really be a dusk, just a darkening of the grey until it was imperceptibly transformed into black.

There weren't many people about, though a little way up the beach Amy could see a group of Girl Guides struggling against the wind to erect some tents on the shingle. She remembered the girls' leader Greta Knox telling her they had some camping exercise planned, though it didn't look much fun on a cold March evening. She recognised Greta's stocky outline amongst the girls, and waved vaguely in her direction. Whether Greta saw her or not, she couldn't judge.

Amy also saw, lingering on the edge of the group, trying to avoid doing anything useful, a girl called Tracy Crofts to whom she had more than once refused service at the bar of the Admiral Byng. In spite of her protestations, Amy knew the girl to be underage. There was a general view in Crabwell that it was only a matter of time before Tracy Crofts, a seething mass of teenage hormones, came to no good.

Amy Walpole lived in a dilapidated little seafront cottage only five minutes' walk from the pub, and she felt a strong temptation to go home, however briefly. Just to put her feet up, have a cup of tea. But she resisted the impulse. She knew how much more difficult it would be to force herself back to work if she succumbed to home comforts.

So she walked determinedly in the opposite direction from her cottage. Towards the end of the beach where, drawn up on the sand, there were a lot of boats. Including the dinghy owned by her boss. No surprise really that its name, picked out in silver stick-on letters across the stern, was *The Admiral*.

More of a surprise, though, that afternoon, was that the boat's owner was standing by it, checking the cords that tied down the tarpaulin cover from which the mast protruded. He wore no overcoat, just his usual blazer.

'Evening, Admiral,' said Amy.

'Hello there.' There was an uncharacteristic air of complacency in his smile, of relief almost, as if he had just achieved something very necessary.

'Problems with the cover?'

'Just checking it, Amy. There have been rather too many thefts from boats on the beach here recently.'

'Have you got much of value in there?'

'Now that'd be telling,' he replied with an enigmatic grin.

'I've hardly seen you today.'

'No, I've been busy in the Bridge.'

'So I gathered. And you haven't talked yet to Ben Milne, the Grand Inquisitor?'

'No. That pleasure is scheduled for tomorrow. Seems to me to be a rather cocky young man.'

'I think if you work in television that goes with the territory.'

He grinned, then his face clouded as he said, 'Also, Amy, you and I need to have a long talk.'

'Really?' She spread her hands wide. 'Well, I'm happy to talk now.'

'No, no.' The Admiral shook his grey head. 'That will keep till tomorrow too. I have other plans for tonight.'

'And what do they involve?'

'Tonight, Amy, is to be my "Last Hurrah". I plan to get extremely drunk.'

'Oh. Drunker than usual?'

'Very definitely.'

'Are you celebrating?'

'Something like that,' replied the Admiral, with a teasing hint of mischief in his voice.

But as it turned out, he never did have an inquisition from Ben Milne. Or his long talk with Amy Walpole. Because, by the next morning, the Admiral was dead.

CHAPTER TWO

'Amy, my dear, another round for everyone, please,' said the Admiral, placing a steadying hand on the bar. His silk handkerchief drooped drunkenly out of his blazer breast pocket, and his silver hair looked as though someone had been running their fingers through it.

Amy knew better than to query her boss's request, however unusual it was. 'What'll it be, folks?' she shouted.

The peace of the late afternoon had vanished. With the return of Stan, Ben's cameraman, word had spread via the usual jungle drums that kept the inhabitants of Crabwell up to speed with the latest developments, and the bar was once again full. Incongruously out of place among the regulars were a bunch of Viking re-enactors, dressed in the full kit and waving rustic-looking tankards. Amy had been a bar manager far too long to find anything strange about their presence. In her line of work you served everyone and didn't ask questions.

She looked around for other locals and saw Crabwell's

GP, Dr Alice Kennedy, who quite often dropped in at the end of evening surgery. She was, as ever, smartly but unobtrusively dressed, on this occasion in black trousers and a navy blue blazer. Amy never quite knew whether Alice came in just for a relaxing drink or to monitor the intake of her patients. Though perfectly friendly, the doctor always seemed slightly aloof from the other barroom regulars. But maybe a level of professional detachment went with the job.

The same could have been said of Crabwell's vicar, the Rev Victoria Whitechurch. She wasn't a regular in the pub, but she had been there for the 'Last Hurrah'. Maybe she was on the lookout to see which of her parishioners over-indulged. Or perhaps she was on a proselytising mission, hoping to enlist more locals into the diminishing ranks of her congregations at St Mary's.

The Admiral was holding court. This was the second of the rounds he'd bought for everyone present. Amy supplied the flood of orders with her usual efficiency, noting that if this kept up, she would have to descend to the cellar and switch to a new barrel of the draught bitter. However, most orders were for spirits, and she rang up the Admiral's tab with a feeling that approached despair. The state of the pub's finances could not justify this random largesse. Then she asked herself, what did she know? The old boy could have come into some unexpected funds. Maybe that would explain the odd procession of folk he'd had climbing to his Bridge throughout the day.

At what time tomorrow, she wondered, would she receive

a summons for the talk he'd promised her? And what would it be about? Amy looked at the happy crowd of villagers and others from further afield, and hoped it was not going to be to tell her that he was selling up. Equally, she hoped that he didn't want to probe into those details of her past life that she wished to keep secret.

'This a common occurrence, your boss pushing the boat out?' Ben, the ever-present television presenter, leaned on the bar and shoved his whisky glass towards her. 'You can make mine a double Glenlivet,' he added.

She didn't answer his question, but looked at his brown eyes, twinkling at her with confident warmth, took the glass and fished out the required bottle, thankful he hadn't asked for the peaty Laphroaig that was the Admiral's favourite tipple. What was it about brown eyes that could melt a little piece of the steel she had built around her badly bruised heart?

Amy pushed the filled tumbler towards the presenter and looked at the Admiral, now climbing up on a Windsor chair and raising his glass.

'My friends, here's to the "Last Hurrah",' he said, and the reckless gleam in his eye did nothing to reassure his bar manager.

'"The Last Hurrah",' Ben murmured, raising his own glass. 'And what's that all about, eh?'

'No idea.' She came around from behind the bar and started clearing empty glasses, lining them up on the counter.

'Tell us,' shouted someone to the Admiral, 'tell us about the time you were stranded in the Caribbean.'

'Ah!' he smiled benignly at them. For the last few weeks he had worn worry like a mother whose son was about to go to war, now it was as though peace had been declared. A slurp of Laphroaig and a long stare into the distance, then he began: 'Antigua was on our port bow and a hurricane was beating up behind us. We would have to anchor down in Nelson's Harbour and ride it out.'

'Was he really ever a sailor?' Ben pushed the flotilla of dirty glasses a little further to the back of the counter to give Amy space for another trayful.

'Thanks,' she muttered. 'How about helping me collect the last of the empties?'

'But I might drop them!' He looked at her with limpidly innocent eyes and leaned back on his stool, surveying the scene. Amy followed his gaze. The Admiral might have been at the wheel of his schooner (a large photograph of the long-gone actual boat was on the wall of the bar, the wind filling its sails, including the spinnaker, the craft leaning forward with the urgency of a greyhound released from the traps). There was the slightest uncertainty in his stance on his chair, his customary drawl wobbled a bit, and the occasional fumbling for a word as he retold the familiar story, suggested he was deep in alcohol's grip.

Then Amy saw that Stan, the cameraman, had his lens trained with steady accuracy on the Admiral Byng's landlord, relishing the opportunity of showing him up. 'You bastard,' she shot at Ben and headed for her boss.

'... and as we hunkered down under a wind wilder than horses freaked out of their senses and a rain that emptied

17

the heavens, we old mariners swapped stories of weird adventures. And that was when…' the Admiral lowered his voice, and his audience waited in gleeful anticipation. 'That was when I heard tell of the Treasure of the Forgotten Island.'

'And it's still forgotten!' someone shouted out as Amy barged into Stan, knocking his camera off its target. 'The island and its gold ingots, all forgotten.' Most of the audience had heard the story more than once.

Stan swore, lifted his camera, and glared at Amy. 'What d'you think you're doing?'

'It's so crowded tonight,' she said cheerfully. 'Can hardly move in here. Having trouble, are you?' She picked up an empty glass and blocked his view as she moved towards her boss.

The Admiral ran a finger over his silver moustache. 'Ah, well,' he said thoughtfully. 'Somewhere there's a map, and some time I'll be going back. And when I get my rightful fortune, it'll be drinks all around every night.'

'What rightful fortune?' demanded one of the Viking re-enactors raucously.

'Ah, wouldn't you like to know?' Fitz replied slyly. 'Let's just say that things here are changing. My fortune has turned around. Money worries will be at an end, family secrets will be revealed, and the Admiral Byng will be saved! Here's to the "Last Hurrah"!'

The vigour with which he raised his arm for the toast nearly overbalanced him. Amy reached out a hand and helped him down from the chair.

Ben appeared. 'Is there really a map?' he asked the Admiral respectfully. 'I'd love to see it. *Treasure Island* has always been one of my favourite books.'

'Has it now? So you like stories of buried treasure, do you?'

'Certainly do,' said Ben. Amy saw him make a subtle sign to Stan that had to mean he should capture this scene on his camera. No doubt he was hoping for more footage of what he'd refer to in his presenterese as 'Fitz's lovable eccentricity'. 'And you say the treasure is buried somewhere in the Caribbean?'

'*That* treasure is,' the Admiral replied judiciously. 'Though you might do better looking for ill-gotten gold rather nearer to home.'

'What do you mean?' asked Ben eagerly.

'What indeed?' The Admiral's eyes gleamed with what Amy recognised as his mischievous look. It did her heart good to see it back. She had been worried by Fitz's lack of animation over the past few weeks. 'Well, perhaps we can have a talk about that tomorrow,' he went on. 'I think tomorrow is going to be full of all kinds of revelations.'

'Guilty secrets about Crabwell's drug fiends, illegitimate children, and rich old people murdered in their beds?' suggested Ben Milne.

Really, thought Amy, was this how he tried to get his interviewees onto the scurrilous gossip tack? She'd thought he would be more subtle.

The Admiral, however, was too canny to give any response that might provide titillation for Ben's viewers.

'That kind of thing, yes,' he said, his intonation firmly suggesting that the subject was closed.

Ben looked as though he would like to keep grilling Fitz, but instead he was nobbled by the Reverend Victoria Whitechurch. 'Mr Milne, we need to have a talk about spreading the word of God. If you want to get a full impression of what life in the village is like, you and your cameraman will, I hope, be with us in church next Sunday?'

'I'm afraid we'll be finished with filming and back in London by then.'

'But maybe you could come and visit St Mary's tomorrow? It's in terrible need of repair, and if its condition was seen on national television, it might—'

'I'm sorry,' said Ben quite brusquely, 'the subject of my documentary is the pub, not the church.' The vicar recoiled, suitably snubbed.

Amy went back behind the bar and started washing up the dirty glasses. Someone came and asked for the bar menu. 'Sorry,' she said. 'Last orders were twenty minutes ago. The kitchen's closed.' It was a shame. The pub hadn't been this full since Christmas, and a little earlier she'd asked Meriel if she'd be prepared to take orders beyond the usual cut-off point.

'Ah, now, that's a pity,' the cook had said. There was no hint of regret in her smile, indeed it could only be described as smug. 'Business has been so *good*, food's run out. I'll have to be on the phone *first thing* tomorrow morning to restock. Now, if you'll forgive me,' she said with heavy emphasis, 'I've an order for steak and chips to send out.'

Quietly furious, Amy had gone back to the bar. The two women had always riled each other, and sometimes Meriel's attitude was downright offensive.

For the rest of the evening she wished she had organised extra staff. Ted, the odd-job man who helped out, was drinking in the corner, but she knew asking him to serve behind the bar was more trouble than it was worth. He was old, not a bad cook, and fine for bringing in logs from the outside store, but managing the electronic till was beyond his capabilities.

So, ever conscious of costs, she had decided not to draft anyone else in, but battle through on her own. How was she to have known they'd have so many customers? What in heaven's name was it about the possibility of being caught on camera that attracted people so? The pressure made it difficult for her to keep an eye on Ben and his cameraman. Though the Admiral continued to be at the centre of a jovial crowd, all prompting a continuous string of reminiscences, the television duo now seemed to be concentrating on a series of 'vox pops', short interviews with the locals on their opinions of the Admiral Byng.

She knew an interview with the Admiral himself was scheduled the next day. She stood for a moment watching Ben and his cameraman in action. A sense of anger began to fill her as she realised how the presenter was drawing out his interviewees, all of them well under the influence of alcohol. Whatever they were telling him was likely to reflect badly on themselves as well as the pub. The Admiral Byng was certainly not going to be shown as somewhere viewers were going to flock to for a good night out.

'Ooh, that Ben Milne is a caution,' said Joan, one of their regulars, plonking her tankard on the bar for a refill of her 'special', a small brandy mixed with a large fizzy orange. Her best wig was worn at a slight angle, its glossy black curls tip-tilted over one ear. 'Makes me feel twenty again. Understand he's staying here.' She gave a loud cackle filled with meaning. 'If I were your age, sweetie, I'd be in there without a second thought.' The washed-out blue of her eyes twinkled.

'There you go,' Amy said, resisting any response and drowning the brandy in orange. 'Any jobs coming up, Joan?'

'Ah, now there's a thing. Got a call this morning. Did you hear there's a new version of *Far from the Madding Crowd* being shot here in Crabwell? They'll be at the Tithe Barn next week and I'm down for an old lady selling eggs. "Little less of the old," I told them.' She gave Amy a broad grin. 'With those wide hats they put us in, I could pass for forty.' The tankard was picked up, and Joan looked back at Ben, now affecting close attention as he listened to the local bookseller, who would be sounding off about planning permission difficulties. Without it, Amy knew, the bookshop couldn't be sold as perfect for conversion to a private dwelling. After all, who wanted to buy a bookshop these days? 'Looks as though our brown-eyed boyo needs rescuing,' said Joan. 'He'd love to hear about my filming.' Off she sailed, navigating her way through the crowded room with the ease of a small tug.

Amy smiled for a moment; when she was eighty years old, she hoped she'd have Joan's verve and optimism. At the moment she lacked any of either. But it was good news about the *Far from the Madding Crowd* filming. Maybe the crew would need accommodation. Though if they were coming next week and hadn't made a booking by now, they'd probably found somewhere else to stay.

Suddenly the Admiral was leaning towards her over the bar. 'Amy, my dear, that talk we must have. I think tomorrow morning, yes?'

'Of course, Fitz.' After a moment's hesitation, she added, 'Can you give me some idea what it's about?'

He ran a hand over his rumpled hair without much effect, and for a moment looked embarrassed. 'Some unsettling information has come to my ears...' He seemed about to go further, but then changed his mind. 'No, I shall say no more. Let us leave it until tomorrow. Tonight has gone well, has it not? My "Last Hurrah"?'

Then he was gone, leaving Amy tied in a tangle of unpleasant thoughts.

'Some unsettling information has come to my ears.' The words echoed uneasily in her mind. What could the Admiral have found 'unsettling'? Somehow it didn't seem to apply to anything connected with the pub. But surely it must be?

Unless... For a moment Amy's spine turned to ice. Surely nobody could have told him? Nobody here knew. And all that was in the past, left behind when she moved here. And she would do anything to make sure that was where it would remain.

But there had been something in the Admiral's eyes as he looked at her. A subtle redrawing of their relationship.

There was a bustle at the door that led up to the bedrooms, and in came a whirl of woman in a mock leopard-skin coat, dirty blonde hair all over the place, and thigh-length leather boots. Amy recognised her immediately and remembered her melodramatic arrival earlier that evening.

'I rang yesterday and booked a room,' she had barked out in supremely confident tones. 'Ianthe Berkeley.'

Who could forget that name?

'Of course,' Amy had said smoothly. 'I think we've had the pleasure of your company before, Miss Berkeley, or is it Mrs?' She looked innocently into the woman's bleary eyes and forced herself not to recoil from the unsettling, easily recognisable odour that clashed with Dior's *Poison*. Amy remembered vividly the previous occasion. Claimed to be newly married, though there was nothing uxorious about either of the couple. Spent the time fighting with each other, and with the pub. Complaints about a damp bed, a mattress that should be condemned to the tip, noises in the night, and who knew what else. Nothing was right for them, though as they both spent most of the time drinking, with him watching football on the TV, and her flirting with any half-decent looking man who crossed the threshold, Amy hadn't taken their complaints too seriously.

She did, however, on their second meeting recognise a difficult customer when she saw one, and waited behind the bar for the obnoxious woman's drink order. That turned out to be a pint of the local cider, but of course it wasn't just alcohol she wanted. She also demanded food. She was a resident, she said, and she had been assured that she'd be able to get something to eat whatever time she arrived.

Amy didn't know who had made these assertions – she certainly hadn't – but the woman was getting embarrassingly loud. Once again the bar manager mentally cursed Meriel for stopping the food service early. But, taking the line of least resistance, she sent Ted into the kitchen to knock up an omelette to appease Ms Berkeley's demands.

Glowing from her small triumph over the catering system, Ianthe had then caught sight of the TV presenter. 'Ben, darling!' she cried, and flung herself – there was no other way to describe it – at him; arms an octopus would have envied snaking around his neck, her sagging body pressed against his admirably taut figure. Amy had trouble stopping herself from smiling at his horrified reaction. For a moment Amy wondered what had brought the woman down to the Admiral Byng. Some connection with Ben Milne...? Or maybe with Fitz...? Yet another secret in his past...?

'Have we met?' Ben managed to get out, extricating himself from the octopus embrace.

'Darling, it's Ianthe! You remember our days at uni?'

Amy had difficulty in imagining this woman was anywhere near Ben Milne in age. Perhaps she had been a mature student? Calls for more drinks from other customers claimed her attention elsewhere.

* * *

25

Finally Amy was able to sing out 'Last orders'. She looked towards where she had last seen the Admiral, hoping he wasn't going to ask for another round for everyone, but he seemed to have disappeared. No doubt he was back on his Bridge upstairs. He must be tired. All those chats with people during the day, and then the conviviality he had enjoyed in the bar. At least, she thought, pulling a couple of final pints of bitter, he had had something of a triumph this evening. Fancy bringing out that old Treasure Island story again!

The closing time message seemed to have been received; only a few hard drinkers were left, and they all had charged glasses. She wiped down the bar with well-practised efficiency, and picked up a tray.

'How about we film you clearing up?' Ben appeared at her side. 'After all, it's a vital part of pub life.'

Amy could just imagine what the editing room would make of the shots of her clearing tables, her hair lank with sweat, her top sticking to her body, the ribald remarks that would follow her progress around the room. 'I'll get Meriel, and you can film her,' she said. Meriel should have cleaned her kitchen by now, and their usual practice was for the cook to help clear the bar. And, boy, would she enjoy being filmed!

Only Meriel wasn't in the kitchen, nor were any of the long streaks of pimply-faced teenagers who helped her at the busiest times and were supposed to clean the cooking utensils and keep the washing-up machine charged.

'We'll settle for you,' Ben said, looking at the fat-stained

stove, encrusted stainless-steel bowls for prepped ingredients, and the sink piled with dirty saucepans.

Amy forced him back to the bar. 'You've got quite enough
material to feed your nasty sub-text. Now tell your cameraman to get back to his B & B. I'm sure his union won't
allow him to film any more today.' But when she looked
around for Stan there was no sign of him; he seemed to
have given up for the evening.

'"Nasty sub-text", what are you talking about, Miss
Walpole?' said Ben, seemingly untroubled by his colleague's
departure. 'All we are doing is shining a light on the problems that pub-owners face in these troubled times.'

'Don't give me that injured puppy-dog look.' Amy
announced loudly that the bar was closing, that it was time
customers left, and started to load more dirty glasses on
her tray. 'I know exactly what you are up to, and it's
disgraceful.'

'Disgraceful? What talk is that? We're shooting actuality
here, making a documentary. There's nothing disgraceful
about our activities.' She seemed to have shaken him out
of his usual complacency.

'The way your programme makers lull your victims into
thinking they will get a fair hearing in front of the nation!
Instead they are made to look like fools. Your programme
won't save the Admiral Byng. By the time you've finished
with us, it's more likely to close our doors for good.' This
last was hissed in an undertone; Amy had no intention of
spreading the word before the TV programme did it for her.

She wouldn't have been surprised if Ben had turned his

back on her and gone up to his room. Instead he shoved his hands into the pockets of his jeans (they had 'Gucci' stamped all over them), leaned back against the bar, and fixed her with an injured look.

'The camera cannot lie.'

'Don't try and get sanctimonious with me.' Amy was now so angry she could hardly speak. But she seemed to have punctured his smug carapace, and something approaching a human being who had genuine emotions was emerging. 'You know perfectly well that the camera lies and lies and lies. You seem to think it's the duty of TV to pander to all the worst impulses of your audience. That they need to feed on the weaknesses of their fellow men and women to feel comfortable with themselves.'

'You seem to have a higher opinion of your "fellow men and women"...' he repeated her words with a sarcastic twist, '... than I do. But perhaps you lack my experience of the common man.' His eyes narrowed, his self-importance was back. 'Though how you can keep pulling pints for the sort of customer you get in here without wanting to hit them over the head for the petty-mindedness, bigotry, and basic ignorance they display every time they open their mouths, I find it hard to understand. I seem to have been giving you credit for more intelligence than you obviously have.'

'I'll hit you over the head if you aren't careful.' Amy picked up an empty tray and shoved it at him. 'Now pick up the remaining dirty glasses. It's all due to you and Stan that there are so many. Or is doing something useful beneath your dignity?'

He actually flushed, and after a moment started to move around the now almost deserted bar collecting empties.

'Just as well Stan has gone,' he said ruefully. 'He'd give a day's wages – and they're no mean sum – to capture me doing this.'

'You know,' said Amy, clearing tables behind him, 'that's what your programme needs, a touch of realism.'

Ben worked in silence for a couple of minutes. Then, 'What's he really like, your boss? He doesn't seem your usual sort of landlord.'

'And what does that mean? How much experience of pub landlords do you have?'

'Well...' he made a vague gesture with a pint tankard. 'They're either sharp-eyed management types, keen to build up the business so they can sell on at a massive profit, or chaps with dreams in their eyes who've always yearned to run a pub, but without a clue what it entails. Your Admiral I'd put in the second category... except he's had the nous to get someone like you to keep the ship from sinking.'

Despite her doubts about Ben Milne's sincerity, Amy couldn't help warming towards him ever so slightly.

'How long have you been here?'

She had to think for a moment. 'Just over three years.'

'So you must have got to know the Admiral pretty well.'

'He's a very nice old boy.'

'Is that all?'

She put the full tray on the bar, picked up a cloth and started wiping down tables.

'What about family?'

'His? There isn't any.'

'None at all? Did he fall out with them?'

'We don't all come provided with a full set of parents, brothers and sisters, cousins and aunts.'

Ben had given up collecting empties, instead he'd taken up position on one of the bar stools and was fiddling with a smartphone. Amy was certain, though, that his attention was on the answers to his seemingly idle questions.

He looked up. 'Which are you missing from that cast list?'

She continued wiping down tables.

'Parents still alive?'

'Ben, shouldn't you be renewing your relationship with Ianthe?'

'Ianthe who?'

'The over-the-top blonde who draped herself all over you earlier this evening.'

'Oh, her! I was hoping you could tell me who she was.'

'You mean, you weren't at uni with her?'

'Amy, Amy, how could you! Do I look her age?' Ben suddenly paused and his expression changed. 'She could, I suppose, have been a mature student? There is something familiar about her...' He rubbed his chin in the manner of one who has had to change his mind about something, and Amy thought he looked guilty enough to have remembered being in bed with her. Surely not! Still, she paused for a moment in her task of putting chairs upside down on the tables so she could sweep the floor. No edge-to-edge carpeting at the Admiral Byng. Her head on one side, she considered Mr Ben Milne. 'In a way you look, well, sort of ageless.'

'Thank you very much.' He obviously did not consider this a compliment. 'Have I got bags under the eyes, frown lines, lips that have disappeared?'

'Mr Milne, you can't be as self-obsessed as that comment makes you sound!'

'If we were in a novel, at this point I'd give a rueful laugh. Consider it laughed. You're right, of course. I am your average simple male who hates the fact that the years are slipping by and he can't kick a football as far as he used to.'

She gave him a closer look. If you reckoned that Ianthe had aged beyond her years, and that he had managed to off-load his excesses on a portrait in the attic, maybe, just maybe, they had been at uni together.

'You, on the other hand, have been on the go all the evening, and look as though you are good for a marathon.'

'So what is it you want? Bar's closed.'

'Come on, have a heart.' He looked quickly around the saloon. 'The place is empty. We could have a quick snifter together and no one would know. Unless you think the old boy is likely to descend?'

Amy shook her head. 'I think he's retired for the night. I haven't seen anyone go up to the Bridge for some time.'

'So?'

She ran hot water into the bar sink and started washing glasses.

'Sweet, pretty Amy, please?' He put his elbows on the bar and gazed into her face.

She couldn't help laughing. 'You could sell snow to an Eskimo.'

'Tut, tut,' he said. 'Don't forget your political correctness. We call them Inuits today.'

'So we do. I had this lovely book as a child; all about a little girl helping to build an igloo and fishing through a hole in the ice, so the name Eskimo stuck with me. I've always wanted to go to Alaska.' She wiped her hands and turned to the bottles lined up behind her. 'OK, what'll it be? As you're a resident, it's legal and can go on your tab.'

He grinned. 'My work tab.' He scanned the shelves. 'I had a Chilean Merlot earlier. That wasn't bad.'

Most of the time Amy made it a rule not to drink at work. She had seen too many in the hotel and catering trade end up full-blown alcoholics. Once in a while, though, couldn't harm. And she knew the Chilean Merlot was good.

She gave one of the filled glasses to Ben and raised hers. 'What shall we drink to?'

'"The Last Hurrah", surely!' He drank, then said, 'Just what did he mean by that?'

'I have no idea.'

'Come on, you must have some clue.'

Was he trying to get her drunk so she'd let her tongue run away with her?

'After all, it couldn't be a big surprise if he wanted to sell this place, surely?' Ben gave an expansive gesture that took in the shabby nature of their surroundings. 'And you, your title might be bar manager, but you seem to be in charge of everything. You must know exactly how things stand with the Admiral Byng, financially speaking.'

Amy drank some more of her wine and considered the TV presenter over the edge of her glass. What sort of person was he, really? Pushy, cynical, and quite, quite ruthless. And could be unutterably charming. When he wanted.

One of the few maxims Amy followed in her life was to beware of charming men. In her experience they brought nothing but trouble.

CHAPTER THREE

By the time Amy had finally managed to persuade Ben to
quit the bar, and convinced him she was not going to accom-
pany him up to his bedroom, it was well past midnight.

She took another look at the dirty kitchen and hoped
that Meriel would be in early. There was no way she herself
was going to deal with it at that hour. Then she shrugged
her way into her Barbour and fished a pair of woollen
gloves out of the pocket. Roll on spring, she thought.

She checked that the key to Ianthe Berkeley's room wasn't
hanging on its hook behind the reception desk. The fact it
wasn't there was no guarantee, of course, that the woman
was in her room. Or even in the pub. But the room keys
opened the side door, a fact that was always explained to
guests on arrival, so Amy locked both that and the front
door, then let herself out of the back.

In the act of using her key to secure that door as well,
she stood for a moment fighting an unexpected urge to
return and go upstairs to Ben's room.

He'd put his empty glass down on the bar, and, just as she was preparing to tell him that had definitely been his last one, he'd run a finger along her right eyebrow. 'I love the way you raise this whenever you think I've gone too far,' he said. 'And your nose is enchanting.' He'd leaned forward and placed a soft kiss on its tip.

Amy had felt something melt within her. If he'd been silent then, she would probably have been in his bed before you could say 'reality show'. Instead, 'Up the stairs with you,' he had said, and had given her behind a quick smack.

So that had been that. It was the nearest thing she'd experienced to: 'Wham-bam-thank-you-ma'am'. Hadn't the man a smidgen of romance in his soul?

She had pulled down the grille that secured the bar and its contents, snapping the padlock shut. 'I'll see you in the morning.'

'Amy!' He had reached for her, but she wasn't going to let him get that near to her again.

'Mind the stairs, they're tricky for anyone under the influence,' she called on her way out to her coat. She had not looked back.

For a few moments there had been deep satisfaction at the strangled cry of frustration that had reached her as she left.

Now, though, she remembered that moment of tenderness and felt something approaching regret.

The air was chilly outside after the warmth of the bar. Amy drew the ancient but serviceable Barbour around herself as she set off along the shore to her little cottage. The moon was full, flooding the beach with silver light.

Phrases from the captivating duet from *The Pearl Fishers* sang in her mind as she crunched her way over the pebbly beach. Was true romance confined to fiction? She had thought her decision never to fall in love again was as sensible as her shoes. Love, true love, had done for her. Amy shivered. The door she had shut on that relationship, one that had brought such delight and such despair, must remain closed. Closed, barred, locked, secured.

How could she have let a pair of brown eyes switch on a set of electric currents, making her tingle in ways that brought back so many memories? It wasn't as if she even liked the man! Or could respect him!

Amy forced herself to put any thought of Ben out of her mind. Instead she considered the unusual behaviour of her boss, the Admiral. Buying drinks for everyone like that, telling them all it was a 'Last Hurrah'; what had the man been thinking of?

And what did that constant procession of people up to the Bridge mean? One by one they had climbed the stairs, and one by one they had returned. There had been the occasional order for a pint or some other tipple. None of them had seemed talkative; some had left in a hurried, almost furtive way. What had been their business with the Admiral?

Once again Amy wondered what it was he wanted to talk to her about. It must be something to do with the pub. She almost managed to convince herself that he had decided it must be sold. Yet he had seemed so uncharacteristically cheerful. And there had been that look he'd given her; surely, though, she was reading too much into it? Thinking that it said something had made him change his mind about her?

Ever since she had started work at the Admiral Byng, its landlord had been a constant support. She'd arrived in Crabwell on a wickedly rainy winter's night, her woollen coat soaked right through. She had sat in it on the long bus ride, shivering, not knowing where she was going. All she knew was that she was leaving the past behind her. The bus had dropped her in front of a bank. Both that and the shops arranged around a small attempt at a village square were closed tight. Since it was nearly eight o'clock in the evening, that was hardly surprising. 'Crabwell, end of the line,' the driver had said. She had picked up her suitcase, and asked, 'Is there a hotel?'

'There's the Admiral Byng,' the only other passenger left had said as he got off. 'It has rooms,' he had added doubtfully. Then he had cheered up slightly. 'The landlord's a bit eccentric, but a good sort.' He had pointed at the road ahead. 'Five minutes' walk that way.'

Amy had thanked him. She had looked around the square again, but it offered nothing useful, so she had set off in the direction indicated. One of the little wheels on her case had come to grief over a large stone as she tramped down the dark road, trees on either side. She had cursed. The case had begun to feel heavier and heavier, and the rain never let up. Then, suddenly, she had come around a bend, and there was the pub, its lights shining on the wet road. It was as though some fairy godmother had waved her wand and conjured a safe haven.

The landlord had been welcoming. She'd liked his look, his blazer and cravat reminded her of Gramps, the grandfather she had been close to as she grew up, as did the twinkle in his eye. He'd come over the moment she'd entered the bar. He'd taken her case from her, helped her out of the wet coat, and supplied a whisky-mac. 'It's what you need, m'dear,' he'd said, handing the glass over and waving her towards a seat beside the happily burning fire. She'd been the only customer.

He'd shaken out her drenched coat and said, 'Not my idea of a waterproof.' And on the spot he'd found an old Barbour hanging from a hook in the bar and presented it to her. Shabby, but it did keep the rain out, and Amy still wore it. Not really the style for someone her age, but then she'd never been that bothered about fashion.

The bedroom Fitz had shown her to later that night had a cosily sloping ceiling, a fat old-fashioned eiderdown on a brass bedstead, and a deeply comfortable armchair. More comfortable, in fact, than the bed. But she'd been exhausted, and had slept right through to morning. Then she found that her room had a view of the sea, all a-sparkle with the sun shining as though it didn't know what grey, rainy days were. A low windowsill meant she could sit in the chair and look at the dancing waves advancing over a beach where sand gave way to pebbles as it approached the waterline. Small boats were drawn up, their anchors buried safely in the shingle.

They were the same boats she was looking at now, three years later, the moonlight coating them with magic. Beyond them, towards Amy's cottage, well above the tide line, stood three tents. Tents, in chilly March? Then she remembered that Greta Knox, the Girl Guide leader, had said that her troop was going to sample the delights of camping. 'Overnight?' Amy had asked when they had met a few days before in the village shop. 'I thought your girls were too fond of their comforts to mimic Arctic explorers.'

'We'll see,' Greta had said, her tone full of the determination that had corralled every teenage girl for miles around to join her Guide troop. She gave a huffing laugh. 'The girls can surprise one.'

Amy thought now that she would be amazed if any of the tents contained sleeping teenagers. None of them were zipped up, and there was no sound. They must be empty. She looked around. There seemed to be the remains of a campfire, with a discarded scrunch of tin foil suggesting potatoes had been baked in it. Greta must have overlooked that, she was a terror over litter. Nothing else provided clues to the evening's activities. No doubt the Girl Guides were all now safely at home in their warm and comfortable beds.

As if to hasten her in the direction of her own bed, a nasty gust of wind tugged at Amy's hair. She had forgotten her beanie. She took a last look at the light silvering the rapacious tide as it surged in towards the shore and then retreated to gather strength for another attack. It was the only movement in the whole scene. She was alone on the beach.

Afterwards she couldn't say why her attention had been caught by one of the drawn-up boats. Perhaps it was the moonlight shining on the stuck-on silver letters on its stern, identifying it as *The Admiral*, Fitz's dinghy. But it shouldn't be there. Its usual place was in the other direction. When had it been moved? She remembered seeing it earlier in the day, safely where she'd expect it to be.

Had the Admiral moved it this afternoon? But when would he have had the time, and why would he want to? Or had he gone out into the moonlight after ordering the last round and brought it here? If so, why?

Maybe someone else had moved it. The Admiral was known to be highly selective about who he allowed on his beloved dinghy. Never anyone without him, and only allowed to take the tiller after they had proved themselves seaworthy, as he called it. Once some pranksters had taken the boat out and then left it swinging drunkenly from its anchor in the far reaches of the bay. The Admiral had not been amused.

Amy reached the anchor and checked the way it had been set in the shingle. Right and tight it looked. The chain stretched down to the boat itself, now beginning to wallow drunkenly on the incoming tide. There was something not quite right about its movement. The beach shelved steeply down from where she was standing, so that it was almost possible to see inside the craft. Amy caught her breath. It looked as though... But surely it couldn't be...

Without hesitating, and heedless of her sensible shoes, she ran down the beach and through the water to the dinghy. As she got closer, she saw that the waterproof cover had been rolled back and stuffed into the prow.

The boat was half-full of water – that was why it was wallowing. But there was more than water in there. Amy took hold of the dinghy's side, forcing it towards her so that she could scramble aboard. With horrible squelches she managed to find a steady footing. A man was slumped on his front in the bottom of the boat, his face beneath the water. Supporting herself on the gunwales, Amy shuffled her way alongside the collapsed figure to the boat's stern. Then she bent and slipped her hands beneath the shoulders and tried to pull whoever it was up far enough to bring his head above the water that slopped about as the boat veered from side to side with her movements, threatening to capsize.

In her heart Amy knew her efforts were hopeless, but still she struggled, lifting and pulling the shoulders, cursing her weakness, looking along the shoreline for help. But the beach was empty. With a final effort, using unexpected reserves of strength, she managed to pull the heavy body up, then to turn it so that the drowned man sat supported by the mast, his feet caught up in the oars that lay along the boat's bottom.

For a moment she stood holding onto the mast, gasping, her eyes closed as she tried to recover from her efforts. Then she opened them and looked at the sorry remains of the man who had been lying in the bottom of the boat.

The grey hair was soaked, plastered to the skull, the eyes that had been so bright such a little time ago were staring sightlessly. All personality had been stripped away by death. Only the blazer with its brass buttons proclaimed the corpse's identity.

Exhausted by her efforts, struggling not to fall as the dinghy moved with the rapid surges of the incoming tide, Amy looked at the body of her boss. What on earth had the old man been up to? What could have made him move the dinghy so late at night? And just how had he managed to fall and drown himself in his beloved boat?

CHAPTER FOUR

Amy was surprised by the tears running down her cheeks. She knew it wasn't just shock at discovering the body. It was an overwhelming sadness at the thought that she'd never hear the Admiral's voice again. Maybe, somewhere deep down in her psyche, she had felt love for the old bastard.

She decided, rather than ringing the police from her cottage, she would have to go back to the pub and prepare herself for a long night of disruption and probably questioning.

Her basic knowledge of police procedure, gleaned from endless television cop shows, told her that she should touch as little as possible at a crime scene, but when she looked closer at the boat she saw something white, stuffed into the folds of the crumpled boat cover.

An envelope. Printed on it the words: *'TO WHOM IT MAY CONCERN'*.

Sod not touching anything at a crime scene. No power

43

could have stopped her from opening that envelope. Fortunately the flap was just tucked in, so she didn't have to tear it.

She read what was written on the folded sheet inside.

I'm sorry. All the pressures were just getting too much. I've had my Last Hurrah and it's better to go out on a high. Apologies to anyone who's going to be upset by my death (though I don't think there'll be many).
  Fitz

The text was not handwritten. It had been typed and printed. Possibly using the computer in the Admiral Byng's downstairs office.

In other words, whoever had composed the suicide note, it certainly hadn't been the computer-illiterate Fitz.

Which, to Amy's mind was proof positive that the old boy had been murdered.

And made her absolutely determined to find out who had committed the crime.

A car in the blue and yellow livery of the Suffolk Constabulary was heading rapidly towards Crabwell.

'Watch your speed, laddie,' the DI in the passenger seat told his driver, Detective Constable Chesterton. 'This isn't life or death.'

'It's death, isn't it?' Chesterton said. 'Death in my book, anyway.'

'Come clever with me and you'll find yourself back in

uniform.' DI Cole didn't take lip from fast-track graduate detectives. 'It's only a suicide. There was a note beside the body, and it couldn't be more plain.'

A suicide was difficult to envisage as anything other than a death as far as Keith Chesterton was concerned, but he knew better than to argue with 'The Lump', as Cole was known to everyone who worked with him. He cut their speed to fifty-nine and gave thought to the strange circumstances of the incident. They had collected the suicide note from the local bobby called to the scene overnight, who had told them the victim had been found on Crabwell beach lying in a dinghy partly filled with water and anchored in the shingle. A young woman out walking had made the grim discovery and then suffered a worse shock by recognising the corpse as that of her own employer, the owner of the pub that overlooked the beach.

'So there's no rush,' Cole said. 'It's not like murder or a robbery, rounding up suspects. The perpetrator was the corpse, and he isn't going anywhere.'

Only on the most momentous journey any of us will ever make, Chesterton mused. He had a spiritual side he kept to himself. 'Where is the body right now?'

'The mortuary, of course. They wouldn't leave it in the open for all and sundry to gawp at. That wouldn't be fitting.'

'They could have put a forensic tent over it and taped off the area so nobody could get near.'

'What would be the point of that?' Cole said. 'I keep telling you, there's only one person involved in a suicide.'

'But if it was suicide, how did he end up in the boat?'

'You know what boat-owners are like. They have love affairs with the bloody things. When they die they can't think of anywhere they'd rather be.'

'Like a ship burial?'

'I didn't say anything about a burial, cloth-ears.'

'So how do you suppose he managed to kill himself and end up there… sir?'

'We'll have to wait for the post-mortem, won't we? My guess is that he had a supply of sleeping tablets and mixed them in with a bottle of grog from his pub, then swallowed the lot. Best way to go. He took the short walk to his dinghy, and crashed.'

'Remembering to take the suicide note with him?'

'Naturally.'

'First tucking it carefully into the folded tarpaulin where it wouldn't get wet?'

'You're making sense at last.'

'And crashed. But we won't know for sure until they test his body fluids?'

'Right.' Cole grinned to himself. 'Have you ever attended a post-mortem?'

When Amy Walpole answered the insistent knocking and saw two strangers at the pub door she told them at once that she wasn't open for business. There had been a bereavement.

'We know about that, my poppet,' the older of the two men said. He was grossly overweight, and dressed in a brown suit with a windowpane check that wasn't just loud, it was bellowing. 'It's why we're here.'

Amy wasn't anyone's poppet, least of all this clown's. She decided they were journalists and slammed the door. Well, almost. The younger of the two placed the palm of his right hand against the wood before it closed. He was strong.

'If you want trouble,' Amy said through the narrow gap, 'I'll call the police.'

'No need,' the first man said. 'It's me and him.' He held up an ID, and it didn't look like a press-card. 'Cole and Chesterton, detectives, here about the man found dead in the boat last evening. May we come in?'

The second man also dipped in his pocket with his free hand and produced his warrant card displaying his photo, and the insignia of the Suffolk Police. He was not bad looking, quite a dish, in fact, but Amy wasn't in any mood to be friendly.

She opened the door fully and jerked her head to let them know they could enter.

'Are you the barmaid?' DI Cole asked.

She eyed him as if he were something the dog had coughed up. 'Bar manager.'

'The table by the window will do us nicely.'

'For the time being,' said DC Chesterton. 'We'll need to set up an Incident Room in here soon. Is there anywhere suitable?'

Cole's look at his subordinate showed that he didn't think an Incident Room would be necessary for such an obvious case of suicide, but Amy's presence stopped him from voicing his objection. It wouldn't do to let her know yet that he'd already decided what had happened. Perhaps they would have to go through the charade of setting up an Incident Room anyway.

'Well, there's the Bridge,' Amy replied. 'Fitz used it as an office. That'd probably be the best place for you.'

'Thank you,' said Chesterton politely.

Cole thought he had been silent for quite long enough. 'You don't have to offer us a drink, but a coffee wouldn't come amiss.'

'The machine isn't on,' Amy said. She could have boiled a kettle and given them instant, but she wasn't feeling hospitable.

'And isn't that fried bacon I can smell?'

'Breakfasts have to be booked.'

'You could make an exception for Suffolk's finest, couldn't you?'

'We cater for our guests, not casual callers.'

'Ooh! That was below the belt,' Cole said. They'd already seated themselves at the table. 'Let's see if we can soften your heart. Why don't you join us, my love?'

'Let's get one thing clear,' Amy said, remaining standing. 'Call me Miss Walpole, if you wish. Anything else is offensive or patronising.'

'Whatever you wish,' he said. 'We know a lady manager when we meet one.'

Amy took this as compliance, and drew up a chair.

'Are we speaking to the same Miss Walpole who reported the incident on the beach last night?'

'You are. After I found him I came up here directly and dialled 999.'

The younger of the two, DC Chesterton, had produced a notebook and was writing in it. 'This was at what time, Miss Walpole?' They were the first words he'd spoken, and he had a voice that went down warmly, like the breakfast Amy hadn't provided.

'Late, after midnight, towards one a.m. I'd closed the bar and was on my way back to my cottage.'

'Hold on,' Cole said, eager to regain control. 'We'll do this from the beginning. You were here in the pub all evening, I take it?'

'Yes.'

'Quiet, was it?'

'Actually, no,' Amy said. 'The place was packed.'

'On a perishing Monday night in March?'

'We had the TV people in, making a documentary, and the locals got wind of it and wanted their five minutes of fame – well, five seconds more likely – so just about everyone was in, and some we never normally see.'

'And was Mr Fitzsimmons present?'

'No one calls him that,' Amy said. '"Fitz" or "The Admiral".'

'Served in the Navy, did he?'

'I can't say for sure. He'd been to sea, that's certain, and once owned a schooner. He was full of stories, but I got the impression they improved in the telling. He was at it last night for the TV, going on about lost treasure in the West Indies, or some such.'

'So he didn't appear unduly depressed?'

'Quite the opposite. He was in his element, buying drinks and playing to the crowd. You had to admire him. He could work an audience like a professional, and he was making mischief, too.'

'In what way?'

'He talked about "treasure closer to home" and said they could look forward to all kinds of revelations the next day.' She sighed. 'That would have been today.'

'What did he mean by that?'

'I've no idea. Earlier he'd been holding court upstairs in his private apartment that we call the Bridge, receiving a steady stream of visitors. He wanted to see me as well, but my turn was coming today.'

'You don't know what it was about?'

She shook her head. 'I can only speculate, and you don't want that.'

DC Chesterton said, 'We don't mind you speculating, Miss Walpole. You must have known him better than anyone else.'

She glanced across the table. Young Chesterton's eyes were as remarkable as his voice, the colour of the sea off Crabwell on a bright May morning, and he didn't seem aware of their power. She was willing to speculate for Chesterton. She wouldn't need much urging to speculate *about* him. 'I wondered if he'd decided to sell up. We've had falling sales all winter. Until this week.'

'Familiar story, sadly,' Chesterton said.

'So he *was* depressed,' Cole butted in.

'Not at all,' Amy said. 'He obviously had plans for some new project. He was one of life's survivors.'

Cole said with a leer. '"Was" is the operative word.'

Amy said, 'I was asked for my opinion. You seem to have made up your mind he took his own life. I'm not so sure. I've known him three years.'

Now Cole blinked and straightened up. 'Do you have any evidence that he didn't kill himself?'

'Quite a bit,' Amy said. 'Earlier in the evening I went for a breath of fresh air along the beach. I'd been run off my feet until then, but it had gone quiet in the pub because the TV people were on a three-hour break. I happened to meet the Admiral. He was beside his boat, checking the cover, I think.'

'Really? And did you speak?'

'Of course. I enquired what he was doing and he said there had been too many thefts from boats. I remarked that he'd been extra busy with the visitors to the Bridge all day, and I asked if he'd spoken to Ben Milne, the TV man. He said ironically that he was reserving that pleasure for tomorrow.'

'Ironically?'

'He called Mr Milne a cocky young man, and he was right. Then he added that he wanted a long talk with me, but it would have to wait till the next day because he planned to get extremely drunk.'

Cole held up a finger. 'Got you. You're thinking he drank himself to death.'

'Not at all. I've seen him drunk before and he was always

51

fine the next day. My point is that he had definite plans for today. He wasn't suicidal.'

'The facts prove otherwise,' Cole said. 'There was a suicide note in the boat.'

'I know,' Amy said calmly. 'I found it and showed it to the policeman who answered the 999 call.'

'So?'

'So I don't believe the Admiral wrote it.'

'Oh, come on,' Cole said. 'It's the clincher. What are you going to tell me now – that he was illiterate?'

'Couldn't use a computer,' Amy said. 'The envelope was printed – "*TO WHOM IT MAY CONCERN*" – and Fitz hadn't the faintest idea how to work the printer. Have you seen the note?'

'It's in an evidence bag in the car. We picked it up this morning,' Chesterton said. 'Both the note and the envelope were computer-generated.'

For that, he got a glare from his superior.

'It's no big deal,' Cole said. 'Any fool can learn how to use a computer.'

'And print off a page – and an envelope as well?' Amy said. 'The Admiral was no fool, but he wasn't capable of that.'

'The wording couldn't be more clear,' Cole insisted, and did a rapid recap. 'All the pressures getting too much, he'd had his "Last Hurrah" and was going out on a high, with apologies to anyone upset by his death. No arguing with that.'

'If he actually wrote it,' Amy said. 'If he didn't, your so-called clincher is a busted flush.'

'We'll see about that, Miss Walpole. We need to speak to the people who were called up to the Bridge. Did any of them tell you what the Admiral wanted?'

'Not one. They were remarkably tight-lipped, almost as if he'd asked them to keep a secret.'

'We'll winkle out the truth, don't you worry. That's our job. I'd like you to make a list of those concerned.'

'I didn't see them all. I was busy serving while it was going on.'

'Jot down any you remember.' His eyes slid upwards. 'What was that?'

A sound had come from upstairs.

'A guest, I expect. We do let rooms, you know.'

Ben Milne appeared at the top of the stairs. 'How's my breakfast coming along?'

Amy called back, 'I'll tell Meriel. Is it the full works, Ben?'

'With a large mug of black coffee.'

'No problem.' She turned back to the policemen. 'That's the TV guy, Ben Milne. Excuse me a moment.' And she was off to the kitchen.

Cole looked at Chesterton and muttered, 'No problem, my arse. What about "the full works" for you and me, then?'

Ben had come downstairs and walked straight to their table. 'Have we met? I don't think so. Ben Milne. Are you from the village?'

'Police,' Cole said, 'enquiring into the death of the landlord.'

53

'Dire, yes. Woke me up, all the comings and goings in the small hours. Why did he do that, do you suppose?'

'That's what we're in process of finding out, sir. You're making a TV show, I understand.'

Ben winced as if he'd been stung. 'A "show" it is not. This is for real. Documentary filming. We point the cameras and go with the flow. You never know what you'll get. So far, it's been better than I could have hoped, and now we've struck gold with the Admiral dying.'

'Struck gold?' Even Cole's jaw dropped.

'Put yourself in my position, filming a failing business just at the moment the head honcho tops himself. A tragedy played out as we watch. I just wish my dozy cameraman had been here last night to shoot the beach scene. We might do a mock-up, now I think about it. The boat's still there, isn't it?'

Chesterton nodded. 'But if this is a reality programme—'

Ben was too hyped up to listen. 'The networks will break their balls to buy this. I see world-wide sales. It's got Emmy written all over it.'

'Who's Emmy?' Cole asked.

Chesterton saved him from embarrassment by saying, 'There may be legal complications.'

'How come?' Ben asked, frowning.

'If – for the sake of argument – a court case ensued from this, they could stop you from airing the programme.'

'What are you on about – a court case?'

'You could prejudice the legal process.'

'Bugger that,' Ben said. 'I'm on a roll. I'm not stopping

54

for anything. Are you going to question the witnesses? I need it all on film.'

And now Cole waded in. 'You can get stuffed. You're not filming us.'

'However,' Chesterton added in an inspired moment, 'we need a copy of every frame you've shot up to now. It could be crucial evidence.'

'No way,' Milne said.

'No? Obstructing the police is an offence under section 66 of the Police Act, punishable with six months' imprisonment. We need that film by noon tomorrow.'

Cole eyed his assistant with surprise. There was more to the young man than he'd supposed.

Ben looked at his watch. 'You've buggered my schedule.'

Amy returned with a tray bearing Ben's breakfast: a large mug of coffee, orange juice, toast, marmalade, and a plate stacked high with bacon, egg, sausages, mushrooms, tomatoes fried bread.

'I don't have time for this,' the TV man said. 'I've just been given a whole new heap of work.'

For a moment Amy stood holding the tray, at a loss.

But Cole said, 'Leave it with us, Miss Walpole. It mustn't go to waste. Are you off the coffee as well, Mr Milne?'

Feeling better after their fortuitous breakfast, the two detectives went upstairs to look at the Bridge, the function room adjacent to the owner's living quarters. Presumably all the private consultations had taken place here the previous day. Dusty pictures of sailing ships crowded the walls. A dusty glass cabinet was filled with a collection of razor shells, conches, scallops, and clams. Lines of small dusty flags were suspended from the ceiling like Christmas decorations. At the far end, a huge desk that could have doubled as a poop deck was filled with as many bottles as the bar downstairs, but most were empty. There were some unwashed glasses as well. Beneath them, acting as coasters, were numerous sealed letters, some heavily stained.

'From his energy supplier,' Chesterton said, picking several up and leafing through them. 'Gas, the bank, a brewery. Most of these look like unopened bills.'

Cole was sitting behind the desk in the Admiral's padded armchair under a ship's figurehead of a topless blonde woman. 'It just confirms the obvious. He'd given up. He was desperate.'

'There's no computer up here, and no printer. There isn't even a filing system.'

'An old-fashioned phone,' Cole said, lifting an upturned waste-paper basket to show what was underneath. He opened the desk drawer and saw that it contained one item: a corkscrew. 'Even his bottle-opener is out of the ark.'

'Makes you wonder if Miss Walpole had a point about him being technophobic,' Chesterton said.

'Techno what?'

'Unable to use a computer.'

'We've only got her word for that,' Cole said with irritation. 'She told us herself his stories grew in the telling. The man was living a lie, pretending he'd spent his whole life at sea. Bloody fantasist, if you ask me. All this seaside tat around us – the stuffed swordfish and the old lamps and the ships in bottles – is just props. Anyone can pick them up in local junkshops and furnish a pub with them. In reality, I reckon he was a failed businessman or a bloody civil servant, perfectly capable of printing that suicide note. You may be sure there's a computer somewhere in this pub.'

'I spotted one downstairs, in the little office behind the bar,' Chesterton said. 'They'd need it to bill the overnight guests.'

'There you are, then.'

'But I was impressed by Miss Walpole. She's worked with the guy for three years, and she doesn't buy the suicide theory.'

'It's more than a theory, sunshine,' Cole said. 'It's what happened. And you'd better stop being impressed with that bimbo. I saw the way she was batting her eyelashes at you. She's the sort who picks up DCs and drops them from a great height. I'll show you how to deal with a woman like that. Watch me when we go downstairs.'

'Should we look at his living quarters first?'

'If you like, but I don't expect to find much.'

Up a small flight of stairs they found a sitting room filled with more maritime objects (or seaside tat), as well as a sofa and armchairs. A bookcase was lined with dog-eared paperbacks by C.S. Forester and Patrick O'Brian. Beyond that was the bedroom and a small en suite.

'Take a look in the medicine cabinet,' Cole said.

'What am I looking for?'

'Dangerous drugs, barbiturates, sleeping tablets, anything he could overdose on.'

After a few minutes of searching, Chesterton said. 'Nothing at all like that.'

'Proves my point,' Cole said at once.

'How?'

'Obvious. He must have swallowed the bleeding lot.'

They returned downstairs to the bar, where the sole occupant was a woman at breakfast wearing a white bathrobe and slippers and with her hair in a plastic shower cap. She stared at them in horror. 'Oh my God, don't look at me. I'm undressed, not made up, not for viewing. I thought it was safe to eat my scrambled egg while my hair was drying. Go away, whoever you are.'

'It's a public bar, ma'am,' Cole informed her.

'Residents only at this hour.'

'Do you live here, then?'

'A paying guest. Go away. Vamoose. Shoo.'

'We're on an investigation.'

'You're not the…?'

'We are, following up the tragic event of last night.'

'Oh my God! Then if you won't leave, I will. Don't you dare try and stop me.'

With that, she got up, dashed across the room and upstairs, leaving a slipper on the lowest step.

'There's your chance, Prince Charming,' Cole said with an evil grin. 'Why don't you go up and see if it fits?'

Chesterton rolled his eyes and said nothing.

In a moment Amy Walpole returned. 'Didn't Ianthe finish

her breakfast either? You two won't be popular with Meriel, our cook.'

'Is that who she was – Ianthe?' Cole asked. 'Ianthe who?'

'Berkeley. Another guest. Publishing person.'

'Were she and the TV man sharing a room?'

She frowned. 'Not unless…' Then she reddened. 'Is that what she told you?'

Cole shook his head. 'Deduction. First the man appears from upstairs, looking like the cat who found the cream, then the woman in a state of disarray.'

'That's observation, not deduction, and they had very good reasons for looking like that, unconnected with each other. Anyway, all the guest rooms are on the same landing.'

'I'm broad-minded,' Cole said. 'The only thing that interests me is that they were both here yesterday, when the Admiral was still alive. We'll need to question them about his state of mind.'

'I keep telling you he was in excellent spirits.'

'Yes, eighteen-year-old malt. There are some empties on his desk. Did he take anything to help him sleep?'

'He never mentioned it.'

'It makes a deadly mix, alcohol and sleeping tablets.'

'He wouldn't do that.'

'There's no denying he ended up dead, Miss Walpole. We weren't informed that he shot himself, and I doubt if he drowned in a few inches of water.'

'He might have, if he was already unconscious.'

'True.'

'Is concussion a possibility?'

'A knock on the head, you mean? Self-inflicted? No chance.'

'I didn't say self-inflicted.'

Cole grinned. 'You watch too much crime on television. It isn't like that in the real world. Don't forget we've got the suicide note.'

'The questionable suicide note,' Amy said.

'All right. Let's play it your way. The only people who know about the existence of this note are your good self and the officer who attended the scene last night. Have you mentioned it to anyone else?'

She hesitated for a nanosecond. She had mentioned it to Ben. But she didn't want to complicate things, so she said, 'No.'

'Then don't. This is how we root out guilty parties. If someone else concocted the note, as you seem to be implying, they'll give themselves away at some stage. Clever, eh?'

'I hadn't thought of that.'

'And just to be quite certain, we'll be fingerprinting the paper the note was written on. Forensics can get prints off anything these days.'

Amy caught her breath. 'Mine could be on it. I lifted the envelope from the tarpaulin.'

'But they won't be on the letter inside. The only prints we can expect to find are those of the person who wrote it and the officer who opened it. If, God forbid, we find any others, that individual will have some explaining to do.'

Amy was silent.

'So this will be our little secret, Miss Walpole. Are you with me?'

She gave a nod, but her mind was in turmoil. *Touch as little as possible at a crime scene.* If only she'd listened to her own inner voice.

'Another thing,' Cole said. 'I want you to print something now on your computer. We noticed you've got one in your office.'

'Print what?'

'A notice in large letters saying the pub is closed until further notice owing to the sad death of the owner.'

Having printed the note as requested, and closed the door on the detectives, noting incidentally that the younger of the two looked as good from the back as he did from the front – then scolding herself for even thinking that when she'd seen Fitz dead not twelve hours ago – Amy let Meriel know that she might as well have the day off.

'With the pub closed until the police decide otherwise, there's nothing else we can do.'

Meriel was not happy, and, looking around the kitchen, half a dozen dishes seemingly on the go at once, a massive number of vegetables already prepped, Amy could see why.

'You don't usually work this hard on a Tuesday, Meriel.'

'We don't usually have a film crew in the bar dragging in all and sundry, and hungry with it. We don't usually have detectives eating my full English. And I don't usually have the chance to... to... oh never mind. Get out of my way and I'll try to salvage some of this. They're going have to let us open once they confirm it's suicide.'

Amy turned in the door. 'How do you know about that?'

Meriel smiled. 'Little pitchers, big ears. And that,' she pointed to the extractor above the big catering oven, 'still leads into the old chimneys, they're all connected. When it's turned off, I can hear half the conversations in the bar, clear as day. Now if you don't mind, you may not have anything to do with the bar closed, but I have no intention of letting this lot go to waste. It'll do for funeral-baked meats, if nothing else.'

Amy used the locked front door as an opportunity to give the bar a good clean. The old chairs, the scuffed walls, the tables with their ingrained sticky beer would also be put to use for the wake, she was sure of that, it wasn't as if there was anywhere else to go after the funeral – once they were allowed to have the funeral – she might as well make the bar as presentable as possible. She shook her head, feeling tears coming on again, smarting at the back of her eyes. No, she would not cry. Last night was bad enough, she wasn't going to let it all get to her in broad daylight as well. A deep breath, a bucket of hot water, and a brutally effective and pungent spray cleaner, that was more use than tears right now.

As Amy got to work she thought how odd death was, the way someone, anyone – loved or hated, it didn't matter – just suddenly stopped. The incredible cessation of life. No wonder people had invented religion to make sense of it, nothing else did. She scrubbed harder, as old memories, unbidden, threatened to well up. She'd trained herself to be tougher than this, not to look back, not to dwell. It wasn't even as if Fitz had been a good boss, his business skills were appalling, but he had been kind to her when she'd needed help, and she'd not forget that. The arrival of not one, but two, good-looking men in town was not going to let her forget Fitz's kindness, even if most people had been all too ready to consider him a bit of a joke. There had been much more to Fitz than most people saw, Amy wasn't even sure she knew what that more might be, but she knew he wasn't just the village drunkard, the old buffoon. And he was no suicide. Whatever he'd been planning for his 'Last Hurrah', it had been something he'd personally found thrilling, something that had generated that twinkle in his eye. She threw away the second dirty bucket of water and rinsed the sink. Fitz had been planning something all right, but it most certainly was not suicide.

Amy was halfway back to her cottage, the wind no less brutal than it had been in the middle of the night, the sky only slightly less lowering, when a new thought occurred to her. Ben Milne and his cameraman Stan had been filming most of yesterday afternoon. Cutaways of the pub, close-ups of the dust caught in the nautical ceiling decoration – 'for atmosphere only, love', Stan had assured her, with a wink to Ben – long shots of the desolate seascape beyond the small windows, and plenty of vox pops, where Ben – as producer-presenter – had his own style, simultaneously enthused but also laid-back, just this side of too cocky, yet not quite as charming as he no doubt thought himself. They must have taken at least a couple of hours of video footage, and not all of it could have been her own or Meriel's cleavage, despite Stan's obvious interest in the female form. She'd been too busy with the influx of non-regulars, all of them keenly hoping to get caught on camera, to pay much attention to the people who'd visited Fitz yesterday afternoon, but Amy was aware that the stairs up to the Bridge had been busier than usual. And somewhere in all that footage there might well be a clue to what else had been planned yesterday, something that would make the police look more closely into their suicide theory, something that would help her help them – even if they clearly did not want her help.

Amy turned on her heel and headed back to the pub. The last she'd seen of him, Ben was stomping upstairs to his room, with dire threats about suing the pub if the promised Wi-Fi didn't work, and how the hell was he supposed to copy all their film in the time the police had given him. Amy knew enough about technology to know he needed neither Wi-Fi nor a great deal of time to copy from the camera memory card to his own laptop's hard disc or a memory stick, but she'd assumed he was using the tantrum to get himself off and back into bed, making up for lost sleep and last night's hangover.

She let herself back into the pub and checked in the kitchen. She was pleased to see Meriel appeared to have tidied everything well enough, and then went upstairs to

Ben's door. She knocked, and was surprised when Ben opened up almost immediately.

'About bloody time,' he said, walking away, neither looking at her, nor removing his headphones, 'just put it on the bed, I asked for that over an hour ago.'

'Asked for what?' Amy said, standing in the doorway.

'Huh?' Ben turned and was clearly surprised to see Amy. His frown burrowed even further into his forehead for a moment, until he remembered he was frowning at Amy, and he fancied her, or he would do if she'd shown any sign of fancying him back, as most women did. He tried – too late – to offer his lopsided grin, the one his viewers seemed to find so attractive.

'Who were you expecting?' Amy asked.

'That woman, in the kitchen, the one who thinks she's the next voluptuous telly cook.'

'Meriel,' Amy prompted

'Merry hell, yes.' Ben chuckled, pleased with his own joke, no doubt planning something similar for the documentary voiceover. 'I went down over an hour ago, you were scrubbing hell out of that old table in the corner, I asked her if I could have a sandwich and a cup of coffee. If I have to waste good filming time copying stuff for the police, I might as well have some food after all. She said she'd bring me something up.'

'She must have forgotten.'

'I thought she wanted to get a series out of me?'

'Maybe she's realised you don't do "shows",' Amy said with a grin, copying Ben's earlier tone to the policemen.

'Yeah, or maybe she's gone off to kill a fatted calf and present it to me, apple in mouth and fat glistening.'

'When I last saw her she was putting the stuff she'd been prepping into the freezer. The police have insisted the pub's closed for business.'

'They're not about to turn me out of my room, are they?'

'No. Actually, another thought… Fish market.'

'What?'

'Tuesday. Fish market, well, more of an old transit van, comes all along the coastal villages, Tuesdays, Thursdays, and Saturdays, around about this time of day. That's where Meriel'll probably be.'

'Whole poached sea bass I'll be getting then?'

'More than likely.'

They both smiled, and then Amy was suddenly aware that she was standing in Ben's bedroom, the unmade bed astonishingly inviting, no doubt due to her lack of sleep, not at all to the lopsided grin Ben was trying out on her again.

'I was wondering…' she said.

'Yes?'

The grin again; Amy wondered if his cheek ever ached. 'The police are pretty sure Fitz committed suicide.'

'The note's a bit of a clue there.'

No grin this time, and Amy ignored him. 'But I doubt Fitz even knew where the envelopes where in the office, let alone how to type and print a note as well as an envelope. He is – he was – a complete technophobe. Actually, worse than that, not phobic, he honestly didn't care, one way or the other, he wasn't interested in learning. I don't believe he wrote that note.'

'Then...'

'Then someone else did. And that someone else may well have visited Fitz yesterday afternoon, the place was heaving, I have no idea who went up and down those steps to the Bridge. But what I do know is that Fitz was very much himself, and truly excited about what he had planned for his "Last Hurrah" as he called it. Something happened between him and one of his visitors – maybe more than one of them, I don't know – but something must have happened. Either something that did make him kill himself – even though I can't see him doing that, or...?'

'Or indeed. And you think some of my footage might show who went up to see the old man?'

'I do.'

Try as he might, Ben just couldn't stop his dark eyes lighting up. Amy watched him as he worked it all out, in the sharpest televisual terms, she was sure – a derelict old pub, a 'character' of a publican, a potential suicide that segued neatly into murder. She couldn't really blame him, he'd come all this way hoping to make a perfectly ordinary little programme that gently mocked local characters and made people up and down the country feel better about their own stolid lives from the safety of their own soft sofas, and now he'd been handed a real life actual drama. No wonder his dark eyes gleamed. To his credit, he didn't leap up and punch his fist in the air – not that the low beams of the room would have allowed it – he simply nodded.

'Good point. We can have a look if you like – as soon as I've given the copy of the footage to the police. And maybe we could have a coffee and a bite to eat while we do it?' He looked around the bedroom, perhaps thinking of it as a suitable venue for their investigation, but something he saw in Amy's eye prevented him from making the suggestion. 'I'll bring the laptop down to the bar and get set up, while you go and see what treats the lovely Meriel might have left in the fridge.'

Amy went back down to the kitchen, while Ben quickly gathered together his gear. At least her suggestion had wiped the lopsided grin off his face.

CHAPTER FIVE

Greta sighed as she put the final tick against Cherry's maths homework and added the sheet to the pile on the right of the desk. This was a time of day Greta usually liked. Alice – Dr Alice Kennedy – was conducting her Wednesday evening surgery; the shoulder of local lamb was roasting, with a selection of Moroccan-spiced vegetables softening under it, and sending delectable vapours upstairs; a particularly flavoursome Cabernet Sauvignon was breathing; and the setting sun was driving a magnificent, red-gold track across the dark sea.

Marking Year Nine's maths should have been a reassuring task. Here in these dog-eared books everything was either right or wrong. Nearly right, as she always told her pupils at the start of the year, was wrong. But tonight the familiar satisfaction just wouldn't come. Too many uncomfortable ideas were swilling about Greta's mind.

The Admiral was dead. You couldn't forget that if you had any sort of human kindness in you. And Greta had quite a bit. He'd turned into a buffoon in the last few years, but there had never been any malice in him; and in the old days he'd been generous and funny, as well as reasonably good-looking. Now he was dead.

In the village they were all saying the Admiral had done it himself because of the pub's debts, but that was bonkers. In spite of the buffoonery, Fitz had never lost his essential decency, and no one who cared about other people would commit suicide without leaving a note. No way, as the girls would say. And so far the police hadn't revealed whether there had been a note or not.

You'd have to be incredibly angry to kill yourself in a way that would land unjust suspicion on everyone you'd left behind. You'd have to be incredibly unhappy, too. Greta gazed at the heavenly view outside the small attic window of her study and couldn't really bear the thought that Fitz's bluff public manner might have hidden dreadful suffering.

Don't think about it now, she told herself. It won't do you any good. And you've got to finish the marking before supper or you'll never be able to relax. And that wouldn't be fair on Alice, not when she's dealing with so many patients on the brink. She needs you calm and supportive just now.

Greta reached for the next worksheet and shuddered at the name written on it. Calm and supportive were not likely characteristics in anyone who'd become one of Tracy Crofts' victims. Even so, Greta made herself pay proper attention to Tracy's proof of Pythagoras' theorem. However irritating the child was, her work deserved to be taken seriously. It wasn't bad. Tracy had a brain, which made her shenanigans even more irritating. And dangerous.

In normal circumstances, Greta wouldn't have wasted a second's anxiety on Tracy's idiotic threat. After all, Greta and Alice had been a fixture in Crabwell for the past seven years, most people knew they were a couple, and no one bothered about them. As Fitz himself had once said, they didn't frighten the horses. Besides which, Alice was the best GP for miles around, and Greta had earned a great reputation for getting her girls through GCSE maths and on to higher things. There was no one else around here who'd bother to run the local Girl Guides either, and someone had to do something to keep the girls occupied and thinking of something other than...

She dropped Tracy's work on the desk and covered her face with both hands, rubbing the palms up and down her cheeks. The gesture did nothing for her headache, or the sore patch inside her cheek, where her grinding teeth so often caught the soft flesh.

Someone needed to save Tracy from herself, and her feckless parents weren't likely to do it, so Greta had tried. She'd talked to Tracy in a quiet moment on the last camping trip, but the attempt had failed.

Greta understood the difficulty without any trouble at all. Tracy was being driven to a quite unusual degree by her teenage hormones, or evolution, the selfish gene, or whatever you wanted to call it. All her instincts were telling her to polish up her charms and display them as clearly as she could until a suitable sperm donor picked her as his chosen receptacle. She had already got a reputation around Crabwell for being at it like a rabbit. But Tracy wasn't a rabbit, or a praying mantis, or even a fur seal. She was a human being with seventy or eighty more years of life to come. If those years were to be remotely happy, she was going to have to learn to know herself, find fulfilling work of her own, and only then choose the mate with whom she could reproduce her genes.

All Greta's recommendations of keeping her options open, getting good enough results to gain access to a good university and so have the chance of an interesting career made Tracy laugh like the hyena she wasn't. Greta could almost see the thought bubbles coming out of Tracy's head about poor old bags and disappointed lesbians. She offered Tracy her copy of *Gaudy Night*, hoping that Dorothy L. Sayers's demonstration of the importance of doing your own work and not confining yourself to life as someone else's helpmeet might do the trick.

She herself had found such succour in Sayers's good sense when she'd been faced with an awful decision years and years ago that she couldn't believe anyone would reject it. But that attempt had been a failure too. And it was after Tracy had spurned the novel that she'd made her silly threat. Silly but horrible.

'If you tell anyone about me,' she had said, 'I'll tell them all that you're just jealous because I wouldn't let *you* touch me.'

No one in Crabwell would pay any attention. But if the sleazy man from the telly encouraged Tracy to say it on camera there could be real trouble. These days no one would – or should – ignore any suggestion of paedophilia, and the fact that there was no evidence could make everything worse. The police would have to be involved, and, as far as Greta could see from the various stories that had recently emerged in the news, they'd publicise her name and the accusation in the hope that other victims would come forward. She could be on police bail for years until they realised that there were no victims at all, and never had been, and that they'd been manipulated by a naughty little trollop, who needed to distract attention from her own carryings-on.

Alice would hate it. Come to that, Greta would hate it too. And it could ruin their reputations and the careers to which they'd devoted everything.

But that didn't change the one crucial fact: someone had to rescue Tracy before she let her instincts dump her in a dead-end under-age relationship, perhaps with a baby, and no chance of using her brains or creativity, or anything else. And what future would that baby have?

'Stop it!' Greta shouted at herself, just as the front-door bell rang. She'd be worrying about that baby's baby and the one after that if she didn't get control of her imagination.

She looked down at her watch. It couldn't be Alice, having lost her key. Evening surgery still had another half-hour to run, even if it didn't over-run, which it usually did. Crabwell's inhabitants weren't great droppers-in, thank goodness, so someone must need something.

Greta pushed herself up out of the chair and ran down

the narrow stairs, revelling in the scent of the roasting lamb. Good food and drink couldn't change the awfulness of life, but they could give you comfort on the way.

Hoping the smile she'd manufactured would look welcoming and helpful, she opened the door.

'Oh,' she said, letting the smile go as she saw Amy Walpole and the egregious Ben Milne on her doorstep. Greta's dark, almost black eyes offered them no encouragement.

'Can we come in?' Amy said, trying to be charming. 'Ben and I need to ask you something.'

Greta allowed herself to look at her watch again. 'I don't want to be unwelcoming, but I haven't much time. I'm doing some marking.'

'It won't take long.'

'OK.' Greta flattened herself against the door and allowed them to walk past her. Amy headed straight for the living room, where the fire was crackling.

'Come on, Ben. You must see Greta's paintings. She and Alice have been collecting for years. They're amazing.'

'I must say something to Mr Milne straight away.' Greta stood in the doorway, feeling sure that Ben was about to sneer at her cherished artworks.

'Yeah?' he said, stuffing his hands in his pockets, to make his jeans even tighter.

'I will not take any part in the film you are making.'

He laughed, as though the very idea was ludicrous. She was tempted to tell him why: that in her view reality television was designed to make the stupid and malicious happy by allowing them to laugh at the even greater stupidity of the fools who agreed to be paraded on their screens.

'That's not why we're here, Greta,' Amy said quickly. She wasn't a bad woman, her unwilling hostess observed, just not particularly clever or particularly interesting. 'We're in such a state about poor Fitz. I know we won't any of us know anything for sure until the inquest...'

'If then,' Greta said, giving up the attempt to embarrass them into leaving the house by waiting at the door. She sank into her favourite armchair and felt the cushions rising up around her.

'And so you see, we were wondering what you saw when you were with your Girl Guides on the shore last night. I mean, it must have happened while you were there. Practically.'

'It couldn't have.' Greta had spent so long fretting over how and why Fitz had come to die that she was sure of that much. 'We were alone on the beach. We struck camp at eight o'clock, packed up all the stuff except for the three tents, and left.'

'Why did you leave the tents?'

'Too heavy for the girls to carry. One of the fathers has a pick-up truck. He was going to fetch them this morning.'

'And you say you all left at about eight?' asked Amy.

'Yes. And, according to everything I've heard, Fitz was buying drinks for everyone in the pub by then.'

'How do you know that?' Ben's voice had a nasty suspicious tone to it. Greta breathed carefully to control her irritation.

'Because my partner, Doctor Alice Kennedy, was having

75

a drink there. It's our custom to support the pub when one or other of us has a solo engagement elsewhere. Alice goes when I'm with the Guides. I go when she's at a conference – or anything like that. She filled me in on all the local gossip when she got back a little after nine o'clock.'

'And what about the Guides?' Amy asked. 'Were there any stragglers, who could've seen something?'

Tracy's threat was so vivid in Greta's mind that she might have believed the other two could read it. But she was a rational mathematician, and she knew that wasn't possible. Even so, she didn't want to raise any suspicions by mentioning Tracy's name.

'Everyone left together,' she lied.

All the darkness in her mind lifted as she heard the engine of Alice's beloved vintage MG outside the house. Everything would be all right now. These unwanted visitors would go, and she and Alice would solace themselves with lamb and Cabernet Sauvignon, and all would be right with the world – for tonight at least.

CHAPTER SIX

'You started filling up about one o'clock, right?' They had just returned from their encounter with Greta – the pub was, temporarily at least, closed for business by the police – and it was the first opportunity Amy and Ben had had to look at what had been filmed on the Monday. At a table in the corner of the bar, hunched over his laptop, Ben was fast-forwarding through Stan's footage of the Admiral's last day alive, pausing occasionally to check the timings. He *is* attractive, Amy thought wistfully – but then, men often are at their most appealing when they're absorbed in something. If only he didn't fancy himself *quite* so much… But it didn't matter who he fancied, because she wasn't interested, was she?

Peering over his shoulder at the blur of speeded-up images, she caught glimpses, whenever Ben slowed down, of desolate stretches of beach, the scrubby village green with its single, wind-blasted tree, the grim row of deserted shops, a lone cottage, mud-splashed and crouched under sodden thatch, and distant container ships on the grey sea. 'You've made it look like one of those post-apocalyptic things. Like there's been a… I don't know, a nuclear winter or something.'

'What did you expect?' Ben sounded irritable. 'It's March and the weather's crap. It's hardly going to look like a tourist brochure, is it?'

'No, but did you have to make it quite so dreary and miserable? There isn't a soul about, and—'

'There will be in a second. Look at that.'

Amy looked. On the screen, the bar of the Admiral Byng was heaving with people, and she caught a glimpse of herself, head bent, pulling a pint. 'If I pause it, can you see how many you recognise?'

Pulling up a chair, Amy said, 'OK. Left to right: that's the guy who has the local newsagent's – Sam, don't know his other name – but I'm fairly sure he just stayed at the bar. I've seen that lot before.' She pointed at a gaggle of ruddy-faced pensioners. 'I think they live somewhere around here – not Crabwell village, but not far away. They don't come in much, so I suppose they must have heard about you. They had a couple of bottles of Pinot Noir from Burgundy. It's thirty-six quid a pop – first time I've ever sold more than a glass.'

'They do look pretty well-heeled,' said Ben. 'All that mail-order cashmere. That's what a final salary pension does for you.'

'Don't! The way I'm going, I'll be working till I drop. I'll be the barmaid equivalent of Miss Havisham, stuck to the pumps by cobwebs, and surrounded by bowls of mildewed peanuts.' Why was she telling him that? Shut *up*, Amy, she told herself. Don't give him ammunition.

Seeing Ben's grin, she braced herself for a clever riposte, but he contented himself with looking pointedly up at the ceiling. The fishing nets, lobster pots, and other bits of nautical tat decorating the wooden beams were a dust trap, all right, but Fitz had always been adamant that nothing must be changed. It was just a pity she'd not had time to have a proper go at cleaning it all before the film crew arrived. Before she could explain any of this – or even decide whether she wanted to explain any of it – Ben nodded at the screen and said, in a neutral tone, 'What about the Boden twins over there?'

'Second homers,' said Amy, relieved. 'Two glasses of Merlot. We get the ones who can't afford places like Southwold. Last time those two were in here, she spent ten minutes moaning to me about how there wasn't a Pilates class in Crabwell. They're not usually here in the week – not at this time of year, anyway, so that's the attraction of you and your camera again – but neither of them went upstairs. *He* did, though.' Amy pointed at a shabby, balding blazered figure hunched over the bar. 'Bob Christie. Edits the local rag.'

'This place has a *newspaper*?' Ben looked incredulous.

'Newspaper's putting it a bit strongly – six or eight pages of not a lot, and I doubt we'll have it much longer.'

'No wonder the poor sod looks miserable. Boozer, is he?'

'He enjoys a tipple, yes,' said Amy, repressively. 'Gordon's, mostly. When he'd had a couple of those, he went up to see Fitz. I think he was up there for about half an hour, perhaps a bit more.'

'So that brings us up to, say, two o'clock... Let's see what happens then.'

They spotted Bob Christie coming down the stairs at ten past two, looking, Amy thought, as if he might have had his glass refilled a few times from Fitz's private supply. He didn't return to the bar, but made his way, slightly unsteadily, towards the exit.

Ben fast-forwarded, with stops and starts, through the next twenty minutes of film, until they spotted someone else going up the stairs to the Admiral's office: a short, plump, figure wrapped in a puffa jacket with a hood, who moved furtively as if he was deliberately trying to avoid identification.

'Any idea?'

Amy shook her head. 'I'm pretty sure I didn't serve him, and he scuttled up there pretty sharpish, didn't he?'

'Like a rat up a drainpipe. Hoping no one'd notice, do you think?'

'Certainly looked like it. Let's see him again.'

Ben ran the few seconds of film several times, but Amy was none the wiser. They fast-forwarded a bit more, until, twenty minutes later, the man in the puffa jacket descended as rapidly as he'd gone up, his face still averted from the camera. The speed with which he moved suggested he might be a young man. He made his way through the throng and – they assumed – out of the pub.

'So,' Ben took a notebook out of his laptop case, 'Bob Christie, editor of the... what's the paper called?'

'*The Crabwell Clarion.*'

'Bloody hell. I really didn't think any local papers like that still existed.' Ben made a note. 'Followed by an unknown chubby rat-up-a-drainpipe male – let's call him Rat Man for the time being – who went up at approximately two thirty and left at...' he peered at the screen, 'two fifty-four. Let's see who's next.' They watched the next twenty minutes, during which plenty more people came in, the majority of whom were unknown to Amy, but no one went upstairs. Then, with the timer showing 15.24, Amy pointed out a willowy forty-something ash blonde in jeans and a fleece. 'The Reverend Victoria Whitechurch, our vicar.'

'Oh yes, I met her. Doesn't look very clerical, does she?'

'Well, perhaps the clergy have dress-down Monday or something. Anyway, she definitely went up to see Fitz.'

They watched until they saw her go upstairs, and Ben paused the film. 'Did she have a drink?'

'St Clements.'

'What's that?'

'Orange juice and lemonade. Like the nursery rhyme.'

'What? Oh, yeah, course. Do you remember what everyone drinks?'

'Pretty much. Hardly surprising, given what I do. You had a double Glenlivet and a Merlot.'

'So I did. But why would the vicar go up there? Was Fitz religious?'

'Not as far as I know. I certainly don't remember him

going to church, or even mentioning it, but – as I've already told you – I didn't know much about him, and I'm not sure that anyone else did, either.'

'You must know *something*. Come on, Amy…'

'I don't. And stop doing that melting brown eyes thing.'

'What melting brown eyes thing?' Ben did it some more.

'You know perfectly well what. And I really don't know any more than I've said.'

'Let's go back to Fitz and the suicide note. Suppose he did write it…?'

'I've told you exactly why there's no way he could have—'

Ben raised a hand to silence her. 'I said "Suppose…" Let's just play with the scenario. What reasons might Fitz have had to top himself?'

'I told you, he would never—'

'Play Devil's Advocate for a moment. What motive could he possibly have had to end it all?'

'The business wasn't doing well,' Amy replied grudgingly, 'but I don't know the details – about that, or about him. It was all the act – the booming voice, the tall tales, you know… He didn't let anyone get near enough to see what was behind it.'

'The bigger the front, the bigger the back.'

'What do you mean?'

'Something my grandma used to say. You know, a nice big facade, such as being a…' Ben flexed the index and middle fingers of both hands in air quotes, '*character*, to hide the stuff that you don't want to acknowledge yourself, or let other people see.'

'I suppose. But,' Amy added, feeling protective, 'he was always good to me.'

Ben sighed and turned back to the screen. 'All right. What about her with the gilet, next to the vicar?'

'No idea. I've never seen the man with her before, either. Or them,' Amy pointed to the group of what looked like students behind the cluster at the bar.

'Probably thought it would be a laugh, getting on TV. Not likely to know Fitz, are they?'

'Doubt it. They were all drinking halves, and one or two of them went outside – for a smoke, I should think – but I'm positive none of them went upstairs.'

'OK. So, the Rev Whatsit—'

'Whitechurch.'

'Whitechurch comes in at twenty-four minutes past three, goes upstairs at three-thirty and leaves at...' Ben fast-forwarded again, until they saw the vicar descend the stairs, looking, Amy thought, a lot less sanguine than when she'd come in '... three minutes to four. Shall we go on a bit?'

After stop-starting through another ten minutes of film, Ben hit the pause button and jabbed his pen in the direction of a lugubrious-looking individual in a dark suit who was standing at the bar. 'Who's that bloke? The local undertaker?'

Amy shook her head. 'We haven't got one – at least, not actually in the village. Have to go to Lowestoft or Southwold for that. I don't recall ever seeing that man in the dark suit before, but he must have been there a while, because I remember him talking to those second-homers – the ones you called the Boden twins. He had a sparkling mineral water. But I don't remember seeing him go upstairs.'

They watched a bit more, and, after five minutes, he did go upstairs. 'Seems official,' said Ben. 'That suit, and he's carrying a briefcase, look. Do you think he could be a rep from the brewery?'

'No, because I'd have known about anything like that.'

After fifteen minutes, during which a party of hearty, rosy-cheeked types, several of whom Amy identified as being stalwarts of the local branch of Young Farmers – 'God, it's *The Archers* now,' was Ben's comment – piled into the bar, the man in the suit came downstairs again, and left.

'Four twenty-six.' Ben made a note.

They watched some more, but no one else went up before five o'clock, which was when Stan the cameraman had taken his statutory three-hour break, and the customers had begun to leave.

'I think we've earned a drink, haven't we?' said Ben, glancing at the locked-down bar. 'On me, of course.'

'Of course.' Amy got up and fished her keys out of her handbag. 'What would you like?'

'Ooh... a nice sexy red, I think, don't you?'

Ben picked up his glass of Argentinian Malbec and stared at it intently. For a moment, Amy thought he was going to go through one of those annoying sniff-and-slurp tasting routines with a lot of jocular blather about body and being taken from its mother too young and needing to settle down, but instead he took a hearty swig and said, 'Jolly good. Let's get on with it, shall we?'

What they were watching on the screen was fairly quiet during the first twenty minutes after Stan's return at 8 p.m., but then things began to gee up a bit, with a party gathering around Fitz, who was now seated at the end of the bar. 'He wasn't downstairs all the time, though,' said Amy. 'I know, because at one point I looked around for him, and he'd gone.'

'Are you sure? I thought you told me he'd said his plan was to get roaring drunk. Perhaps he'd just nipped off to the loo or something.'

'Possibly – they're on the ground floor, and I didn't actually *see* him go upstairs,' Amy conceded. 'I just thought he might have.'

'Fair enough. Let's fast-forward a bit, shall we?'

At 8.45 p.m., Fitz could still be seen at the end of the bar, now partially obscured by a group of Viking re-enactors, still in their tunics and helmets. Several had axes tucked in their belts, and one held a large spear, the tip of which was perilously close to the fishing net swagged across the top of the bar. 'I remember them all right,' said Amy. 'Never seen them before, though. I suppose they'd heard about the programme, unless they were mustering somewhere—'

'That's Scouts.'

'Well, whatever it is Vikings do.'

'Rape and pillage, I think.'

'Well, they were raping and pillaging,' Amy avoided Ben's eyes, 'but they gave up because it was too cold. They brought their own tankards,' she added. 'Leather and horn things. They wanted mead, but we don't stock it, so they had to settle for the Old Baggywrinkle instead.'

'What the hell is that?'

'The local cider. It's a nautical term, apparently – something to do with covering up cables to stop them chafing.'

'Well, it sounds disgusting.'

'Not disgusting, exactly, but certainly an acquired taste.'

'This, on the other hand, is delicious.' Ben took another swig of his Malbec. 'We interviewed a couple of the Vikings. Didn't get much sense, but they looked good. Oh, look – there's that old girl who kept rabbiting on about being an extra talking to them. Perhaps they wanted to be in her film, as well.'

'I think Vikings are a bit thin on the ground in *Far From the Madding Crowd*.'

'Oh, was that what it was? Never mind. Do you know that woman?' He indicated a blazered woman with a glass of white wine.

'Alice Kennedy. *Dr* Alice Kennedy. She's the local GP. Sometimes drops in after surgery for a Chardonnay. I'm pretty sure she didn't go upstairs to the Bridge.'

'Who's he?' Ben pointed at a stout man with a battered Barbour jacket and a cocker spaniel.

'That's Treacle.'

'Really? He doesn't look the type.'

'The dog, idiot. I think the man's name is Simon.'

'I don't remember him.'

'He's not the type to want to be on TV. He's a regular – comes in and sits in a corner by himself for an hour, nursing a pint, then goes off home. The dog's a bit of a menace, though – lifts its leg if he doesn't keep an eye on it – look, there it goes.' They watched as Stan's camera dipped to the floor, and, through a thicket of bodies, saw Treacle directing a sly jet at an immaculate pinstriped trouser leg. The owner of the pinstripes – which ended in a pair of smart black shoes – stepped back sharply, colliding with one of the Vikings, but Stan's camera lens was still trained on the floor, so they couldn't see his face.

'Huh,' said Amy. 'I suppose you'll keep that in – for your precious programme, won't you? Nothing like a dog peeing to raise the tone, is there?'

'The viewing public will love it,' said Ben smugly. 'Do you know who he was – the one who got peed on?'

She shook her head. 'I was vaguely aware of someone in a pinstriped suit. I didn't really take in his face.'

'Nor me. Though I do recall someone in pinstripes who looked vaguely familiar.' The skin around Ben's brown eyes wrinkled with the effort of recollection. 'Someone I might have seen on television, some political programme possibly…' But the name wouldn't come. 'We'd better check this footage with some of the regulars. They may recognise him.'

'They'll be clever if they can do that from a shot of a trouser leg being peed on.'

'Some of them may have known who he was.'

'Maybe,' said Amy dubiously. 'All I know is that he had a large glass of this Malbec.'

'A man of discrimination. So... if Fitz did go back upstairs at some point, perhaps he went up for a meeting...?'

'With Mr Pinstripe?'

'It's possible. Let's see if we can spot him.'

They watched more, but most of it was Ben's vox pops, so the camera wasn't pointing at the stairs, and the pinstriped man seemed to have disappeared. When Stan panned back to the bar, there was the Admiral again, sitting in his customary seat and regaling his audience. 'He's about to tell that story,' said Ben. 'About the treasure map. Anything in it, do you suppose?'

'I shouldn't think so.'

'When I asked you if he'd really been a sailor, you didn't answer.'

'That's because I honestly don't know. He was certainly keen on the sea – you've only got to look around here to see that – and I suppose he could have been in the Merchant Navy or something, but...' Amy shrugged.

'Oops,' said Ben, as Stan's camera, clearly knocked off target, turned its gaze on some chairs and a pool of spilled beer. 'You did that deliberately, didn't you? I saw.'

'I didn't want you making a fool of old Fitz,' said Amy. 'Especially when he'd had a few.' They watched as Stan pointed his lens once again at the seated figure of the Admiral, who, making to lean his elbow on the bar, missed and slopped Laphroaig across his corduroy trousers. Behind him, Amy could see herself, harassed and sweaty, shoving dirty glasses into the washer.

'Ten to ten,' said Ben, making a note. 'So, by my

calculations, the Admiral could have gone upstairs for another meeting – possibly with Mr Pinstripe – at any time between nine fifteen and nine forty, which was when we picked him up at the bar again, telling his rollicking seaman's yarn.'

'I think it was about then that Meriel told me she'd run out of food,' said Amy.

'Meriel's the one who wants to be TV's next culinary sex-bomb, right?'

'That's the one. She's all right, really,' Amy added, defensively, forgetting how cross she'd been with the cook. 'And it was quite soon after that that your *friend* from university arrived. Ianthe Berkeley.'

'There's no footage of her actual arrival. Stan must have had his camera focussed somewhere else.'

'I'm sure she managed to get on film later in the evening. No shrinking violet, that one.'

'You speak as though you've met her before.'

'She's stayed here before. On her honeymoon, I believe, although I had the impression it wasn't exactly a love-fest. *He* spent the whole time either watching football or talking about it, and *she* made a beeline for pretty much any man who crossed the threshold, up to and including Simon.'

'Simon with Treacle? She must have been desperate.'

'She might have got somewhere with Treacle. If any dog is over-sexed, that one is – if he's not pissing on people's legs, he's humping them.'

Ben grinned. 'Ooh, *mee-ow*.'

'Yes, well… Anyway.' Amy took a drink of her Malbec,

which really was very nice. 'She had a pint of Old Baggywrinkle, and I managed to persuade Ted the odd-job man to make her an omelette, and she was talking to Fitz, and to you...'

'Mm.' At least, Amy thought, Ben had the decency to look abashed. 'She was going on about some book or other.'

'Yes, she left it on the bar. She didn't stay long after that, though. I'd sent Ted up to the room with her bag, so I assumed she'd gone to bed.' Amy raised an eyebrow at Ben.

'If she did,' he said, firmly, 'it was on her own, and it stayed that way.'

'None of my business,' said Amy, dismissively. 'You don't think she had a meeting upstairs with Fitz, do you?'

They watched some more of Stan's film – at 10.55, when Amy was calling time and people were straggling out of the bar, they saw that Fitz's stool was unoccupied, and they couldn't see Ianthe, either, but as Stan's camera wasn't pointed at the staircase, they couldn't see whether or not the pair of them had gone up to the Bridge.

'That's it, then,' said Ben, as the screen went black. 'So, we've got Bob Christie from the *Clarion*, then Rat Man, then the vicar, then the chap who looked like an undertaker, and then, in the evening, possibly the pinstripe man and Ianthe Whatshername.' He leaned back, stretching his arms above his head, then looked at his watch. 'Almost seven o'clock. I'm starving. I don't suppose your sex-goddess left anything stashed away in the freezer, did she?'

'She might. I haven't looked.'

Ben picked up a bar menu that was lying on the next table. 'Looks OK. What the hell are duck fingers? Ducks don't have fingers.'

'Neither do fish.'

'Fair point. Why don't you go and see if you can find something, anyway? Failing that, we can always make do with olives and crisps. Then we'll have another glass of that lovely Malbec, and work out how to proceed.'

He did the melting brown eyes thing again, and, utterly failing to think of any response that was remotely challenging to his easy assumption that he was a) irresistible and b) in charge of things, Amy got up from the table and did as she was told.

CHAPTER SEVEN

The Reverend Victoria Whitechurch parked her old Escort next to Crabwell Vicarage and scooted inside as quickly as she could. All that Thursday there had been a raw wind blowing from the sea, and she was in a hurry in any case: her hospital visits had taken longer than she'd expected. If she was quick about it, she would just be able to manage a cup of tea before it was time to go across to the church to say Evening Prayer.

She paused in the hallway only long enough to drape her fleece jacket over the newel post at the foot of the stairs. A moment later she was in the kitchen, switching on the kettle, then warming her icy hands on the radiator before opening a tin of cat food, scooping it into Maggie's dish, and plonking it on the floor in the appointed place. 'Maggie!' she called. Maggie – short for Magnificat – stalked in and began nibbling daintily, ignoring her mistress.

There had been a time, a few years back and in her last parish, when Victoria Whitechurch had borne more than a passing resemblance to a fictional woman vicar well known on television, dark of hair and rotund of body. Since then, though, she had lost a fair bit of weight, grown her hair out, and lightened it to a becoming ash blonde. Sometimes when she looked in the mirror she scarcely recognised herself. The comforting thought was that other people from her past might not recognise her either.

The kettle came to a boil. Victoria bunged a teabag into her favourite mug, poured in the water, stirred it a few times, then fished the bag out and dropped it in the bin. A splash of milk from the jug in the fridge would cool the tea down enough to drink quickly. After the first scalding sip, she moved around the kitchen, drawing the curtains against the chill that struck through the glass, and the draught sneaking in around the ill-fitting window casements. There would still be an hour or so of what passed as daylight on this murky March afternoon, but it was more important to retain what little heat the room possessed.

In Victoria's last parish she'd had a snug modern vicarage, purpose-built at the bottom of the garden of the Old Vicarage before that desirable Georgian residence had been flogged off to an aspirational couple from London. What her former dwelling had lacked in atmosphere, it more than made up for in comfort. Now she had atmosphere in spades, and more rooms than she knew what to do with – or could afford to heat. Unfortunately, selling Crabwell Vicarage wasn't a viable option: years of neglect by the diocese meant that it was quite literally mouldering away in the damp sea air. And aspirational Londoners weren't exactly queueing up to move to Crabwell, for that matter. Maybe they would be, once this reality programme about the Admiral Byng was broadcast...

Victoria glanced at her answering machine and saw that it was flashing. With a sigh she put the tea mug on the counter and reached for the phone.

There was just one message.

'Hello, Vicar, this is Amy Walpole. From the Admiral Byng, you know.' The voice hesitated. 'I'd really like to see you for a few minutes. The sooner, the better. If you could ring me...'

Victoria grabbed a pen and scribbled down the number.

The church was even colder and danker than the next-door vicarage. Victoria shivered as she tugged the heavy oak door open just far enough to squeeze in while keeping out the draught from the chill sea breeze. She switched on the lights at the back, and moved through the nave to the chancel, where she slipped into her stall and dropped to her knees on the mouldy hassock.

'Dear Lord, forgive me,' she whispered, before reaching for the well-thumbed prayer book and turning to the section for Evening Prayer. Although no one would be joining her – no one ever did – Victoria never failed in her duty to say the daily offices, here in the church she loved.

There was no logical reason why Victoria should love this particular church so much. Both of the other churches under her care were far more distinguished: Sutton Magna had magnificent stained glass, while West Underwell boasted one of the finest medieval fonts in East Anglia. No, St Mary's Crabwell was small and rather ordinary, with cramped Victorian pews and a leaky roof. Its chief treasure was the wooden medieval painted rood screen, badly damaged during the Reformation. The figures of saints on the panels on either side of the screen had evidently offended the reformers, who had gouged their eyes out and scribbled over their faces in an act of deliberate vandalism. Victoria suspected that her special love for that screen was because of, rather than in spite of, its literal defacement.

Now she was in danger of losing the screen, or the church, or both.

Only last week the bad news had come, in the form of the archdeacon's official visitation.

'St Mary's Crabwell just isn't viable,' the archdeacon had pronounced. 'Not in its current condition, or its financial state.'

The leaky roof was no longer patchable: it would require a complete re-roofing job. The lead had been nicked a few years ago – hence the leaks – and replacing that alone would cost a fortune. Congregational numbers were at an all-time low. They hadn't even come close to meeting the cost of their assessed parish share last year.

Victoria had known it was bad, but she hadn't been prepared for this verdict. This death sentence, even.

St Mary's would be made redundant, said the archdeacon.

That would be his recommendation. The diocese might be able to sell it for use as a community centre, a youth club, or perhaps for conversion to two flats. They would naturally sell Crabwell Vicarage as well.

And Victoria? She'd found the courage to ask the question. 'What about me?'

There was plenty to keep her busy at her other two churches, the archdeacon opined. Sutton Magna had flogged off its vicarage years ago, when the three parishes had been amalgamated into one benefice, but the diocese still owned the one at West Underwell. Yes, it needed some work, and it was rather small, but he was sure she would be comfortable there.

The rest of his thinking on the matter hung unspoken between them: she was a single woman. Not a family man, or someone with anyone but herself and her cat to worry about. She would cope. She would have to.

'Is there nothing else we can do?' she'd asked in desperation.

He'd hesitated for just a second, as though unsure whether he should hold out even a scrap of hope.

'Well, we might sell the rood screen,' he said begrudgingly. 'The V&A have expressed some interest in it. They might give us enough to keep the church going for another year or two.'

St Mary's Church without the screen? Without her faceless friends? Unthinkable. And yet, if that was the only way...

Victoria stared at him helplessly, her eyes filling with tears.

The archdeacon smirked.

For the first time in her life, Victoria Whitechurch hated someone enough to wish him dead.

Victoria had always believed that God answered prayers, though she'd come to realise that the answer was not necessarily the one desired, or that it would be delivered in the expected way.

In the case of St Mary's Crabwell and its future, the answer to prayer had come in the form of a rather ordinary-looking young man who arrived on the doorstep of the vicarage just a day after the archdeacon's visitation. He was wearing a cheap, shiny suit without a tie, and carrying a clipboard.

Victoria could see his quick glance at her dog collar.

'Vicar?' he said.

'Yes, that's right.' Inwardly she sighed.

It was one of the hazards of her job: you couldn't just slam the door in someone's face because you didn't like the look of them. Door-to-door salesmen, religious nutters, con artists, people down on their luck and looking for a handout of cash or a cup of coffee – she was obliged to give each of them a fair hearing and help them if it was at all possible. It always surprised her how many of these people found their way to the vicarage.

'I wondered if I might have a word.'

She'd heard that before. But this time the word had surprised her.

He was, he told her, representing a well-known mobile

phone company. They were seeking ways of improving their coverage in remote areas such as Crabwell, which suffered from notoriously bad reception. In other villages, they'd had great success in siting phone masts in church towers. He'd had a look at Crabwell church, and as far as he could determine, it would be an ideal location for a mast. It wouldn't be obtrusive, he assured her – either it could be completely concealed within the tower, or it could be disguised as a flagpole.

And then had come the thunderbolt.

They were willing to pay, he said. Handsomely. A cheque every year. Ten thousand pounds per annum, minimum. Maybe more.

Ten thousand pounds. It was enough to pay the parish share, with change left over.

'I can see that your roof is a bit... in need of attention,' he added tactfully. 'On installation of the mast we would be willing to cover the cost of necessary repairs to the roof, to compensate you for the inconvenience.'

Victoria had felt her eyes welling with tears for the second time in as many days. This time, though, they were tears of gratitude.

Victoria was reciting the third Collect as the west door of the church blew wide open. Only momentarily distracted, she continued to the end of the service and finished with the Grace, then closed the prayer book, crossed herself, and stood to face her visitor.

The woman had closed the door and now stood

with her back to it, hands shoved deep into the pockets of her Barbour jacket. Victoria recognised the tall outline of Amy Walpole, the bar manager at the Admiral Byng.

'Sorry,' said Amy. 'I hope I didn't disturb you.'

'No, it's all right.'

'I got your phone message, and took a chance that you'd be back a bit earlier than you said. When there was no answer at the vicarage, I saw the light in the church, and guessed you might be here.'

She sounded nervous, Victoria thought. 'It's all right,' she repeated. 'Shall we go back to the vicarage? I can put the kettle on and make us a cuppa.'

Amy shook her head. 'The thing is, I need to get back and open the pub for six o'clock. The police have given us permission to reopen today. This won't take long. I just wanted to ask you a couple of questions.'

Now Victoria was intrigued. She knew Amy Walpole by sight; it was a small village, after all, and the Admiral Byng was pretty much at the heart of it. But though the two women were of a similar age, the bar manager was not a churchgoer and had never made any effort to get to know the vicar. Victoria, for her part, didn't believe in forcing church down anyone's throat. She was available if people wanted to talk to her, and was always happy to make time for her parishioners, but she wanted it to be on their terms rather than hers.

'Take a pew,' she said with an ironic gesture and what was meant to be a welcoming smile.

Amy Walpole relaxed visibly and folded her long body into one of the cramped Victorian pews. 'Thanks,' she said.

Victoria slid into the row in front, twisting to face her. 'How can I help you?'

The other woman averted her gaze. 'It's about the Admiral.'

'The pub?' Victoria asked, confused.

'No. I mean Fitz. The Admiral.'

Victoria flinched involuntarily, glad that Amy wasn't looking at her. 'Yes?'

Now Amy raised her head. 'There's something about his death that's... not quite right.'

'But... he killed himself.'

'That's what they say.' Amy's face scrunched up for just a second. She was tempted to divulge her reason for not being convinced by the suicide explanation, but again decided to keep her theory about the printed note to herself. 'But I don't believe it. I *can't* believe it.'

'You mean you don't want to believe it.'

Amy's red hair flew around her in a wild cloud as she shook her head vehemently. 'I knew him,' she stated. 'I worked with him for over three years, for God's sake.' Looking abashed for just a second, she added, 'Excuse my French, Vicar.'

'But I've heard... I mean, the police seem to think—'

'They didn't know him. He just wasn't capable of it. You have to believe me.' Amy folded her arms across her chest and challenged Victoria with a stare.

Victoria took a deep breath, hoping she appeared calmer

than she felt. 'Supposing you're right. What did you want to ask *me*?'

The other woman hesitated for a moment, as if framing her words with care. 'You saw him that day. The day he… died. You came to the pub to see him. In the Bridge. I was just wondering… why? What was it about?'

Victoria's eyes widened, but she held herself still and managed not to betray her agitation by any other movement. How did Amy Walpole know about her meeting with Fitz? She supposed the bar manager had seen her coming or going from the Bridge that afternoon, though she herself had been too upset to register much about who else might have been around the place.

She ran her finger along the top of the pew, buying a few seconds while she decided what to tell Amy Walpole.

Honesty, said a voice inside her head.

She had nothing to hide. She would tell the truth.

'He rang me,' she said. 'He asked me to come and see him.'

'What about?' Amy asked.

'Church… matters.'

Amy looked sceptical. 'Church? Did Fitz go to church?'

'He's… he *was*… one of my churchwardens,' Victoria stated.

The other woman's mouth dropped open; she gasped for air like a landed fish before she was able to get her next words out. 'I had no idea. He never said.'

'Well, no reason why he should mention it, I suppose.' Not so good for his street cred in Crabwell, Victoria surmised – he rather liked cultivating the image of the crusty hard drinker, as opposed to pillar of the church. 'But he was here most Sundays. Quite conscientious in his duties, as well,' she added.

'Well, I never.' It took Amy Walpole a moment to process the information, shaking her head and frowning. The idea of Fitz being a believer was somehow incongruous, but the alternative, that he'd gone to church for social reasons, seemed equally unlikely. Granted, she'd never asked him how he spent his Sunday mornings. She was too busy enjoying her precious weekly lie-in before she had to get to the Admiral Byng in time for the twelve o'clock opening. But being a churchwarden... It was once again forcibly brought home to her how little she had known her boss.

It had started to rain, Victoria noticed in the ensuing silence. Water was streaming down the windows and would be coming through the roof soon.

'OK. So he went to church,' Amy said at last, still sounding doubtful. 'What exactly did he want to talk to you about, that last day?'

Victoria sighed. 'Let me back up a bit.' She swept her hands around, indicating the church. 'It's not in the best of shape, this building. We've all been working hard to keep it going – the churchwardens, the PCC, the congregation, and me.'

As if on cue, a fat drop of rainwater detached itself from a roof beam and splatted on her outstretched hand. Amy recoiled.

'See what I mean? The roof has had it, and if something doesn't happen soon, the church has had it as well. There are so many things...'

Amy looked at her watch.

Victoria could sense that the other woman wasn't following her, was in fact impatient for her to tell her what she wanted to know about that last day so that she could get back to the pub. 'Anyway,' she said quickly, 'last week we pretty much got a death sentence. And then, out of the blue, a ray of hope.' As concisely as she could, she outlined the archdeacon's pronouncements, and the visit from the young man from the mobile phone company.

'After that, I talked to both of the churchwardens. I was so excited – it finally looked like there might be a way out. An answer to a prayer, really.'

Amy flared her nostrils, clearly disbelieving.

'It seemed that way to me, anyway,' Victoria amended. 'And Greta Knox agreed with me – she's the other church-warden. We even opened a bottle of wine to celebrate.'

'Then what happened?' Amy prompted. 'What about Fitz?'

This was the hard part, or at least the beginning of the hard part. Once again Victoria sighed, shifting her eyes to the runnels of water on the windows. It was beginning to get dark. 'Fitz... didn't agree,' she admitted. 'I told him that God had sent us a way to save the church, and he said that was... rubbish.'

'What?' Now she had Amy's full attention.

'He was... old-fashioned,' she said. 'Old school.'

Amy frowned impatiently. 'Yes, I know that.'

'He said it would be making a pact with the Devil, to sign a contract with the mobile phone company. He said that we still don't know whether it's safe to be around those things, that we would be exposing ourselves and our children to harmful rays, and we'd all end up dying of cancer.'

'That seems a bit extreme. But it *does* sound like him. Fitz was never one to be at the forefront of new technology. In fact he hated all of it.'

'I told him that we didn't have a choice, really – that it was the phone mast, or the church would almost certainly be closed. But he wasn't buying it.'

'When was this?' Amy wanted to know. 'This conversation? Was this when you went to see him?'

'No, it was on Sunday, after the morning service. I asked him to stay behind for a few minutes.' For a moment she re-lived her feeling of shock at his unexpected reaction: she'd thought he would be as pleased as she was – as Greta Knox had been – that there was a possible way out of their dilemma. But he'd been vehement in his opposition.

And then, on the Sunday night, she'd had the phone call: 'Come and see me tomorrow afternoon. In the Bridge. Half three.'

Now that it was time to tell Amy Walpole about the meeting, Victoria began to have second thoughts. After all, what business was it of the bar manager's? What did it have to do with her?

'I know he was difficult,' Amy said into the momentary

silence, in a surprisingly conciliatory voice – as if sensing her doubts. 'He could be a right sod, and no mistake. But I did care about him, in a funny way. And he didn't deserve to die like that.'

'No, he didn't.' Victoria went on with renewed resolution. 'Anyway, he rang and asked me to come on Monday. He seemed so cheerful on the phone that I thought he'd changed his mind – that he wanted to tell me he'd realised it was a good thing after all, an answer from God rather than a pact with the Devil.'

'But he didn't change his mind?'

'No.' Victoria closed her eyes, remembering. 'He was surer than ever, he said. He wanted to tell me that he'd done his research. And he now knew how he could put a stop to this nonsense, as he called it. If I was mad enough to think I could go ahead without his approval, that is.'

She *had* thought about it – how he might be circumvented, if he persisted in his opposition. A word from the archdeacon, perhaps? A letter from the bishop?

Then he'd lobbed his bombshell. As churchwarden, he would refuse to sign the necessary papers of agreement for the work to be done. And if somehow he was overridden, he would lodge a formal complaint, and, as was his right, take the matter to Consistory Court. Where he would win, beyond the shadow of a doubt.

And if she didn't like it, she could lump it.

She explained all of this to Amy, whose eyes began to glaze over at the necessary elucidation of ecclesiastical procedures.

'So what you're telling me,' Amy interrupted her, 'is that Fitz called you to the Bridge to tell you that he wouldn't play ball about the phone mast?'

'That's it, in a nutshell.' Victoria unclasped her clenched hands and turned them palm upwards.

'Well, I'm buggered. That's all it was?'

Victoria felt wounded by the dismissive tone. She'd confessed all, she'd been honest. It might not seem like a big deal to Amy Walpole, but Victoria's whole future was at stake.

'OK, then. Thanks for your time.' Amy Walpole was unfolding herself from the pew, checking her watch.

She went to the west door and yanked on the iron ring, then turned back to face Victoria. The vicar certainly seemed to have had a motive to want the Admiral out of the way, but Amy wondered who else might be in the frame. 'Oh, one more thing. Can you think of anyone who might have had a grudge against Fitz? Anyone who had had a row with him? Anyone Fitz ever mentioned that he didn't get on with?'

Victoria wasn't expecting that. The words popped out before she had a chance to think about them. 'Bob Christie,' she said. 'The newspaper editor. Fitz couldn't stand him. I think it might have had something to do with that article in the *Clarion* last year, but I couldn't say for sure.'

'OK, thanks.'

'I hope I've been of some...' Victoria's voice tailed away as Amy slammed the door behind her.

*　　*　　*

She should have locked up the church, turned out the lights, and gone home to her cat and her supper. But there was unfinished business to be taken care of.

Victoria returned to her stall in the chancel and knelt once again on the mouldy hassock. 'Lord, be merciful to me, a sinner,' she whispered.

Yes, she'd been honest with Amy Walpole. She'd told her the truth. Up to a point. At least, everything she'd told her was true.

But was it the whole truth?

No. She hadn't told Amy how she'd felt when she'd heard that Geoffrey Horatio Fitzsimmons was dead.

She had been... relieved.

She had even been glad.

He could no longer stand in the way of saving St Mary's Crabwell.

And, God help her, no matter how hard she prayed or tried to repent of her wickedness, she was still happy that Fitz was dead.

Victoria lifted her eyes to the carved wooden figure on the cross, high above the rood screen. 'Forgive me,' she said. 'I'm so... sorry.'

CHAPTER EIGHT

When Amy got back from St Mary's on the Thursday evening, the Admiral Byng was empty. Clearly the news that the police had given them permission to reopen had yet to filter through the village. However, she did find Ben hanging around the bar, clearly waiting for her. He had the smug smile of someone with good news to impart.

'I've remembered who he is! Mr Pinstripe.'

'Oh,' said Amy, determined not to sound impressed by his cockiness.

'It just came to me. I thought he looked familiar in the bar, but I was busy with the filming and, you know how it is... Anyway, I knew there was a political connection. He's an MP. Willie Sayers. I did some research on him once for a programme that never happened. His constituency includes Crabwell. In fact, he grew up and went to primary school here. Shifty bugger, like most of them. I've put a call through to his office to fix up a meeting.'

Amy was not so churlish as to refuse him a 'Well done.'

'And…' Ben beamed complacently, 'I've also identified the miserable-looking bastard with the dark suit and the briefcase. The one who went up to the Bridge at four ten.'

'Oh? And how did you do that?'

'Showed the footage of him to some of the people who were in the bar at lunchtime.'

'Very sophisticated technique,' said Amy coolly.

'Don't mock,' said Ben with another annoying smile. 'Funny how often the obvious approach can be effective.'

'Thank you for that. So who is he?'

'Local solicitor called Griffiths Bentley. Office right here in Crabwell. He's quite well known around the village, but never uses the Admiral Byng. Teetotaller, I believe.'

'Ah. Hence the mineral water. So presumably he came to see Fitz on a business matter?'

'Well done, Watson. That was my deduction too.'

'Two down, one to go,' said Amy. 'So… did you get anywhere on Rat Man?'

Ben's brow furrowed. 'No, I haven't got anywhere on him. He's so wrapped up in that puffa jacket. Almost like he was deliberately avoiding being identified.'

'Perhaps he was.'

'That would figure.' Ben fixed his brown eyes on her. 'You got any ideas of how we might get a name for him?'

'Just the one.'

'Oh? And what's that?'

'I thought we could see if there were any appointments

109

for Monday in Fitz's desk diary. That is, if we can get into the Bridge.'

'Why shouldn't we be able to?'

'One of the policemen – you know the big hunky one, Constable Chesterton – said they were going to take the Bridge over as an Incident Room.'

'Well, if they are, I don't think they've moved in yet.'

And so it proved. Amy and Ben encountered no problems getting into Fitz's office, no 'Keep Out' notices, no door sealed with police tape, nothing.

She went straight to his desk, picked up the appointments diary, and flicked it open on the page with the ribbon marker still in position.

'Monday,' she read. 'Two thirty p.m.'

'That's when Rat Man came up here.'

'Yes.'

'Is there a name?'

'Of course,' replied Amy, deliberately infuriating.

'Then what is it?' came the testy response.

'Greg Jepson.'

Ben's smartphone was immediately out of his pocket as he started to search for the name. Then he looked at her and offered a grudging 'Well done.'

'It's amazing how often the obvious approach can be effective,' said Amy.

No nightingales were singing in Berkeley Square that Friday morning, but a cold-looking pigeon was picking at an empty

Prêt à Manger sandwich wrapper in front of a Bentley dealership. Ben aimed a kick at it, and then looked up at the bland office building overlooking the grand square. Somewhere in there was Mamba Capital.

It turned out that Gregory Jepson was 'something in the City'. With further digging, it transpired that the firm Jepson ran wasn't even in the City, but rather Mayfair, the home to the bulk of London's hedge funds.

Ben didn't know much about hedge funds, except that the people who ran them had way too much money. His quick online researches into Gregory Jepson demonstrated that that was definitely true of him. Thirty-four and he was supposed to be worth eighty-two million pounds. Eighty-two million! It made Ben sick. With envy.

Yet although he could discover how much Jepson was worth, nowhere could Ben find a visual image of the man. He had heard hedge funds could be secretive about their activities, but he still found something odd about the complete absence of photographic records. Maybe Greg Jepson was always as camera-shy as he had shown himself to be at the Admiral Byng.

Mamba Capital was on the fifth floor. The receptionist was stunning: blonde, late twenties, grey silk blouse that clung in all the right places. The smile that she gave Ben when he introduced himself made his heart skip. And when she stood up and he saw her figure, he knew he had to act. Legs like those didn't often go with a chest like that. Combined with the more-than-friendly smile, and Ben had to strike. He knew he was attractive to many women, and being recognisable from the television made him even more attractive, so it was worth a shot.

'Nearly lunchtime,' he said. 'Can I buy you a drink somewhere around here? After this.' He gave her his best grin: a sideways effort with a hint of danger.

The receptionist glanced at Ben's jeans and denim shirt. Her smile disappeared. 'I'm sorry, I have some filing to do at my desk.'

'Well, if you have important filing…' said Ben, unable to keep the irritation out of his voice. He didn't like being rejected.

'Oh, it's not *important* filing,' said the woman, and led him through a glass door into a trading room where half a dozen men and women were staring at rows of computer screens on their desks. In a small glass corner office with a great view of the square on one side and the trading room on the other, a short man with slicked back dark hair wearing an expensive suit waited for him. An IT geek was fiddling with the huge computer screen on the large black desk.

Ben tried to visualise the suited man skulking up the stairs at the Admiral Byng obscured in a puffa jacket. Yes, it was possible. He held out his hand. 'Mr Jepson? I'm Ben Milne. Thank you for meeting me.'

The man shook it. 'I'm Stephen Torrington from Devonshire Communications. This is Mr Jepson.'

Ben glanced at the IT geek. He was short, had mousy brown curly hair, and unnaturally white teeth. He was staring at his array of split screens, occasionally jabbing with his mouse. He didn't look a day over twenty-five.

At first Ben thought he was having his leg pulled, but the smooth PR guy in the suit seemed deadly earnest.

'Sorry. Mr Jepson?'

Jepson, if that's who he was, ignored him. Ben glanced at Torrington, who nodded ever so slightly, suggesting that they wait. Which they did, for a full minute, until Jepson wiggled his mouse violently, clicked twice, and pushed his chair back from the computer with a flourish.

He turned to Ben, and stared at him. He had dark, intense eyes, almost black. He was wearing black jeans and an orange, un-ironed shirt with a Ralph Lauren polo player on its chest. Probably a knock-off, Ben thought. Could this man really be worth eighty million quid?

On the other hand, his slightly jumpy body language fitted with the unidentified visitor filmed going up to the Admiral's Bridge. Greg Jepson was definitely Rat Man.

'Well?' Jepson said. He pursed his small lips into a disturbing little pucker.

Although he hadn't been asked, Ben sat down in one of the chairs in front of the desk, and Torrington sat at another to the side.

'Thank you for seeing me, Greg,' Ben said, opting for the matey touch.

'I'm very careful to preserve my privacy,' Jepson said. That fitted in with the absence of any visual images of him online. 'If you're planning an exposé on me, don't. And forget trying to film in here.'

'It's something I would like to discuss with you alone,' Ben said.

'And I'd like Stephen to be here,' said Jepson.

Ben didn't want the PR guy hanging around. 'It's to do with the Admiral Byng.'

Jepson stared at Ben. Ben held his gaze. 'Could you leave us, Stephen?' Jepson said.

The smooth PR man looked as if he was going to protest, but then left the office, and stood alone in the trading room, staring out of the window.

'What have you got to do with the Admiral Byng?' Jepson asked.

'Have you heard Geoffrey Fitzsimmons is dead?'

'Suicide, I hear,' said Jepson, his eyes flicking to his screens.

'Maybe,' said Ben. 'I understand you saw him the day he died? Monday.'

Jepson ignored him and turned his chair towards the screens. He swore under his breath. 'Gaston has no balls.' He tapped a message furiously on the keyboard, presumably sending a little missile to the luckless Gaston in Paris or Geneva or wherever. Then he turned back to Ben.

'Why on earth should I tell you who I saw on Monday afternoon?'

'My company is producing a reality television show. We were filming in the Admiral Byng on Monday, the day the Admiral died. Naturally we are interested in his death.'

Jepson's eyes flicked to the screens beside him. 'OK. I get why you want to see me. But why should I tell you anything?'

Ben was ready. 'We have you on film going up to meet the Admiral that day. It would really make our programme if we could show a wealthy hedge-fund manager going to speak to a murder victim the day he died.'

'I'm not that wealthy,' said Jepson.

'Net worth eighty-two million last year?'

For the first time Jepson smiled, a swift rearrangement of those puckered lips. Ben almost missed it. 'It's a bit more than that now,' he said.

'I'm sure,' said Ben, flatly.

'And if I tell you what I was doing, you'll leave me out of the programme?'

'Oh, yes,' said Ben, thinking the opposite. He should be able to manufacture some 'public interest' justification to go back on his word, once he found out a little more about what was going on.

Jepson's eyes flared at him. Pure aggression. He was a little guy, but he reminded Ben of a drunken football hooligan on a Saturday night looking for a fight.

'Do you know why my fund is called Mamba Capital?'

'You liked the song?'

'That's *mambo*. The mamba is not only one of the most venomous snakes in the world, it's also the fastest. I like to strike fast. That's my trading style, that's how I have made all that money.'

'And your point is...'

'My point is that if you put me in your little film, you are finished. I'll finish you. Professionally. No one will want to touch you or your work.'

115

Ben looked at the geek in the fake designer shirt threatening him. How could he be scared of a loser like that? On the other hand, if the loser had that much money and was willing to use it, maybe he should be.

Jepson turned to his screen again, swore, and typed something furiously. As he watched, Ben wondered whether the geek was sleeping with the gorgeous receptionist outside. Surely not; she looked like she had too much taste, even though the guy was loaded. Surely not.

But the thought, once sparked, began to burn.

Ben tried to regain control. 'Well, let's not just threaten each other, shall we? No doubt whatever you were doing at the pub was perfectly harmless. How did you know the Admiral?'

Jepson didn't answer for a few seconds, and then turned to face Ben. 'I was brought up in Crabwell, my mother still lives there. My parents were old friends of the Admiral, I've known him since I was a child. He's always shown an interest in my career. I was seeing my mother for a brief visit, and I thought I would drop in and say hi.'

'I see. So what did you discuss with him?'

'I said "hi".' Jepson's lips puckered.

'Is that all?'

'That's all.'

'Did he seem agitated about anything? Excited?'

'Not particularly,' said Jepson.

'Because he told other people that he was going to get drunk that night. That it was his "Last Hurrah".'

Jepson shook his head.

Just then the door flew open and a young man of about thirty burst in. Like Jepson, he was wearing casual clothes, but unlike Jepson's, they looked like they had cost a lot of money. Ben took in the watch, the carefully trimmed stubble, the expensive haircut, the Italian shoes.

'Greg, the market is still being bid up! We're twenty million under water. We have got to cut our position now!'

The accent was strong and French.

'Did you sell those four million shares, Gaston?'

'Sell four million? Of course not! We need to cover our short, and we need to do it now!'

'Calm down, Gaston,' said Jepson. 'Just calm down. Then sell four million more shares like I told you.'

'This could destroy our performance for the year, Greg!'

'It could, but it won't,' said Jepson. Even Ben was impressed by the geek's authority. 'This stock is way over-valued, and it will go down. All we have to do is be patient. And sell four million more shares.'

The Frenchman, his chest heaving, stared at his boss. He looked tense. Frankly, he looked scared. 'Are you sure, Greg?'

'Am I ever wrong?' said Jepson.

'Sometimes,' said the Frenchman. 'Sometimes.'

'But not this time, eh?'

The Frenchman shrugged. 'OK,' he said. 'I'll sell four million more.' He left the room.

Jepson glanced at his screen and then turned back to Ben. 'You didn't hear any of that,' he said.

'Certainly not,' said Ben, thinking about just how much

damage he could do to the financial markets with the hundred and fifty quid he had taken out of the cash machine that morning. 'Do you have any idea why the Admiral might have killed himself?'

The lips puckered. Jepson gave a tiny shrug.

'Or why anyone else would want to kill him?'

Jepson snorted. 'You must be joking. No one would ever kill anyone in Crabwell. I doubt there has been any major crime since the outbreak of cow-tipping in 2000. Now if you want to know who was behind that, I might be able to help you.'

Ha bloody ha, thought Ben.

'Nothing ever happens in Crabwell, Ben,' Jepson continued. 'That's why I got out of there as soon as I could, and rarely go back.'

'Except on Monday?'

'Except on Monday,' said Jepson.

'I don't understand why a busy guy who hates the place should suddenly decide to return on a working day and say hi to the alcoholic friend of his parents.'

A pucker. A shrug. 'Somehow, I suspect that there is a lot you don't understand, Ben.'

Ben decided to try one last tack. 'OK. There was a whole procession of people who went up to see the Admiral that day. We have the names of some of them, but not all. Did you see anyone come and talk to him?'

Jepson thought a moment and decided to throw Ben a bone. 'Yes. After I left the pub that afternoon I was sitting in my car with my iPhone, checking up on some trades.

And while I was there in the car park I saw Griffiths Bentley going in, carrying a briefcase.'

'Griffiths Bentley?' said Ben, feigning ignorance.

'He is my parents' solicitor. Well, my mother's, since my father died.'

Ben smiled. 'Thank you. Possibly the Admiral's solicitor too?'

'I wouldn't know about that.'

Jepson turned back to his screen, squinted at it, and tapped out a message.

Ben watched, waiting for him to finish, and trying and failing not to think of Jepson sleeping with the receptionist. How could such a loser have so much money? It wasn't right. It wasn't right at all.

'Are you still here?' said Jepson, his eyes not leaving his screen.

Greg Jepson waited a couple of minutes for the TV scumbag to get out of his office. Gaston had sold another two million shares of the ailing pharmaceutical company short, and was working on the last two with the broker Bloomfield Weiss. Although the share price was still ticking up, Jepson was confident. He had a good feeling about this one.

He was a little nervous about Ben's threat to put his visit to the Admiral Byng on TV. Stephen the PR guy had said Ben could be dangerous. Jepson was confident he could find a way to spend money to intimidate him, even if he wasn't quite sure how. Maybe he should talk to Stephen after all. He glanced out into the trading room, but Stephen had left.

The talk of the Admiral's death reminded him he needed

to call his personal banker. He picked up the phone and speed dialled.

'Rupert?… It's Greg Jepson… About that funds transfer I made on Monday afternoon, have you checked whether it went through?… The name of the account was Geoffrey Horatio Fitzsimmons, and the amount was two million pounds, I told you that!… It must make some difference if he's dead… Well, find out and get back to me!'

Jepson slammed down the phone. He stared at the rows of numbers blinking at him, and switched one of the screens to the high-quality colour CCTV feed of Jemima bending over the filing cabinet out in reception. It never failed to soothe him.

Jepson saw her straighten up and turn to the lift doors. The journalist appeared, said something cheery to her, and then swept out of view.

Jepson quickly switched the screen back to equity prices, and hunched his shoulders in intense concentration. A moment later, there was a quick knock on the door. Jepson decided to ignore the journalist.

'Sorry. Forgot my bag. Won't keep you.'

Jepson ignored him, but with his peripheral vision, he saw the journalist bend down and pick up a canvas shoulder bag, which was hidden almost out of sight beside the chair Milne had been sitting in.

'Cheers, Greg,' Milne said, and he was gone.

Outside, in Berkeley Square, Ben sat on a bench and lifted the digital voice recorder out of his open bag. It was a trick he had been taught by an old documentary maker, who had now passed on to the great boozer in the sky. It only worked one time in ten. Usually someone pointed out the bag, or the subsequent conversation was irrelevant. But every now and then when a journalist left an interview having asked some awkward questions, the interviewee decided he wanted to discuss those questions with someone else right away, and it was worth it just for those times.

Ben turned on the machine and listened.

Bingo!

CHAPTER NINE

Amy wasn't at the pub when Ben came in off the lunchtime train, in fact there was no one in the bar other than Meriel, who asked him if he fancied anything on the menu. Backing out of the door as swiftly as he'd come in from the rainy afternoon, Ben assured Meriel he'd eaten on the train, but oh dear, he'd forgotten to post a letter. Ignoring Meriel's plaintive cry that the day's only collection in Crabwell went in the morning, Ben hurried back along the seafront. Amy was the only person he wanted to share this news with, and Stan had pointed out her cottage the other day. It was cold, and wet, she couldn't turn him away if he arrived on her doorstep, could she?

She hadn't, though she hadn't seemed too pleased to see him either. Nevertheless, he'd got himself across the threshold with the promise of a revelation, and when he'd played her the recording Amy sat back in the tired old armchair, suitably impressed.

'Shame I can't whistle.'

'Sorry?' Ben asked. 'Whistle?'

'Two million. It's worth a whistle, at least. No wonder Fitz was so cheery.'

'And now dead.'

'Yes, thanks, I hadn't forgotten.'

Ben kicked himself. He'd rather enjoyed spending the afternoon in this cottage – warmer since she'd banked up the log-burner, wanting to set the scene for his revelation. The wind and rain beating against the windows, a whisky each – Amy had at least been forthcoming there – it was all quite cosy, and he was a fool for forgetting she clearly had a very big soft spot for the old man.

'I'm sorry, that was crass of me. He was your friend.'

'Fitz was kind to me at a time when I very much needed kindness, I arrived here...'

'Go on.'

Amy looked up from her drink and studied Ben for a moment, maybe she could tell him, maybe this was someone she could trust after all, and then she looked down at the recording gear on the battered coffee table sitting between them, and remembered what he did for a living. Puppy dog eyes or no, she wasn't ready to tell that story yet.

There was one thing she was prepared to reveal however. Ben was clearly good at this investigating lark, he'd found a key piece of the story – though neither of them had any idea where the money might fit in – it was only fair she shared her latest thinking too.

'I've been thinking about the note.'

'The suicide note?'

'Yes. The one that Fitz definitely didn't write.'

'You are absolutely certain about that? Because Cole and Chesterton seem pretty convinced that he did write it.'

Amy tutted contemptuously. 'Well, that says everything that needs to be said about the competence of Cole and Chesterton. I've seen a lot of Fitz over the last few years, and I know he didn't know one end of a computer from the other, he couldn't tell a PC from a Mac, refused to get a mobile phone – not that reception's great in the pub anyway. He hates... hated,' she added, correcting herself, 'technology of any sort. He had an old wireless radio.'

'For the shipping forecast?'

'Exactly, and the same landline telephone he's had since the seventies, that's the closest he got to anything from the twentieth century, let alone the twenty-first. The idea that he could suddenly teach himself how to print up a suicide note – and address an envelope – is just nonsensical.'

'All right, I'll buy that. In fact, I had already bought it. You told me before. So what are you telling me now that's new?'

'Well, I'd been thinking... if Fitz didn't write the suicide note, then who did?'

'A reasonable question.'

'And I've decided it couldn't be anyone who knew him very well.'

'Because they'd have known about his aversion to computers?'

'Exactly.' Amy was impressed by how quickly Ben caught on to ideas. He was bright all right. But that still didn't make him trustworthy. She hurried on. 'And the person who planted the note hadn't thought things through, anyway. He or she had just plonked it on the rolled-up cover of the dinghy. It wasn't even damp, though. Nobody would be fool enough to imagine that Fitz had written the note and put it there himself.'

'Unless that "nobody" happened to be DI Cole or DC Chesterton. I get the impression they'd be fools enough to do anything.'

'Yes,' Amy agreed glumly.

'Incidentally,' said Ben, adroitly changing the direction of the conversation, 'I think we should keep doing this.'

'Keep doing what?' asked Amy suspiciously. If Ben thought she would welcome him making a habit of dropping around to her place, then he needed to be quickly disabused of the idea.

A sly smile showed that he had anticipated her thought. With an expression of brown-eyed innocence, he replied, 'Keep telling each other of any advances we make on the investigation. Keep pooling our information.'

The suggestion was not one with which she could disagree. But part of her wondered why he had made it. Was his main concern an altruistic search for the truth about how Fitz had died? Or did he have a different, more personal agenda? With people like Ben Milne, it was always hard to be sure what they were up to.

But for the moment his behaviour was impeccable. 'I

must go,' he said, rising from his seat. 'Thank you for the drink.'

'My pleasure.'

'Yes. Do you have plans for who you're going to talk to next?'

'I thought I should have a word with Bob Christie.'

'Crabwell's very own intrepid boy reporter? Good idea.'

'What about you?'

He looked at his watch. 'Maybe Griffiths Bentley will still be in his office at this time on a Friday afternoon.'

'Good thought.'

Then he took her hand with more warmth than was perhaps strictly necessary. His empathetic brown eyes were working overtime. 'Don't worry, Amy. Between us, we'll find out who killed Fitz... who of course we now know, thanks to Greg Jepson, was on the verge of becoming a very rich man—'

'A very rich man who was murdered. Yes.'

'So how was it for you, sunshine?' Detective Inspector Cole said to DC Chesterton above the crunch of the pebbles as they progressed along Crabwell beach.

'How was what?'

'The post-mortem on the Admiral yesterday.'

'You mean did I enjoy it? Not particularly. But I didn't pass out.'

'That's a relief. I'd be worried if you had. That pathologist dissects whatever is stretched out in front of him. I've lost more DCs that way than I care to remember.'

Black humour goes with the job in CID. Chesterton tried to appear amused.

'Did he come to any useful conclusion?' Cole asked.

'Not while I was there. Various bits and pieces had to be sent to the lab for analysis.'

'The usual story. And the white coats won't be hurried. We could go for a Caribbean cruise before they report back. That's not a bad idea, in fact, researching the Admiral's background. Legitimate travel expenses. I wonder if the chief constable would sanction it. Did he drown? The Admiral, I mean, not the chief constable.'

'Apparently not.'

'Thought so. Bullet through his brains?'

'No.'

'Severed an artery? Swallowed caustic soda? Self-strangulation? Tripped over a rock? Struck by lightning? What's the point of an autopsy if you don't find out the cause of death?'

'If it had been as obvious as that, he'd have said.'

'Did he have any opinion at all?'

'He found some bruising on the top of the head that he said was consistent with a fall.'

'The *top* of the head?'

'He called it the cranium, but that's what he meant.'

'How would anyone get a bump on the top of his head from falling down?'

'By cracking it on the mast.'

Cole pictured this for a moment before nodding and saying, 'Possible.'

'Or one of the thwarts.'

This triggered a longer pause while the detective inspector decided whether to claim he knew about thwarts, he'd grown up with thwarts, he'd seen more thwarts than Chesterton had had hot dinners.

Chesterton finally said, 'The seats that go across the middle. It's a nautical term.'

'You don't have to explain. And that knocked him out?'

'Subdural haemorrhaging was what he called it. Old people are prone to it if they hit their heads.'

'Ties in nicely with what I said from the beginning. He staggers to his boat, high on a lethal cocktail of drink and drugs, crashes into it, bashes his head against the mast, and goodbye sailor.'

'The pathologist didn't venture an opinion.'

'They're cagey buggers. I happen to know he's been on the phone to the coroner.'

Chesterton was impressed. 'Really?'

'Really. The only reason you and I are back on this godforsaken beach is because of an email I found in my inbox this morning. The coroner isn't entirely happy with the suicide explanation, so would we take another look? "Isn't entirely happy." As if it was our job to make him happy. Who wants a happy coroner, laughing and joking all the way through the inquest? He's paid to be serious, not happy.'

'What's he on about? What else could have caused the death?'

'Accident – but then there wouldn't have been a suicide

note. Anyway, we now know the old salt was up shit creek. The pub has been leeching money for months, if not years. Amy Walpole, the manager, hasn't been paid a penny in wages for nearly a month. It's a lost cause, and the captain has to go down with the ship. If this wasn't suicide, you can have my job and welcome to it.' Cole grimaced. 'I'll get back to the coroner pronto and tell him to get a move on. I want the suicide verdict tied up with a bow on top as soon as possible.'

'Is that his boat – the dead man's?' Chesterton was pointing to one of several small craft hauled up on the stretch of beach in front of them. This one had a mast and was mostly covered with a tarpaulin.

'Looks like it to me. What's the name on the side?'

'*The Admiral*, in silver letters.'

'Ridiculous name for a thing that size,' Cole said. 'A proper admiral wouldn't be seen dead in a tub like that. Wouldn't be seen dead – geddit?'

'I heard the first time, sir.'

They went closer. It was, indeed, a pitifully modest vessel for a top-ranking officer, even compared with some of the other boats drawn up nearby.

'Why is the front end facing out to sea?' Chesterton asked.

'Front end? Please! The bow.' Cole paused before adding, 'Nautical term.'

'Shouldn't it be the other way around from when it was last dragged out of the water? All the others are.'

'Don't ask me. I'm no sailor,' said the man who knew

what the front end was called. 'I daresay the tide turned it around. Untie the cover and let's look inside. When I last checked there was a fair amount of water. It may have drained away.'

Chesterton started loosening the ties and unfurling the cover. 'Plenty of water still here. Pity we didn't bring wellies.'

'Neither did the Admiral. Take off your shoes and socks and have a paddle. I want you to examine the bilge.'

'The what?'

'Another nautical term. You've got a lot to learn. There could be a vital clue under the water in the bottom of the boat.'

Chesterton did as he was told, rolled up his trousers and stepped in. 'Bloody freezing.'

'Get your hands in and have a feel around.'

But the constable's attention was elsewhere. 'Don't look now, sir, but isn't that someone filming us from the top of the shingle bank?'

Cole looked directly to where a man with a hand-held camera was pointing the lens straight at them. 'Bloody hell, you're right. Collar him, Chesterton. He's a spy.'

Chesterton was a fit man. He leaped out of the dinghy and started at quite a sprint, but his bare feet and the steep shelf of pebbles slowed him. The spy had seen him coming and hared away in the direction of the Admiral Byng. With such a start, it was no contest.

'We know where to find him,' Chesterton was able to tell Cole when he returned, breathing a little harder.

'Did you get a good look?'

'Never seen him before. It wasn't Ben Milne, the TV guy.'

'Probably Stan the cameraman,' Cole said. 'We'll demand that film and destroy it. I'm not having us exposed to ridicule on the box. It's their favourite game, portraying decent people in undignified situations. We'll continue our forensic examination of the boat. Step inside again and see what you can find.'

'What am I looking for?'

'You don't want to know. Could be his false teeth or a glass eye, or something he threw up.'

A voice interrupted them, female and very close. 'What's he doing?' A girl in her mid-teens had approached them from behind. In a miniskirt and thin sweater, she made quite a provoking spectacle. She wasn't dressed for an east-coast beach in March.

'Never you mind,' Cole said with all the dignity he could muster. 'On your way, young lady. We're busy.'

She showed no intention of moving off. 'Busy doing what?'

If Cole had learned one thing in the police it was not to answer questions like that. Not truthfully, anyhow. You have to think of a cover story. 'He's on two hundred hours' community service cleaning out the boats. Move on, now.'

'Are you his probation officer?'

'Watching his every move, yes. He's the sort of monster your teachers tell you to stay away from at all costs.'

'You made that up,' she said with scorn. 'That was a catch question. I know who you are. You're the policemen who came here on Tuesday, and that's the Admiral's dinghy. He's dead.'

'How do you know that?'

'Miss Knox told me. I'm Tracy, one of her Girl Guides, and she's our leader, and we're trained to observe things. We were camping here on Monday. Some of the young ones are trying for their camper badge. I'm an advanced camper already, got the badge. Each patrol shared a tent, and there was a fire and baked potatoes. It was cool.'

'I bet it was, this time of year.'

'We didn't stay all night. We broke camp quite early, around eight, but I made sure we left no mess.'

'I'm glad to hear it. Now shove off fast, Tracy, or I'll be forced to speak to your Brown Owl.'

She poked out her tongue and moved away with a hip movement she must have perfected some time ago. She was advanced in more skills than camping. Cole wondered what else she'd got a badge for.

While this was going on, Chesterton had been dredging the bottom of the boat with his curled fingers. 'Found something,' he announced.

Cole glanced at the shiny circular object resting on his assistant's damp palm. 'Money?'

'A button. A blazer button, and it's still got some cloth attached to it, as if it was torn off quite violently. If we didn't know he'd committed suicide, I'd say he'd had his blazer grabbed by someone.'

'Caught one of the rowlocks as he fell, more likely. Rowlocks, constable. D'you know what I'm talking about?'

Chesterton said, 'Rollocks.'

Cole's blood pressure rose to danger point. 'I beg your pardon?'

'It's the right way to say the word.'

After some uncomfortable heart-searching the inspector decided his only option was to ignore the insubordination. 'Good find, though. I knew there had to be something, and now we're going to reward ourselves. Put on your shoes and socks and we'll step up to the Admiral Byng and make ourselves known to that cook woman.'

'Meriel Dane?'

'You don't need much encouragement, do you? I saw her bedroom eyes all over you when we were questioning her about her movements on the night of the suicide.'

'Really? That's news to me.'

'This time we won't ask that mean bitch Amy Walpole. We'll go straight to the kitchen – or you will. Tell sexy Meriel you're up for it.'

Chesterton's eyes were the size of the rowlocks. 'She's old enough to be my aunt.'

'And when she asks you "Up for what?" say "Late lunch. Mixed grill with all the trimmings and kindly make that two".'

'Do you really think it'll work?'

It did. For once, Cole was spot on with his analysis, and two policeman-sized late lunches were swiftly served. Meriel brought them to the table herself, having first removed her apron and unfastened the top buttons of her blouse.

'Phew. Extra helpings, constable,' Cole remarked.

Once Meriel had returned to the kitchen, Chesterton took the opportunity to ask what else needed to be done to make the coroner happy.

'Your guess is as good as mine,' Cole said. 'We interviewed almost everyone who spoke to the Admiral on his last night.'

'His "Last Hurrah".'

'Yes – that's the phrase that kept coming up. It was even in his suicide note.'

'The Admiral wasn't interested in politics, was he?'

'What's that got to do with it?'

'*The Last Hurrah* was a book about an elderly politician in his last campaign. It was a film, too. That's where the phrase comes from.'

This smart-arse DC was skating on thin ice. Cole forked up another mushroom and chewed it viciously.

'I only mentioned it because one of the witnesses said she thought the local MP was here that night,' Chesterton added.

'Have you typed all the statements on your laptop yet?'

'I haven't had time. I was at the mortuary yesterday.'

'Make time. With the coroner breathing down our necks we can't drag our feet.'

'We didn't get much from all those witnesses. Did you notice how guarded every one of them was about what the Admiral said when he spoke to them on the Bridge?'

'That's understandable,' Cole said. 'It was personal stuff, *The Long Goodbye*. Or, if you prefer, *Farewell My Lovely*. That's two books, by the way, and two films.'

'Right. I suppose he'd made the decision to do away with himself and wanted to tie up the loose ends, settling any unfinished business and letting them know how much he valued their friendship – if they were all his friends.'

'I'm not sure they were,' Cole said, 'but he may have thought they were. You never know what other people truly think of you.'

'How true,' Chesterton said.

Meriel Dane came from the kitchen again and asked if they wanted extra of anything.

Cole winked at her and said, 'DC Chesterton here might welcome a bowl of cereal. He likes his oats.'

She giggled. 'Me, too – and not just for breakfast.'

Chesterton was quick to put police tape across that route. 'We were meaning to ask if a man with a camera came in a short time before us.'

'He did, yes. That was Stan, Ben's cameraman. He's upstairs now. He isn't staying here, but he reports to Ben each morning, and they plan their day's shooting.'

'We need to have a word with him,' Cole said. 'He's been filming things he shouldn't.'

'Naughty, naughty,' she said. 'In Crabwell? I thought nothing like that ever happened here.'

CHAPTER TEN

It was that same Friday evening that Amy interviewed Bob Christie over a gin and tonic in the snug (nicknamed the 'Mess') of the Admiral Byng. There weren't many customers in the main bar, but she wanted a level of privacy. She had seen Christie often enough in the pub, but could not claim to know him. She couldn't claim to like him that much either. And she certainly had no idea what went on beneath his bluff, gruff exterior.

Christie was by nature a mild man. He had had a good relationship with his mother, and as a child had always been willing to help out at her tea parties. He'd always wanted to write – probably novels about young men's rites of passage – and had been a bit surprised to end up as a journalist. Lacking the natural aggression for such a profession, he had assumed it like a disguise, wearing his gruffness throughout his career, along with the livery of a green-eye shade, braces, and carpet slippers. The meekest of men, Christie had trained himself to bark. His bark was almost as good as his bite, and he enjoyed barking into the phone 'Christie, *Clarion* here', on the spurious grounds that that was how a real newspaperman would have spoken.

At times he convinced himself that he was a real newspaperman. He had assumed the front for so long that it had almost become the reality. At times he genuinely believed that, but for a wretched run of bad luck, he, rather than some jumped-up university-educated smart-arse, should be spinning in the editorial chair of a national daily rather than behind the dilapidated desk of *The Crabwell Clarion*.

Since he felt certain that any proper red-blooded hack would have fancied Amy Walpole, he duly acted as though he fancied her. He had seen her often enough behind the bar fending off clumsy compliments from the locals to know that men found her attractive. So he also pretended to lust after Amy, and when she had telephoned suggesting meeting for a drink, just the two of them, at the Admiral Byng, Bob Christie had readily relinquished his true personality, which was timid and gay, and came over all lounge lizard. He had read of such situations involving women like Amy and men such as he wanted to be, and he knew how to behave. Accordingly, he leered. Gone was the real editor of a nondescript local newspaper, and in his place stood a contemporary denizen of Fleet Street, red in tooth and claw. The transformation was, to his mind, wholly convincing. Alas, others were not as convinced as he was. He barked and he leered, but deep down he was still timid, and it showed.

It didn't show, though, to Amy as he asked for a stiff

gin, so she persisted in treating him like the reptile whose image he presented. Unaware of his deep insecurities and experienced in dealing with constant-top-up drinkers, she bided her time. She produced what looked like large G&Ts for both of them, but – an old barmaid's trick – she'd omitted the G from her own. Only after Bob Christie had swallowed down his modicum of Dutch courage (aka a double Gordon's) did she ask him what he and the Admiral had been discussing in the Bridge on that Monday. Instantly he was all a-tremble.

'What makes you think I saw the old thing that afternoon?' he blustered.

'You were filmed going up the stairs in footage for the documentary that Ben Milne's been making.'

It was difficult for him to argue with that, but he very quickly came up with another defence. He explained that he had been in the Bridge that afternoon because the Admiral wanted to see him about having his own regular column in the *Clarion*, to be called 'Through the Telescope – or a Sea-Dog's Tricks – old, new, and beautifully boxed'. Fitz claimed already to have written a number of what he called 'opinion pieces'.

Christie thought there might be something in the idea, but at that Monday meeting they hadn't been able to agree over terms. The Admiral wanted to be paid for his efforts; the editor was in favour of an unpaid contribution, 'at least for the first few weeks until we see how it beds down'.

'Do you think Fitz was keen on the idea because he needed the money?' asked Amy.

'No. And even if I had paid him, the *Clarion* rates are pretty pathetic. No, he was just rather full of himself and reckoned everyone in Crabwell would be interested in his opinions.'

Though the observation about Fitz's character rang true, Amy wasn't convinced by Christie's story. If her boss was seriously going to have a regular column in *The Crabwell Clarion*, she felt sure he would have mentioned the fact to his cronies in the bar of the Admiral Byng, and this was the first she'd heard of it. Also, never shy of expressing his opinions, if he'd got a whole supply of 'opinion pieces' stacked up, he'd have mentioned them too. But she didn't challenge Bob Christie at that point, just waited to see what other embellishments he would add to his lie.

'The column wasn't the end of his ambitions either,' the editor went on. 'He reckoned it was only a matter of time before his weekly musings would appear in book form.'

'Really?' said Amy, sure that she would have heard from Fitz about this idea as well if it were true.

'He was convinced it was a goer. In fact, he'd got some publisher woman there with him.'

'That afternoon in the Bridge?'

'That's right. Well, I say a publisher... a publisher of sorts, and one who might, just might, no promises, nothing as serious as pack-drill, turn next morning's fish wrappings into something altogether more deathless. At least that's what the Admiral was hoping for.'

'What was the publisher's name?'

'Odd one. Not one you're likely to forget. Ianthe Berkeley.

Yes, and she seemed quite keen on getting a book out of Fitz's columns. A book is a book, after all, whereas a newspaper column is just jottings, mere jottings with the accent on the "mere", as it were. Fitz very much liked the idea of his musings appearing in book form.' There was respect in his tone, even a little wistfulness. As a journalist, a producer of 'next morning's fish wrappings', he too aspired to the permanence of one day seeing his work between hard covers.

'And did Fitz appear to know Ianthe well?' asked Amy.

'I wouldn't have said "well", but they'd clearly met before.'

'Hm.' Amy looked thoughtful, even troubled. Christie wondered for a moment whether she was jealous of Ianthe's closeness to Fitz.

He gazed blearily at Amy, trying to fathom her relationship with her boss. She referred to Fitzsimmons as 'Fitz', but then so did virtually everyone else in Crabwell. Whether Amy had ever conducted anything other than a professional relationship with him was a matter of conjecture. Bob Christie, who knew little about the workings of the female heart, assumed that, being an attractive woman, Amy had conducted unprofessional relationships with practically everyone. But her and Fitz... he couldn't quite see it.

Feeling the need for a top-up, he offered to buy Amy another gin, but she said drinks were on the house that evening and fetched two more apparently identical G&Ts (though there was still no G in hers). Taking his drink, the editor settled himself on the sofa and waited for the next part of his interrogation. He thought it was all going rather swimmingly. Just as well that he didn't know what his interrogator was thinking.

Amy was more than ever convinced that Christie was lying. At the time on the Monday that he claimed Ianthe was in the Bridge with him and Fitz, the publisher hadn't even arrived in Crabwell. Still, believing she'd get more out of him by massaging his ego than by confrontation, she pronounced the great untruth: 'You're clearly someone who understands human nature.' He nodded gratified agreement with the compliment. 'Tell me more about Ianthe Berkeley.'

He was more than ready to offer his opinion on the woman. In Bob Christie's view, she was a publisher in name only, even though that was what she put under 'profession' on her CV. She had an office, and a title. Ianthe was an editor at Bone and Spittle, which even had a slogan ('Bone and Spittle – the Home of Books') but, alas, appeared so far not to have edited any books.

'And do you think she really hoped to publish a collection of Fitz's opinions?'

'I don't know. He was clearly of great interest to her.'

'As what? As a potential author?'

'I'm not so sure about that.'

'What do you mean?'

'A few minutes ago you asked me if Fitz had known her well. I said no at the time, but the more I think about it, the more I think there must have been something between them, some shared history.'

Amy was firmly of the opinion that he was making this stuff up, improvising on the hoof, but she still didn't voice her doubts. 'When you use the word "history", do you mean they had been lovers?'

'I'm not sure about that, but there was definitely something. Fitz was a man with a lot of secrets.'

This offered a more promising line of enquiry. 'What kind of secrets?' she asked.

'All kinds.' He smiled smugly. 'I did quite a lot of research on Fitz for a profile I was going to do on him, one of an occasional series I do on local characters. I found out some interesting stuff.'

'Like what?'

'Oh, I'm afraid I couldn't reveal that.'

Then why the hell did you mention it? Amy was tempted to demand. But she restrained herself and said, 'Are you implying that there was bad blood between Fitz and Ianthe?'

'Something like that, yes.'

'You'll have to be more specific.'

'Well, I got the impression that there was something Fitz knew about Ianthe that she wanted kept quiet.'

'Did he actually say that?'

'Not in so many words, but he did kind of...'

'What?'

'Threaten to make what he knew public.'

'And how did Ianthe react?'

'She said she'd kill him to stop him doing that.'

Once again Amy was certain that Bob Christie was making up his part as he went along.

And what was she left with? What admissions had been made? Bob had met Fitz on the afternoon concerned.

They had admitted the meeting – or rather Bob had – without undue pain. But thanks to Ben's documentary footage she already knew that. The second gin at least had been superfluous, maybe the first. What had been discussed at the meeting in the Bridge was, however, anybody's guess because to put it crudely one of the trio who had supposedly attended, had snuffed it.

And as for the other witness, Ianthe Berkeley... Amy decided she had heard enough of Bob Christie's lies.

'I'm afraid, Bob,' she said calmly, 'I don't believe anything of what you've just said.'

'What on earth do you mean?' he asked, affronted.

'I don't believe that Ianthe Berkeley was present at your meeting with Fitz on Monday afternoon.'

'But of course she was.'

'In fact, I wonder if you've ever even met her.'

'What nonsense. How on earth could I know all that stuff I've just told you about her?'

'Fitz could have told you. Or you may have met her in the past, you may have discussed the idea of Fitz's columns in the *Clarion* being turned into a book, but that meeting didn't take place on last Monday afternoon.'

'Are you accusing me of lying?'

'Yes.'

'How dare you? I'm a journalist!'

'So...?' Amy asked coolly.

'Journalists are famed for their integrity.' But the expression on Amy's face told him she didn't fall for such gallant protestations. 'Why don't you believe me?'

'Because your meeting with Fitz in the Bridge took place between one-thirty and two-ten on Monday afternoon, and Ianthe Berkeley didn't arrive in Crabwell until about ten o'clock that evening.'

'Well, I... Well, I...' He was so flustered he couldn't get his words out.

'So what did you and Fitz actually talk about during that meeting?'

'I don't have to tell you that. As a journalist, I must protect my sources.'

'That's rubbish. Journalists always get very po-faced and self-righteous about that stuff, but in this case there are no sources involved. You've just invented a lot of rubbish, and I want to know why. Your pathetic attempt to put Ianthe in the frame as Fitz's murderer I treat with the contempt it deserves... though I do ask myself why you put that forward, unless it was to move suspicion away from yourself. Listen, Bob...' Amy's steeliness was now quite scary. 'You had a meeting with Fitz on Monday – there's no question about that. Fitz is now dead. I want to know what you talked about.'

'And I want you to stop asking these impertinent questions! Bear in mind that you are nothing more than a bar manager. I might be more inclined to co-operate if the police were to question me in the way you have.'

'Oh, I'm sure they will,' said Amy.

Bob Christie looked slightly shaken by this thought, but he said no more. Instead, downing the last of his Gordon's and gathering up his coat, he stormed out of the Mess.

Leaving Amy with a lot of unanswered questions. Like why he had spun out such elaborate lies about his real reason for visiting Fitz? And what was that reason?

Also, why had he been so keen to implicate Ianthe as the murderer?

These were the thoughts of Amy, as she sipped what looked like gin in the snug at the Admiral Byng. She was surprised by the amount of tension she felt draining out of her. Bob Christie really was a very creepy man. The blazer, the eye shade, his other sartorial eccentricities. Amy shuddered. And she really wished that his socks had not been mauve. That was one insult to taste too many.

CHAPTER ELEVEN

Ben Milne was smart enough to keep at a safe distance from the law. His instinctive wariness of police officers (above all those who lurked in unmarked cars on motorway slip roads as he sped past in his sports car) was matched by a deep-rooted distrust of the legal profession. There was nothing personal in this. He'd stayed in touch with several lawyers who were friends from student days, but their tales of professional life did nothing to diminish his prejudices. The criminal defence barrister moaned that everyone he represented was guilty, the personal injury lawyer regarded his whiplash-suffering clients as grasping liars, and the probate specialist only seemed free of the stress that ground down her colleagues because everyone whose estate she administered was dead.

And as a maker of controversial television documentaries, Ben had encountered more than his fair share of pussy-footing lawyers in the broadcasting companies that employed him: overcautious men and women who would always rather cut the best bits of his footage than take the tiniest risk. No, he didn't like lawyers.

Yet into every life a little rain must fall, especially on a Friday evening in March in an English coastal resort. Just about the same time that Amy was welcoming Bob Christie into the Admiral Byng, Ben, taking refuge from the persistent drizzle in a greasy spoon at the end of the village's meagre parade of shops, mastered his reluctance to speak to a solicitor, and found the number for Griffiths Bentley's office in Crabwell. At least the man couldn't charge him for an interview. Perhaps he might even be persuaded to offer a bit of free advice about the validity of the get-out clause in Ben's contract with Tantalus Television.

'Griffiths Bentley and Company.' The voice was mournful and masculine, the accent mildly Welsh.

'Could I speak to Mr Bentley, please?'

'May I ask who is calling?'

'My name is Milne.'

'You're not an existing client.' A statement, not a question. Although how could a receptionist know the name of every client of the firm?

'No, it's about... about a new matter.' Ben had been assured by his personal injury lawyer chum that this phrase equates to *Open Sesame* when trying to get past the gate-keeper of a solicitors' firm.

'A new matter?' The voice definitely sounded a shade less mournful. 'What particular subject?'

'I'm afraid it's rather sensitive.'

'Please hold.'

There was a long silence. Evidently Griffiths Bentley and Company didn't believe in holding music. This was a point in their favour, in Ben's opinion. He had learned to loathe *Eine Kleine Nachtmusik* while spending hours waiting for a human being to answer his enquiry about a glitch with his broadband router.

'Griffiths Bentley speaking.' The voice sounded familiar. Not unlike the receptionist's, actually, if less obviously Welsh and a shade more melancholic. Perhaps this was a family business. Alternatively – and more probably – a one-man business. 'Mr Milne? A new matter, I understand.'

'Yes. I wonder if I could come and see you?'

'Well, you'd need to book an appointment, of course. I could probably make some time early next week.'

'I don't suppose you could spare me half an hour right now? I'm only around the corner, here in Crabwell.'

'Right now?' A shocked pause. 'It is rather late. I was just about to go home.'

'It is a matter of some importance.'

'What's the nature of this "matter of some importance"?'

'It's… personal. I'd much rather discuss it face to face.'

'Personal, you say?' A pause. 'I suppose I could fit you in. No more than half an hour, mind. I need to get home.'

'That's extremely kind. I'll be with you in ten minutes.'

'Very good. May I take your full name, please?'

'Ben Milne.' Ben's middle name was Clint – his parents' first date had involved going to watch a *Dirty Harry* movie – but he refused to acknowledge it. If the opportunity arose, he might even ask Bentley how easy it was to get rid of the stupid monicker by deed poll.

'Ben Milne?' A pause. 'Not the television…?'

'I'm on my way,' Ben said quickly, and cut off the solicitor before he had the chance to remember that he suddenly had a pressing engagement elsewhere.

The first surprise came when Ben, his extremely useful bag over his shoulder, walked down Market Street, a failing thoroughfare full of charity shops, trying to find number 12A, home to Griffiths Bentley and Company. The business occupied the first floor of a building that was also home to a Chinese takeaway, and adjoined by a bookmaker's and a shut-down tattoo artist's parlour. Premises more different from the discreet opulence of Mamba Capital's headquarters in Berkeley Square would be hard to imagine. Did Bentley fear that ostentatious displays of affluence would deter anyone who deduced that the glitzy atriums, marble floors, and fountains found in so many offices these days were ultimately paid for not by the owners of the business, but by the clients?

The vertiginous staircase leading to number 12A was covered in linoleum so ancient that it was probably subject to some sort of preservation order. The door at the top of the steps reminded Ben of the entrance to the domain of Spade and Archer in *The Maltese Falcon*. Judging by the state of the woodwork, the place had last been refurbished around the time that John Huston made the film. He rapped a couple of times, and a man's voice called, 'Come in.'

Ben walked into a waiting room with three empty chairs, a single filing cabinet, and an untenanted desk. The walls were festooned with posters asking questions like *Had an Accident? Not Your Fault?*, and offering occasional words of cold comfort such as *Making a Will Won't Kill You*. A second door on the far side of the room was open, and Ben stepped through it.

The man behind the desk bore no resemblance to Humphrey Bogart, although Ben recognised his lugubrious cast of features from the film footage he and Amy had checked through. The man clambered to his feet, and extended his hand. Tall, balding, and awkward in his gait, he was probably only a few years older than Ben, but he looked nearer fifty. An air of defeat and disappointment clung to him like cheap aftershave.

'Mr Milne? I'm Griffiths Bentley.' His handshake was damp. 'Take a seat.'

Ben gestured towards the empty desk in the waiting room. 'Your secretary's out?'

'She... um... only works part-time.'

Evidently the solicitor answered incoming phone calls himself. No wonder those voices had sounded similar. 'You're a sole practitioner?'

'Indeed. I was in partnership for a while, but it didn't work out.' The solicitor cast a sideways glance at a glossy brochure on his desk that bore the name and logo of the Venice–Simplon Orient Express, and clumsily slid a copy of *The Crabwell Clarion* over it. A photograph of the late

Geoffrey Horatio Fitzsimmons beamed out from the front page. 'I decided to… go niche, as they say. Open a boutique law office.'

'I see.' Ben wrinkled his nose. The aroma of soy sauce wafting up from downstairs was pungent. Griffiths Bentley kept his overheads down to a minimum. The carpet was shabby, and other than a couple of cabinets, a shelf of books, and a framed certificate just to prove that Bentley was indeed a qualified solicitor, the room was bare. No potted plants, no knick-knacks, no family photographs. 'You've worked in Crabwell for a long time?'

'My whole career. I was born close by, though I spent some of my formative years in Aberdyfi. Now, how can I help you? I don't have a lot of time. You said the matter was personal.'

'This isn't a paying job, I'm afraid,' Ben said, contriving an apologetic smile, while privately rejoicing that he wasn't about to embark on litigation with the aid of someone whose demeanour was that of a natural-born loser. 'But yes, it is a personal matter. Not personal to myself, I hasten to add, but in relation to the late Geoffrey Horatio Fitzsimmons.'

'What?' Bentley's tone changed in an instant. He sounded wary, and his eyes narrowed. 'The… Admiral?'

'That's the fellow. I'm a television journalist, and I came to know him through working on a documentary about his pub.'

'I've heard about that.' Bentley's expression was sour, and Ben thought it wasn't because of the smell from the ground floor. 'And about you, Mr Milne. People say you're a muckraker.'

'Is there much muck to be raked in Crabwell?' Ben asked innocently. 'Other than the litter blowing along the pavements of The Parade, that is?'

'This is a close-knit community,' the solicitor said. 'People prefer to keep themselves to themselves. You wouldn't understand. You come from London.'

He made it sound as if Ben were an invader from Mars. The temptation to say: *I come in peace* was hard to resist, but Ben didn't think the solicitor would believe him, and in any event, it wasn't really true. The story was the thing, and he was prepared to fight in order to be able to tell whatever story lay behind the death of the Admiral.

'I understand you knew Mr Fitzsimmons.'

'Who told you that?'

'Ah, Mr Bentley.' Ben risked an ingratiating beam. 'A good journalist never reveals his sources, haven't you heard?'

The solicitor folded his arms. Ben had seldom seen anyone looking less ingratiated. All of a sudden the man seemed almost formidable. 'I think you'd better leave.'

'However, an *excellent* journalist,' Ben said smoothly, 'knows when to share information with a trustworthy individual, such as a representative of your distinguished profession. As a matter of fact, I was told by Gregory Jepson. He was in the Admiral Byng car park when you arrived there. I gather you've acted for his parents for some years.'

Bentley assumed what Ben thought of as a *Finnegans Wake* expression: impossible to read. 'Buying their bungalow was one of my first jobs after I qualified. I've made their wills, I've... but tell me, why on earth have you spoken to Gregory?'

'As I say, it was in connection with the Admiral – Mr Fitzsimmons – and his untimely death while I was working on a documentary about his pub.'

'If your programme has been ruined because the Admiral killed himself, it can't be helped.' The solicitor's smug smile suggested that such an outcome would be very welcome news to him. 'But I'm sure it wasn't your fault. Now if you'll excuse...'

'I hate to say it,' Ben said, aiming for a bashful expression and not entirely succeeding, 'but the death of the man who was the star of the show is bound to boost our ratings out of all recognition. Especially given that the Admiral didn't commit suicide. He was murdered.'

'Murdered?' The solicitor glared at him. 'Is this some kind of joke?'

'For once in my life,' Ben said, with slightly uncharacteristic sincerity, 'I couldn't be more serious. Someone killed Fitzsimmons, and I'd like to find out why. Preferably before we finish filming.'

Bentley blinked. 'You're not recording this conversation, are you?'

'Goodness me, no.' Ben gazed sorrowfully at Bentley. Anything rather than glance at his bag. It had worked all right with Greg Jepson. He hoped he hadn't lost his knack of telling barefaced lies while wearing a mask of innocence. Years ago, in the school sixth form, that same expression had prompted a perceptive careers teacher to recommend a future in politics. 'This is just between ourselves. A private conversation.'

'Hm. Why should I believe you?'

'Please, Mr Bentley. I'm sure you're just as interested in getting to the truth of what happened to Fitzsimmons as I am.'

'What on earth makes you say that? And why do you maintain the man was murdered? It's utter nonsense.' The solicitor waved at the newspaper. 'I have it on the authority of the editor of the *Clarion* that the police are satisfied that foul play wasn't involved. I'd advise you to be very careful about what you—'

'Thanks,' Ben said, 'but I'm not seeking free advice. I simply want to know who murdered the Admiral.'

'You haven't answered me.' Bentley's manner had hardened. He no longer seemed awkward, but sinewy and focused. Was the impression of inadequacy that he conveyed so effectively on first acquaintance no less a charade than Ben's protestations of good faith? 'Why do you say it was a case of murder? And why should I care, even if it was? Let alone wish to discuss the wretched business with a complete stranger?'

Like Amy, Ben didn't feel at this time inclined to mention the printed suicide note. Instead, he argued, 'There was no reason for the Admiral to kill himself. On the contrary. On the last day of his life, he was in high spirits.'

'Suicides don't necessarily flag up their plans to all and sundry.' Bentley's expression darkened. 'Believe me, I know.'

Ben made a note of this rather unusual remark, but didn't pick up on it. 'Things were going well for him.'

Bentley shook his head. 'Everyone in Crabwell was aware that the pub was losing money hand over fist. He didn't have too many reasons to be cheerful, I can assure you.'

'You'd have inside knowledge about that, naturally? Being his solicitor, I mean?'

'I did act for him, yes. He and I… went back a long way.'

'Oh really?'

'Crabwell is a small village, Mr Milne. Only a handful of solicitors practise in the area. And I am…'

'The cheapest?'

Bentley's smile lacked any hint of genuine mirth. '"Well known for offering good value" is how I prefer to put it.'

'Of course.' Ben decided to launch a belated charm offensive. 'People trust you, I'm sure. To be perfectly honest, you and I have more in common than you might imagine.'

'I doubt it.'

'Hear me out. My business requires me to win people's confidence, just like yours.'

'The difference is that you promptly betray it,' Bentley snapped. 'When I heard about this documentary, I looked you up. Found out the details of your *Skeletons in the Cupboard* programme – *huh*. The internet is positively awash with scandalous stories that have your fingerprints all over them.'

'I'm interested in finding out the truth, Mr Bentley. Believe me, I'm determined to discover exactly what happened to that poor bastard Fitzsimmons, and who was responsible for drowning him.'

'*That poor bastard*?' Bentley repeated, with a ham actor's over-emphasis. 'Is that the impression you had of the Admiral?'

'I'm more interested in your impression of him. You've said you'd known him for years. What did you make of the chap?'

A curious glint came into the solicitor's eyes. 'He was an intelligent man, Mr Milne. Some people thought him an overbearing fool, but not me. There was more to the Admiral than met the eye.'

'How much more? Please, I find this fascinating.'

Bentley gave a dismissive shrug, as if irritated that he'd said too much. 'Don't misunderstand me, Mr Milne. We didn't socialise. Ours was a... purely professional relationship.'

'And that professional relationship led you to visit the Admiral a few hours before he died?'

Bentley frowned. 'Certainly. Why else?'

'Isn't it a little unusual for a solicitor to visit his client, rather than the other way around? Surely most people come to this office to consult you, rather than insisting that you call on them?'

'The Admiral was a special case,' Bentley snapped. 'Eccentric, some might say. Unorthodox, certainly. He asked if I would come and see him on Monday afternoon, and my diary was clear, so I was happy to oblige. Client service, you see, takes many different forms.'

'Evidently,' Ben said, although the solicitor's explanation was as clear as the mud in Crabwell harbour. 'So what did he want to speak to you about?'

'That I can't divulge, I'm afraid. You'll appreciate that solicitors need to observe client confidentiality. We have professional rules, quite apart from the implications of the Data Protection Act...'

Ben gave a dismissive wave of the hand. He'd never read the Data Protection Act, and he guessed that was true of almost everyone who claimed to be complying with it. He suspected its principal function was to provide people who had something to hide with a fig leaf that discouraged investigative journalists from seeking out inconvenient truths.

'Your client is dead. He won't complain if you happen to talk to me about your meeting with him.'

'Even so.' Arms folded again. 'I'm afraid I can't help you.'

'I'm sorry about that. I was hoping to present your visit to the pub in a very positive light.'

'There's nothing more to be said about it. It would be of no interest whatsoever to your viewers.'

Ben smiled. A friendly smile tinged, he hoped, with menace. 'On the contrary, a touch of mystery enlivens any television programme. Until just now, I'd presumed the truth about your dealings with the Admiral would be rather banal. But suppose we say something like... "lawyer Griffiths Bentley visited Fitzsimmons only hours before his client was murdered, but refused to disclose what they talked about…" People will be fascinated.'

The solicitor scowled at him. 'Absurd. You must appreciate, it's a serious matter to defame a member of my profession.'

'Of course I appreciate that, just as you will realise that there's nothing in the least defamatory about what I said.'

'The innuendo is that I have something to hide.'

'I can't prevent mischief-making. Thankfully, my programmes attract a discerning audience. Our viewers are deeply interested in reality, to say nothing of reality TV shows. I'm sure they will be sympathetic to the constraints you labour under, especially given the rigours of the Data Protection Act.'

'This really is intolerable.'

'I'm so sorry to have taken up your time.' Ben rose from his chair with a throwaway glance at the telephone on the solicitor's desk. It hadn't rung once during their meeting. 'I realise you're a busy man, and of course you want to get home for the weekend. Who knows? This whole affair may prove a blessing in disguise. You know what they say? No publicity is bad publicity.'

One or two of Ben's lawyer friends were, it was true, as keen on publicity as he was, but he'd calculated that Griffiths Bentley's attitude would be very different, and a glance at the man's pallid complexion proved the point.

'Please, Mr Milne.' Bentley sounded agitated. A spasm crossed his face and he put his hand on his chest as if to wipe away some inner pain. 'I don't think there's any need for you to…'

The solicitor's voice faltered, and Ben found himself secretly hoping that he would be accused of blackmail, giving him the pleasure of a classic rejoinder: 'Blackmail is such an ugly word, Mr Bentley. Shall we just say... you scratch my back and I'll...?'

'... be unduly hasty.'

Disappointed by the anticlimax, Ben murmured, 'So what do you suggest?'

'I am my client's sole executor.' Bentley spoke rapidly; he seemed to be making up what he said as he went along. 'The question is, what would the Admiral wish me to do? I am bound to bear in mind that he was ready and willing to co-operate with you in the making of your programme.'

'Correct.'

'It follows that I can best respect his wishes by affording you a similar courtesy. We could, perhaps, reach an agreement that, if I were to share with you certain information, you would keep my name out of your documentary. I should make it clear that I abhor personal publicity of any kind.'

'A gentlemen's agreement?'

'Absolutely.' Bentley extended his hand; as they shook, it felt as damp as ever.

Ben settled back in his chair. Privately, he believed that a gentlemen's agreement is something made between people who aren't gentlemen, and which is not an agreement. He felt under no duty to voice such an opinion. This man was a solicitor; he must know he was skating on thin ice.

'So what was the purpose of your visit to the Admiral?'

'He had summoned me as a matter of urgency. He wanted to change his will.'

Ben leaned forward. 'Really? Was it out of date?'

'By no means. I drafted the existing will only three years ago.'

'And did Fitzsimmons say that he needed to change his will because his circumstances had changed?'

'No.' The bewilderment with which the solicitor answered meant he didn't know about Fitz's sudden acquisition of two million pounds. And Ben wasn't going to share the information with him.

'Who were the beneficiaries of his previous will?' he asked.

'There was a modest legacy to myself.' Bentley coughed. 'I should say, that was to remain unchanged under the new disposition of his estate.'

'And?'

'The residuary estate was originally divided into two parts. Half of it went to the Reverend Victoria Whitechurch.'

'Really? I had no idea he was a religious man.'

Bentley pursed his lips. 'I'm afraid I never saw any evidence of a spiritual side to Geoffrey Horatio Fitzsimmons, though to my surprise I've discovered that up until his death he did act as a churchwarden at St Mary's. He said to me that he wanted the vicar to have something put away for a rainy day. "In case she's ever defrocked", he said, with a rather impudent laugh. Of course, I didn't include that phrase in the will. It was simply one of those coarse jokes in which he liked to indulge.'

'And the other beneficiary?'

'His cook, Meriel Dane. "For services rendered".' Bentley shuddered. 'He did insist on that phrase being included in the will. Given the years she had worked for him, I did not think I could object.'

'Were there any other legacies?'

'A thousand pounds to a Mrs Rosalie Jepson. "*A la recherche du temps perdu*" was the explanation he gave me. Once again, it was a mark of his peculiar sense of humour to insist on inserting that phrase in the will. A trifle irregular, and undoubtedly otiose, but the client is always right. Or so they must be allowed to think.'

'I see,' Ben savoured 'otiose'. Did anyone other than a lawyer ever use such a word? 'And may I ask – is the "Mrs Rosalie Jepson" mentioned in the will any relation to Greg Jepson, the hedge fund manager?'

Bentley shrugged. 'That I wouldn't know.'

Ben felt sure he was lying. 'But it's a rather unusual surname.'

The solicitor shrugged again. Recognising he wasn't going to get any further on that line of questioning, Ben made a mental note to ask Greg if he was related to a 'Rosalie Jepson' and moved on. 'What instructions did the Admiral give you about drawing up a new will? Was anyone cut out?'

Bentley hesitated. 'No, not exactly. But the bequests to the vicar and to Ms Dane were reduced to the same sum as that for Mrs Jepson.'

'Really?' Well, well. 'Who was to inherit the bulk of the estate?'

'It was utterly extraordinary,' the solicitor said softly. 'The Admiral insisted that he wanted to give it all away to a woman I'd never heard him mention before.'

'Who was that?'

'Her name was Greta Knox.'

CHAPTER TWELVE

On the Saturday morning, Ianthe Berkeley sat in her bedroom at the Admiral Byng, looking out over the slate-grey expanse of the North Sea, and assessed her situation. The death of Geoffrey Horatio Fitzsimmons had certainly changed things, but not necessarily for the worse.

Ianthe was, at least in her own eyes, a 'serious' editor of 'serious' books. She was not exactly an intellectual – she affected to despise academics – but she had a degree of sorts. At least she had not ended up editing silly crime novels like her only friend in the office, Mary Drew. Of course, crime fiction sold very much better than *her* books, as Barry Featherstone, her boss, would often remark. He seemed to enjoy needling her and emphasising that Mary was in line for a bonus. Ianthe had a feeling that without a 'bestseller' her own future in the old-established publishing firm of Bone and Spittle might end in tears – her tears.

That was why she had decided it was worth driving all

the way down to Crabwell to see her potential star author being interviewed on camera by Ben Milne for the documentary he was filming about the Admiral Byng public house. She knew Ben from way back when they had both been at uni. She couldn't quite remember, but she had the feeling she had slept with him once or twice, but then she had slept with a lot of her fellow students, and some of her tutors, which perhaps explained her rather disappointing degree – a poor second, when she had been expecting a first.

However, it had been good enough to get her into publishing, even if she had to settle for one of the small firms, not one of the big ones with names people had heard of where no one spoke of books but of 'units'. Mind you, she liked money as much as the next person. She was not 'ditzy', as one of her authors had hurtfully described her to her boss in her hearing, but she was impulsive. She had an idea that – unlikely though it was – the book Fitz told her he had 'found' in a cellar of the Admiral Byng might be her passport to fame and fortune.

Her original thought had been that if she could get it puffed on Ben's programme to 'encourage the others', as she muttered to herself, that would be a great way to launch the book. She patted herself on the back, metaphorically of course – for 'encourage the others'. As she remembered it, the historical Admiral Byng had been backward when he should have been forward, and had been executed for his lack of initiative. Some French philosopher had made the joke first she seemed to recall, in French naturally, that he had been shot by firing squad... '*pour encourager les autres*'. Who said she wasn't an intellectual? Anyway, no one would ever accuse her of lacking initiative like the unfortunate Admiral Byng.

The one benefit of working for Bone and Spittle was – certainly not her salary, which was ridiculously inadequate – but the car park where she laid her battered Beetle to rest every morning. Her parking skills were rather hit-and-miss though. She thought about the dent she had left in the passenger door of Barry's Prius when she had started out on her journey to Crabwell. He would be furious when he saw it, and he would know who was responsible, but if the book 'went viral' as she believed the expression was, he would have to forgive her. Ianthe claimed to be a good driver, but reverse gear was one direction too far in her manual. She had heard it said by one of her flirtatious male authors that men could reverse park because they had learned to direct their pee into the toilet as soon as they could stand upright – a skill like riding a bike once learned, never forgotten. Whatever the truth of this, she had never been able to navigate her precious Beetle backwards, and it galled her as though it were a stain on her scabbard.

Scabbards were rather on her mind at the moment. The book she had in her neat leather briefcase in the form of an advanced proof was all about scabbards and swords, most with names she could not pronounce like Pendragon and Tintagel, wielded by Arthurian and Templar knights in 'shining armour'.

Oh God! She remembered thinking how badly she needed a knight in shining armour when she had first to face that horrible man Fitz, the author of this book in which she had invested so much. Or perhaps not the author. He had 'discovered' it, so he claimed, and it was vital to the credibility of the book that that was its official provenance. The story that Fitz had 'found' the manuscript under a flagstone in the Admiral Byng's cellar was unlikely, but not impossible, and Ianthe for one was determined to believe it. Perhaps he had been moving a barrel of his famously thin beer, or burying his dog, when he had tripped over it. It really didn't matter. Fitz had found the manuscript, and Ianthe was going to make it a bestseller.

They had decided to call the book, *Dragon Hoard*, but Ianthe still wasn't sure if that was rather too obvious a title. She had checked online and discovered that there were quite a few books already in print called *Dragon Hoard*, but, as she kept reminding herself, there was no copyright in titles. What made her book special was that not only was it a good read – underneath the flowery language there was ripping yarn – but there was also the hint – no, it was more than a hint – the definite assertion that beneath or at least in the grounds of the Admiral Byng there was treasure. She imagined the pub besieged by treasure hunters all carrying a copy of the book – like that one about the golden hare – *Masquerade* she thought it had been called. That had been one of publishing's great successes, and she was certain this could be something similar. The searchers wouldn't find anything, but Ianthe was sure that sales of the book would be enormous. It was a pity the pub could only boast a couple of rooms for the treasure seekers to stay in, and they were squalid, as she had reason to know, but no doubt villagers could be persuaded to put up some of the enthusiasts.

Fitz could have ruined all this with a few ill-chosen words. When she had spoken to him a week ago on the telephone – a very bad line – he seemed to have lost interest in the whole business. He had been quite rude to her. He had said he had more urgent things to think about than 'the bloody book'. Fortunately, half-cut, Fitz had signed a piece of paper Ianthe had scribbled on when he had first given her the manuscript. She didn't quite know if the document was legal, but she had intended to tell everyone she had a contract, and remind Fitz what he needed to do to honour it.

Fitz, she had reckoned, was her one way out of the cul-de-sac she had got into with the two men in her life – her husband and her boss – and she was determined to take it. She had to stop Fitz telling the world the book was all bollocks, a modern pastiche rather than the medieval manuscript it claimed to be. If she judged his character correctly he was perfectly capable of blowing the whole thing apart. He could say there was no treasure, that there never had been a treasure, that he had invented the whole thing himself. She had thought it very important that she should make it to Crabwell and stand by Fitz when he said what he needed to say 'on camera', and if she had to sleep with

Ben to make him include the piece in his programme she would, but that shouldn't be necessary. Anyway, she still had the vague idea that she'd been to bed with Ben before, when they were at uni.

She had felt confident that she could trust Ben to recognise a scoop when he was handed it on a plate. He would see the attraction in being the first to reveal the location of buried treasure. It was what Barry would describe as 'a win–win situation'. After all, it was in Fitz's interest as much as hers that the book should be a bestseller. She knew he was very short of 'the readies', as he phrased it. And Ben ought to be grateful. Who wanted to watch a boring documentary on the decline of the English pub? But a treasure-hunt... that was something else. So why was she so uneasy?

Her mind had been full of such thoughts as she approached Crabwell. She sighed as she turned the Beetle off the main road, narrowly missing a cyclist, who swore at her. She gave him two fingers, but not with much conviction. She had a lot on her mind. If the stuff about the book and Fitz's attitude to it wasn't bad enough, Jerry, her husband of almost a year, had hinted he knew about her ill-advised one-night-stand – it wasn't even that – with Barry after the Christmas party. But how could he possibly know, she wondered, assuming Barry hadn't told him?

She pursed her lips and drove over a pedestrian crossing without seeing the woman with the pram. And Barry could have. That was just the sort of swinish trick he might play on her, telling her husband what he had no right to know. Come to think of it, she thought the post boy, Kevin, might have seen something, but he wouldn't have told anyone, would he? He was a pimpled kid with a red nose and big ears who looked longingly at her boobs. She must remember to be nice to him. But not too nice. She didn't need any further office entanglements.

She regretted the 'Barry incident', as she called it in her mind, but it hadn't really been her fault. She had been drunk and upset about Jerry wanting to go to some bloody Chelsea game instead of taking her out to dinner. She was sure Jerry loved Chelsea more than her. He had almost been late for their wedding, glued to the TV, which he said was more important than being on time for the short walk to the altar. Or 'the short walk to the executioner's block' as he had once amusingly described it to his mates. Barry had taken her into his office 'to discuss her figures' he had said with a smirk. She had cried on his shoulder about Jerry's selfishness, and he had been sympathetic at first. Then he had kicked the door shut and told her he knew how to cheer her up.

He had been forceful – well, quite rough now she came to think about it – and he hadn't used a condom. She'd not even enjoyed it. The telephone on the desk had nearly broken a vertebra in the small of her back. When she had protested, he had told her he liked phone sex, and his breath when he laughed had smelt of cigarettes and beer. That was sexual harassment, wasn't it? Since then he had hardly looked at her, even when she had worn her shortest skirt and positively offered herself to him. She had heard he was shagging that secretary – the one with absurdly yellow hair and blood-red nails – so maybe that was why he had lost interest in her.

The first time she had been to the Admiral Byng, she and Jerry had been on honeymoon – a poor substitute for the week in Venice he had promised her. At the last moment there had been some Chelsea match he just *had* to be at with his mates. So he had wheedled her into agreeing to postpone going away until… well, until it was too late. One of Jerry's mates had recommended the inn at Crabwell, and very reluctantly she had agreed, but, predictably in her view, it had been a disaster.

The weather had been awful, and the bed had been so uncomfortable Jerry thought he had got a hernia. They had spent a truly horrible three days and nights at the Admiral Byng, and had quarrelled the whole time. The sheets were damp, and Jerry said the beer was bad, but the locals were so awful they had just had to get drunk to blot them out. And then Fitz had found out she was a publisher and that was when he had made his commercial proposition to her. He had shown her the beer-stained manuscript he said he had found several years back, and she had seen when she read a few pages in bed with Jerry snoring beside her that it might be worth taking seriously.

Ianthe had been doubtful at first – was it just a competent pastiche or the real thing? But Fitz had spun her such a good yarn about the Knights Templar and how the Treasurer of the Order had been exiled in Britain that she had been quite swept away. According to Fitz, the Treasurer had been a pal of Richard I – the Lionheart. Anyway, Sir Gilbert Fyzeman (as he was called) had ended up in a small castle on the coast long since demolished. It was all rather vague, but according to Fitz the treasure had been inherited – or was it stolen? – by some pirate or other and he had retired to the Admiral Byng, where he had stashed his ill-gotten gains. Ianthe liked the phrase 'ill-gotten gains', but in truth the treasure was not particularly ill-gotten if Fitz's story was true. Fitz hadn't actually found the treasure on his property, despite many years looking for it in a desultory way – 'desultory' had been his word. It was probably all nonsense, of course, but people loved the idea of treasure, didn't they? Look at the success of the National Lottery.

She had been exhausted when she reached the Admiral Byng that Monday evening. Her Beetle, normally so reliable, had broken down ten miles from Crabwell, and she had had to wave down a nice young man in a Morgan who had fixed things. He had said it was a sprocket – or was it a dirty plug? – she wasn't sure, but she had liked him and his Morgan. The long and short of it was that they had sex – very uncomfortably – under some dripping trees – the back seat of neither car being suitable for that sort of caper.

They had agreed to meet the next day 'for a drink', but she quickly forgot about her knight in shining armour when she finally pushed open the door of the Admiral Byng and demanded food and, more importantly, drink. There were not so many people in the bar because it was late and filming for the day was over. And Ianthe was too exhausted to be fazed by the fact that those present included a group of Viking re-enactors.

Fitz had greeted her with a sheepish look and mumbled something about needing to 'have a few words' with her after she had eaten her omelette. And she'd had enough problems getting that omelette. 'The kitchen is closed,' she'd been told. Huh. She's had to really bang on about her status as a resident of the Admiral Byng to that bar manager, Amy Walpole – a dreary stick insect of a girl who needed to wash her red hair – or maybe it was meant to look like that – some sort of fashion statement...?

Amy hadn't endeared herself to her late-arriving guest either by apparently chatting up Ben Milne. And then Ben had hardly seemed to remember Ianthe, which was a bit insulting, especially if she had slept with him at uni (but then again she wasn't sure she had). He seemed much more interested in Amy, which was even more insulting. Ianthe had taken an immediate dislike to Amy. The bar manager seemed to her bony, drab, and distressingly 'bucolic' (a word she had learned only the week before in a pub quiz), and for the life of her, she could not see what Ben saw in her.

Ben *was,* however, interested in the *Dragon Hoard* book when she mentioned it, and asked if she had a proof copy he could read. Tired and rather drunk after a couple of pints of Fitz's very strong scrumpy, the Old Baggywrinkle

– she told him all about it. How it was going to be a huge bestseller and so on. Fitz kept on trying to change the subject, looking ever more embarrassed.

Ianthe had produced a proof of the book from her bag and put it on the bar counter for Ben to have a look at, but to her annoyance she heard Amy say she'd take it 'to read in bed'. The bar manager added that she suspected the whole story was just Fitz's fantasy. Bloody woman.

By that point Ianthe had very much wanted to go to bed herself, but, remembering how beastly uncomfortable the bed was, she decided to stay up for another drink or two. As a resident she could go on drinking until she collapsed comatose, but Fitz wouldn't let her. He said he had something he needed to get off his chest, and persuaded her to come up to his office on the first floor – the Bridge, he called it, as though he was on a pirate ship. Why Fitz needed an office was anyone's guess. Ianthe looked around as she followed Fitz up the stairs. No one seemed to have noticed their departure. Amy was busy washing glasses, and Ben was deep in conversation with the Viking re-enactors. She continued up the stairs, lured by the Admiral's promise that he had 'lots more booze up there'.

So it was that Ianthe – her brain fuddled by drink, sex and weariness – learned in the Bridge that Fitz was going to prevent her publishing his book. She was so appalled she could hardly muster enough energy to protest. He said he had had 'pangs of conscience', though Ianthe was certain he wouldn't recognise a conscience if it hit him in the face. The book was a fake, he told her. He had knocked it off

173

on long wet winter nights a few years back, never really intending to publish it. Although he hardly watched television, he had somehow become fixated by a series full of swords and dragons, and had believed he could write something equally fantastical. But he had never meant for it to be taken seriously. He declared he couldn't live with all the lies and deceit that would follow its publication. Yes, he had wanted the money when they first discussed the manuscript, but his circumstances had recently changed for the better. Besides, there were some things more important than the commercial imperative. He wanted to make his peace with the world.

'But there's a contract!' Ianthe protested weakly. 'We have gone so far we can't go back now,' and, ridiculously, the dent in Barry's Prius came into her mind.

'I'm sorry, Ianthe, but I have decided. That's all there is to it.'

'That's not all there is to it, Fitz. I'm going to make sure you honour our agreement. I mean it, Fitz. I mean it.'

The following morning, the Tuesday – Ianthe had no distinct memory of going up to bed and undressing – she woke up stiff and cold with the most appalling headache. She stumbled across the passage to the toilet to be violently sick.

'You are disgusting,' she told the ravaged face that looked back from the mirror. 'You are nothing but a whore and you drink far too much. You are always being taken for granted by men and you have to snap out of it.'

She wished she could remember how the previous evening had ended. There was a lurking guilt inside her, a sense of shame, as if she had done something she'd come to regret, but she couldn't piece together the details. She had a nasty feeling Ben Milne might have been involved, but she couldn't remember how. She recalled having the thought at some point during last night's confusion of crossing the narrow landing and knocking on his door, though she had no recollection of putting the plan into action. Surely if she had gone to bed with him, she would have remembered that...? Oh dear.

Swilling down copious draughts of cold water and paracetamol while clumsily dressing in her bedroom, not for the first time Ianthe Berkeley promised herself that she would never drink again. In fact, she was going to change everything in her life.

She'd get rid of Jerry – the marriage had been a mistake, they both knew it – and she'd get a new job. With a reputation for bestsellers (which would inevitably follow the success of *Dragon Hoard*) she would have no difficulty. Then it all came back to her. The horror of being told by Fitz that the book in which, rightly or wrongly, she had invested all her hopes and plans for the future was not going to happen. Only – and her lips thinned and her brow furrowed – it *would* happen. She would make it happen, Fitz or no Fitz.

In spite of her grinding hangover, she suddenly had a rather brilliant idea. Forget authentic medieval documents... why not publish the book as a novel? Fitz had more or less suggested that last night. It would appeal to the millions of fans of sword and dragon fantasies. She must find Fitz and see if she could persuade him to agree. It might solve all his problems of conscience – it would be fiction and no one would have to pretend it was true. It would be a bestseller – she felt it in her guts – still churning as they were.

As long as she could retain control of book and author she would gain the kudos for bringing the firm such a big earner. She would make Mary Drew and the sales of her silly crime novels look pathetic. That was it! She would start her own fantasy list. Publish Tolkien rip-offs and dragons, dragons, dragons. She would be the dragon queen. But wait… she was getting ahead of herself. The book would need editing or rather re-writing, and it was already in proof. What would Barry say? He would say 'yes'. He would say, 'Ianthe, you are a genius'.

She must be able to think straight and be persuasive. She had to make Fitz see things her way. God, she was brilliant. If Fitz did not agree she would kill him. She could manage the whole thing without him. She had a contract of sorts, vague enough to cover anything she might do to the book.

A more outrageous thought occurred to her. If Fitz wasn't there – whatever that meant – she could claim to have written the whole thing herself. But hold on, was she going mad? She had left a proof on the bar counter the night before, and she thought she remembered Amy picking it up. If she had read it, Ianthe would not be able to pretend anything. She must get it back as soon as she could without arousing Amy's suspicions. And what about Ben? She had mentioned the book to him. She would just have to tell him a story. Tell him… God knows what, but she could do it. She knew she could. She just needed Fitz out of the way… permanently.

But when she went downstairs to see if she could face breakfast, she found the Admiral Byng full of policemen. And she heard the news that Geoffrey Horatio Fitzsimmons was out of the way… permanently. He had been discovered drowned.

Over the next few days Amy was puzzled by Ianthe's reaction to the news of Fitz's murder. The publisher made all the right noises – expressed her shock in all the right words, but underneath Amy detected an air of triumph that made her uncomfortable. There was a smugness about Ianthe that seemed totally at odds with the tragedy that had shattered the calm of Crabwell. Was she really as shocked as she pretended? The pub and all its habitués were spinning with suspicion, speculation, and naked fear. All but Ianthe, who seemed to take Fitz's death not just calmly, but as if it were… Amy tried to think of the right word and ended up with 'convenient'. Fitz's death was convenient for Ianthe, but Amy could not understand why.

She would have to confront the publisher at some point and find out what was really going on. Fortunately on the Saturday lunchtime, Ianthe came looking for her, asking breathlessly if she could have back the proof of Fitz's book.

'I suppose you won't be able to publish it now?' Amy suggested as she gave it to her.

'Did you read it?' Ianthe asked, not answering Amy's question.

'I didn't have time, but I did flip through it. I thought the bits I read were rather good – all that blood.'

'Did you?' Ianthe was comforted by Amy's commendation. If just an ordinary bar manager could find something good in the book perhaps she was the kind of 'huge untapped readership' Barry was always going on about, that majority of the public disparagingly referred to as 'the people who don't usually buy books'. 'Would you like to read the rest of it?'

'Well, I wouldn't mind.' Amy had no interest in the manuscript's literary merit; she just thought it might contain clues to Fitz's life, and possibly a reason why someone would want to kill him. 'I mean I don't normally like pirates, Knights Templar, and all that Boys' Own stuff, but the treasure... do you really think there is treasure buried somewhere beneath us in the Admiral Byng?'

'I don't know,' Ianthe replied hurriedly. 'Probably not.' She handed the proof back. It wasn't as if she didn't have lots more copies in the office back in London. 'Read it if you want to.'

'Thanks.'

Ianthe grimaced ruefully. 'Fitz was full of shit, wasn't he?'

Amy was rather disconcerted. Should one talk like that of the recently deceased? 'He could certainly tell a yarn,' she said doubtfully. 'You saw him that night, didn't you,

Monday? You went up to the Bridge with him, didn't you?'

Though she hadn't witnessed their departure from the bar, Amy was convinced that such a meeting must have taken place, and rather reluctantly Ianthe admitted that it had.

'Did you discuss the book when you went up there with him? I mean, I suppose it was why you came to Crabwell, to talk about the book?'

'Yes, that was it. He was so interesting,' Ianthe replied, her comment rather at odds with his being 'full of shit'. 'He wanted to add stuff to it, and I had to agree. Between you and me, it would have been rather a bore – the book being in proof and all, but well, anything for Fitz...' She laughed rather theatrically, and Amy guessed the meeting hadn't been quite as amicable as Ianthe wanted her to believe.

'You are going ahead and publishing it then?' asked Amy, suddenly suspicious.

'It was... it would be what Fitz wanted...' Ianthe announced piously 'It was his life's work.'

'It was, was it? I thought it was just a bit of a lark.'

'Oh, Christ no. He was desperate to see it in print. He thought it would solve all his money problems, and I think it will... would have, I mean. It's why he agreed to the television programme – to publicise the book.'

'Hm...' Amy said. Clearly Ianthe knew nothing about Fitz's windfall from Greg Jepson. 'Won't you have to wait for the OK from his heirs and executors?'

'I don't think so. I have a contract. I will have to check

with the lawyers, but I have no reason to think it makes a difference. He wrote the book and we are publishing it. That's all there is to it.'

'But won't it be rather expensive to make changes to the book? You said you were going to "edit it" – add stuff.'

'Not exactly add stuff,' Ianthe sounded flustered, 'but I don't see why you care. It isn't your problem,' she added irritably.

'Sorry! I didn't mean to pry.' But Amy firmly intended to pry. She still couldn't make sense of Ianthe's cool reaction to the Admiral's death – or murder, as she now always thought of it. 'Horrible about Fitz, though, isn't it? It has made us all nervy. Until the police find out who actually did it…'

'Do you think they will?' Ianthe sounded surprised and rather alarmed.

'Well yes, I should think so. There aren't too many of us who had the opportunity and a motive – just those who were in the pub for the relevant few hours.'

'It could have been a burglar. He might have disturbed a burglar.'

'On the beach, Ianthe?'

'No, of course not. He was killed on the beach, wasn't he? Or at least that's where his body was found. You don't think his body was dragged there after his murder?'

'Of course that's possible. No doubt it's the kind of thing the police are checking out.'

'Well I know someone who could have done it!' Ianthe was suddenly excited. 'That creepy politician… always wears a pinstripe suit. What's his name? Ben said he was seen earlier that day going up the stairs to Fitz's room.'

Amy wondered whether Ianthe had just plucked a suspect out of the air, in order to deflect any accusation from herself. 'Willie Sayers? He's an old friend of Fitz's. He was, I mean.'

'Oh no,' Ianthe said excitedly. 'They hated each other's guts.'

'How do you know?' Amy inquired, sceptical.

'It was my boss, Barry Featherstone, who told me when we were contemplating publishing a book by Sayers about Mrs Thatcher. Now what was it Barry said...? I know there was a girl mixed up in it. A girl they both wanted and Fitz got, but... Yes, I remember. She was found dead in the Regent's Canal.'

'What...?'

'Yes, you know, Amy. The Regent's Canal in North London. I believe they both lived around there... I mean ages ago, when they were both young. Barry told me Fitz accused Sayers of murdering her, but he couldn't prove anything. Barry said Fitz was lucky not to have been sued for slander.'

Though she had serious doubts about the woman's veracity and thought she was probably just making the story up, Amy was intrigued despite herself. 'Did they ever find the girl's killer?'

'Never.' Ianthe sounded pleased. 'There you are. I've solved it. Willie Sayers killed Fitz, who... was trying to blackmail him or something. I'd better tell Ben. You know we were… friends at uni,' she added mischievously, trying to get a rise out of Amy but failing.

'Ianthe, please be careful what you say. Mr Sayers is a powerful man. You don't want to have him as an enemy.'

'Like Fitz did, you mean?'

CHAPTER THIRTEEN

Amy walked home that Saturday afternoon with the bound proof secure in a carrier bag against the fine spray being flung at her from the sea. Her mind was full of confusion. She didn't believe the story Ianthe had just spun her, it had all come out too pat, almost rehearsed. But why had the publisher bothered to come up with it? Simply to divert suspicion from herself?

Then again there was the strange behaviour of Bob Christie… What was he trying to cover up with his elaborate lies? She made a mental note that she – or perhaps she and Ben – needed to have another meeting with the editor of *The Crabwell Clarion*.

Entering her cottage, she took off her ancient Barbour and threw it over a seat-back. Then she sat in her armchair, Ianthe's proof lying heavy on her lap. There was a click and scratching from ivy on a windowpane, and it startled her. She turned and stared at the window. For the first time since she'd lived in Crabwell, she was aware of a vague uneasiness. Unbidden, the picture of poor old Fitz lying in the boat, dead, came to her. Maybe the village wasn't as benign as it had always seemed.

Crossing the floor, she locked and bolted the front door, and then, resting her back on the old timbers, she stared about her with a swift assessment of her position here in this lonely cottage, unprotected and unsafe while a murderer lurked... somewhere. She had no safety here, that was plain. In fact there had been no point in locking the front door, she didn't know why she'd bothered. The back door was so rotten that anyone could pull it open by yanking hard, and in any case, all the putty in the windows was perished and falling away. If anybody wanted to break in, they could open a casement without trouble.

Returning to the chair, she stood a moment, staring about her, wondering whether she would ever feel safe again. Then, hoping to set all thoughts of the murder aside for a while, she busied herself opening her log-burner and laying a fresh fire. Setting a match to the paper, she knelt before it and watched the flames licking around the logs.

If she thought about it, she could have been hungry, but she put thoughts of food to one side. She could always get something to eat at the pub later. With the amount she was owed in back pay, she felt entirely justified in eating as well as possible at the pub's expense.

Rising stiffly, she walked back to the table and stared at the bound proof. It was possible that in these pages there was some explanation for the Admiral's death. Poor old Fitz! She dashed away the tears that had threatened, and glared at the manuscript. If there was a motive in here, she would find it.

The Admiral had always made sure that there was plenty of Laphroaig in the pub, and Amy had a bottle secreted in a cupboard. She went and poured a large measure into a tumbler, then took her drink to the table and sat, the book still unopened, considering all that Ianthe had told her.

The bound proof was unsettling. Although Amy would never have confessed to superstition, there was something about the solid mass of paper that made her flesh creep. It was strange to think that the Admiral was dead and that the reason could lie in these pages. She missed the old devil. Poor Fitz! If she could find out what had happened, she would feel happier, as though her employment was itself a debt she must repay.

Good God, hadn't she already paid enough by working without pay for well over three weeks?

The memory of the money she would probably never see now stung her, and she put the glass down violently enough to spill some drops onto the table. Bloody Fitz!

Mopping the spilled whisky with her handkerchief, she set her jaw. He was gone now.

With a swift resolution, she pulled the proof to her. Ianthe hadn't been totally convincing about her own belief in the book, and there was something about the woman that had set Amy's nerves on edge. She flicked through the pages idly while she once again reviewed her talk with the editor. Ianthe had been so – what? Desperate? She was certainly eager to convince Amy that there was real merit in this book, as though it could be an important addition to the history of the Templars or something. Amy had doubts about that. She had once read *The Da Vinci Code*, and it had convinced her early on that the success of the book was due to the astonishing ability of the majority of the population to believe any twaddle that reinforced their own prejudices. The Templars had been just a band of soldiers, surely.

She returned to the first page and began to read.

There was quite a bit of introductory material, a list of Templar Masters in England, maps of Templar sites, and then a short history of the Knights Templar, which told her that they were a group of warrior monks who took the same vows as the Benedictines – in effect, warrior pilgrims. They were the real 'Church Militant', she thought with a grin.

'In their huge circular churches, designed to emulate the great Temple of Solomon, after which their Order was named, the knights would kneel to take their vows. They would swear by the one true God to be faithful to Him, to remain chaste, to donate all their worldly wealth to the Order, and to be obedient to their Grand Master, and to him alone.'

Amy winced and turned more pages. The writing didn't improve. There were more pages of introduction, then the next chapter told of the history of a place in Suffolk. It was Dunwich, not far from Crabwell where, she learned, the Templars had a large farm and storage warehouses. Amy shrugged. Dunwich, she read, 'once was a large maritime port, into which flowed much commerce from Holland. But not only simple trade goods were brought into England from Holland. No, there were other items that were brought in, as well. Some sinister.'

It was enough to make a bar manager sigh, throw the book aside and pour another drink. She groaned, but forced herself to read on. Another page, then two or three were skimmed, until she paused, her brow drawing into a frown as she read:

And so the thief returned to his ancient haunts, determined to retain for himself those profits which should by rights have been returned to their rightful owners. But this man was no 'perfect, gentle knight' like Chaucer's ideal. He was the Devil himself.

She smiled at the overblown language, and could not help reading the paragraph following.

When the townspeople heard of his dark deeds, they instantly called for his arrest. But Gilbert FitzSimon was no coward. He refused to bend the knee to a rabble of raucous peasants. 'Away, churls!' he roared in his clear, deep voice. 'Think ye to challenge a noble knight?'

Amy frowned and turned back the pages until she came to the beginning of the passage, reading the whole section with more care.

There was one there who was so notable for the foulness of his acts, that even in the masses of the Templars, his name became synonymous with evil. Indeed, for centuries after his death and the end of his Order, his acts of blasphemy and heresy became part of folklore. The grizzly truth…

Amy sniggered at that: she wouldn't want to use someone with Ianthe's spelling skills as an editor.

… was that this foul mercenary was so steeped in crime that even a holy and honourable Order like the Templars could do little to mitigate them.

Gilbert FitzSimon became a Templar Knight for a short period in 1278.

Amy stopped reading as a new thought came to her. FitzSimon? Gilbert FitzSimon? And then Ianthe had spoken of 'Sir Gilbert Fyzeman', the Templar Treasurer, friend of Richard the Lionheart. Amy knew that consistent spelling didn't feature much in the Middle Ages. Was it possible that Gilbert FitzSimon and Sir Gilbert Fyzeman were one and the same person? But a quick check with Wikipedia told her they couldn't be. Richard I had died in 1199. There was no way that his friend could have become a Templar in 1278. The names were interesting, though. Was it possible that there was a family line from Sir Gilbert Fyzeman, through Sir Gilbert FitzSimon to Geoffrey Horatio Fitzsimmons…? Well, it was a thought.

She returned to her reading.

FitzSimon served under a contract of only five years, so that he could learn, it was said, how to honourably serve his lord and master. But his service was marked by his dishonourable acts. When at last he was sent to the Holy Land, he was said to have avoided battle when the opportunity presented itself, and was found guilty of raping the wife of a Christian merchant. In disgrace, he was sent back to England. However, the next part of his story shows how violent and dishonest this disreputable man truly was. On the ship home, he learned of a treasure chest. That treasure had been collected by the Templars and was being sent in order to help pay for more soldiers and weapons to protect the Holy Land.

Only a few short years later, the last Christian bastion and stronghold on the shores of the Holy Land was to fall, and her ramparts were thrown bodily down. Who can say, but that this disaster was not largely due to the terrible man who now disembarked upon English soil once more? His very feet polluted the ground he touched.

For Gilbert FitzSimon was the thief and robber who broke into the great hall of the Templars at Dunwich and stole their treasure, taking it for himself.

Amy shrugged. No, it was just a coincidence that the man had a surname so similar to that of the Admiral and to Richard I's treasurer. 'Fitz' meant something, she was sure: that the man was 'son of…' or was it 'bastard son of' Simon…? She would have to look that up. She read on.

According to new documents discovered while researching this book, FitzSimon returned to his manor near Crabwell in Suffolk after his journeys. He had an argument with his father that was overheard by the servants and soon spread all around the village. He was heard to declare that he cared nothing for the Templars, nor even the good name of his family. When his father saw that he was unrepentant, he told his son to leave his house and never return. It is said that Gilbert FitzSimon immediately rode away into the night.

But he rode to a dark moorland. There, he prayed to a terrible figure, a representation of the Devil himself. He swore that he would give up his soul, for he had little use for it. In exchange, he demanded help to steal the Templar gold. That same night he met with certain outlaws, and with their help, he stormed into the Templar preceptory and took all the gold, slaying the Captain of the Templars and three knights. And he slew all but one of the outlaws who had been his accomplices in his dastardly deed.

Not that this atrocious act would serve to provide him with a happy or long life. When he is tempted, the Devil has a way of acquiring much more than his contracts state. Although Sir Gilbert took the Templar gold, he soon learned that there was nowhere he could go with it. With his dying breath, the Templar Captain at Dunwich had called a curse down upon him, saying that he would find no love, no comfort, no peace, and no joy while he possessed the gold. And nor did he. Gilbert FitzSimon was destined to wander, forever seeking the peace his soul craved. It is said that even now he wanders the coast near to the Templar farm at Dunwich, seeking sympathy, or perhaps forgiveness. He buried the gold, and there it remains, somewhere, near to his old home at Crabwell. But woe betide the poor treasure-seeker or adventurer who finds it, for that gold is assuredly cursed. Any man who finds it will soon discover that the Templar's curse is still in force.

Amy pulled a face. Curses, superstitions, all nonsense. Then the wind rattled the window and she almost dropped the book in alarm.

Gold, however... that could explain much. For all the nonsense that this story evidently was, if someone thought the Admiral had found a hoard of gold somewhere, that would be an incentive to kill. Greed was always a good motive, wasn't it? And someone who was gullible might think that because the Admiral shared a similar surname, he might have some kind of clue as to where the gold was buried. There were idiots around who could believe that kind of thing. It wouldn't matter that the silly old fool had made up a story to sell to a publisher.

If he had. Could there be something to the story?

She frowned again, then looked at the back of the proof to see if there was a bibliography or some other reference to the document on which it was based. After all, if Ianthe expected people to set any credence by what was written, there would have to be some kind of evidence to back up the tale. If there was a medieval manuscript, where was it?

All she could find was a footnote in an appendix.

The history of Gilbert FitzSimon has been extensively researched by the author. Although for many years the story of his theft has been held as a myth, certain documents have recently been discovered that shed a new light on the old legend of the Devil-worshipping renegade Templar. These documents have been stored securely against the day that the hoard is rediscovered and their veracity can be confirmed. The author expects to be able to surprise the world very soon with a valuable find of such significance that the world of medieval studies will be astonished.

She put the book down. If the Admiral had found a massive hoard of gold, he would never have been able to keep that quiet. What were these 'documents' though? Where would he have kept them? Surely if they were in his office in the Bridge, she would have seen them? If not her, someone else going through his papers would have found them. If they were truly medieval, they would be obvious, after all. They would have been written on skins, wouldn't they? Vellum, that was the word.

The idea that the Admiral had found a number of new documents was as unlikely as him finding a hoard of gold. He wouldn't have kept it quiet, would he? But even Ianthe would surely never have allowed a manuscript to get so near to publication without checking all the facts, and the most basic facts of all for any editor would be the source material, wouldn't they? She would have to have seen the documents on which the Admiral based his entertaining but far-fetched tale. No publisher could put out stuff like this, not without that kind of verification.

Where would he have hidden the papers, if he had kept them? There was the safe, of course, but Amy had looked inside that every day when cashing up the till. There was nothing else in there. In his desk? Possibly. There were other places of concealment in the Bridge, of course, but none very likely, unless he had found a cubbyhole no one else knew about. The old place was riddled with them, in all likelihood. She had already noted that the panelling on the walls was loose. Perhaps he could have stuffed something behind there? But if he had, the documents would get ruined. He would know that. The whole building was damp. The pub's leaking roof kept the walls sodden.

No. The most likely place was his desk, she reckoned.

Glancing at her watch, she realised she was due back at work. It was time for her evening shift. She hastily closed the book and shoved it away on her shelf before pulling on her Barbour and hurrying to the pub.

The Admiral Byng was almost deserted when she arrived. She served three locals and two men who looked like journalists (not the old-fashioned Bob Christie blazered kind – these two sported expensive branded sweatshirts and jackets, trendy haircuts, one with designer stubble marking his jawline). But after that the bar went quiet and didn't get livelier for the rest of the evening. There wasn't much point in hoping that the pub would keep open, not at this rate. The beer in the barrel was going off, and with so few customers, it would be vinegar before the last couple of gallons were served. And, however sensational Ben Milne's documentary was, any publicity it generated would be quickly forgotten. It was enough to make a girl weep.

If she had the inclination.

Amy did not. She had done her weeping alone when she discovered Fitz's body. Since then she had been made of sterner stuff, and having followed her own course all her life, she wouldn't give up and dissolve into tears now.

The emptiness of the bar allowed her to let her mind wander. There was so much to absorb here, with the information she had gathered from the proof. She wondered whether Ben had managed to glean anything new. He would love the idea of Templar gold, she was sure. The greedy look in his eyes wasn't only avarice for a journalistic scoop with his blasted 'reality' show. He'd be keen for cash, too He probably had an ex-wife or two, and children, to maintain.

She'd have to tell him about the treasure. They had agreed they would share all information they unearthed individually. She wondered whether Fitz's mention during his 'Last Hurrah' of 'ill-gotten gold rather nearer home' referred to the Templar gold. That would make sense.

Gold. She was polishing a wine glass as the thought came

to her. A hoard of gold, perhaps eight hundred years old. That was better than the Lottery. What were the rules about finding treasure? She had heard of something called 'treasure trove', but she didn't know how it worked. Surely it would be safe from the government? If it was gold, and if she were to find it, that would be a nice windfall. She could even forgive the Admiral for not paying her for nearly a month. The book proof said that there had been enough gold to maintain the Templar army in Palestine. If Gilbert FitzSimon had not stolen it, that money could have affected the outcome of the war. So there was enough gold to help fund an army. Perhaps to arm it. That would be enough to cure all her financial problems several times over.

The bearded journalist suddenly called to her, 'Oi, love, give us another round, eh?'

Startled, she moved the cloth too sharply. With a loud snap the stem broke, and she felt the sharp spike of glass stab through the drying-up cloth and into her wrist. Dumbly, she stared at her arm for a moment, then pulled the glass free and felt her stomach clench at the sight of the blood running.

The second journalist took one quick look, turned green, and hurriedly lurched from the room, while the bearded man's face pulled into a sympathetic grimace.

'Oh, oh, I'm sorry, love, Here, you want to get that checked over? I'll drive you to the hospital, right? You got a casualty around here, love?'

She swallowed the first three sharp rejoinders that occurred to her. There was no point snapping that she was

195

not his 'love', nor anyone else's. However, the steady trickle at her wrist told her that she had to go and clean the wound. It was quite a slash, but it wasn't terribly deep, and there was no need to worry about the hospital. It didn't merit stitches, only a plaster.

Amy took the broken pieces of glass and threw them into the bar's bin. 'Be back in a minute,' she said, and made her way to the Bridge, where she knew there was a first-aid box. There was another set of plasters in the kitchen, but she didn't want to have to explain how she'd been startled. Meriel would like that. She always liked to have snippets to store for gossip, and the idea of Amy jumping with fright because a customer asked for a beer would be one she could trade all over the village.

No, in preference she hurried to the toilets and washed the cut. Firmly slapping the drying-up cloth over it, she made her way to the Bridge.

Now there was a 'Police – No Entry' sign stapled to the door. But she couldn't hear a sound from inside. Anyway, if Cole or Chesterton were in there, they could hardly complain about her needing a plaster. She tested the handle. It opened easily, and she closed the door behind her. Though there was evidence of computers and other police impedimenta, the Incident Room was empty.

This wasn't the first time she had been in the Bridge since the death of the Admiral, but it still felt cold without him. He'd been such a lively man, absolutely full of life, never more so than on his last night. Amy felt tears threaten, but would not give in to them.

This was ridiculous, to be so emotional. Where was the box of plasters? She crossed the floor to his desk. The papers piled haphazardly on top could have concealed half a dozen boxes of plasters, but she ignored them and began opening drawers. It took three before she found what she was looking for. She picked up a plaster and ripped the paper wrapper from it, covering the gash in her arm. The blood was already clotting nicely.

The drawer seemed to be the one where Fitz had kept all his medical supplies. There were a lot of small plastic pill bottles with printed labels from the Crabwell surgery. But on each one the name of the drug had been scored out with a ballpoint pen. And all the bottles were empty.

That seemed odd. Fitz had quite often asked her to pick up his repeat prescriptions from the surgery's pharmacy, but she never knew what medication he was on. All she had to do was give his name and address, and sign for the sealed paper bag, which was then handed across to her. Then she'd deliver the unopened package to Fitz back at the pub. She wondered for a moment whether the empty pill bottles might have anything to do with the cause of his death.

But the thought didn't stay with her long, because her attention was drawn to something much more interesting.

It was only a Post-it note, stuck to a thin file inside the first drawer she had opened. Didn't look like a business folder, and then she realised that on the Post-it was the name Gilbert FitzSimon. She pulled it out, feeling a tingling of excitement running down her spine, and opened the blue cover. Inside she found a crumbling, brown sheet of newspaper on top of a number of other documents. Peering closer, she saw that it was a page from the *Dunwich Evening Chronicle*, dated 12 June 1914. She stared at a paragraph ringed in pencil.

Sir Gilbert FitzSimon was, without a doubt, a singularly bold adventurer and outlaw. With the courage and determination of a modern-day Raffles, he went about his nefarious tasks. The vicar of St Stephen's in Dunwich has unearthed a fascinating manuscript that tells of this appalling felon, and has written a short monograph entitled…

'*The Shameful Crimes of the Outlaw FitzSimon*,' Amy read aloud.

It was printed on the topmost page of an ancient pamphlet that was in the file beneath the sheet of newsprint. Browned, just as the news sheet was, and roughly the size of a page of A4 paper folded in half. When she picked the pamphlet up and studied it, she could see that the pages were held together by two rusted staples that had fused themselves into the paper itself, staining the pages. The print was ancient and tiny, but perfectly clear.

'So, this is where you got your story from,' she breathed. 'Where did you find these then, Admiral?'

There were some scribbled notes on the folder's inner surface, and she turned the file around so that she could look more closely.

'Found in attic space of the Sinking Admiral,' she read.

'Hints at medieval document. Called Suffolk Institution, but none known. Vicar was convinced. Gold?'

Amy put the file down again and stared into the middle distance. She was still there when Meriel appeared in the doorway. 'You all right? I heard you'd cut yourself?'

'I'm fine. Just a little nick,' Amy said quickly. She shoved the papers back together again in their file and stood. She felt guilty at being here, and Meriel's sharp little glance didn't make her feel any better. 'Come on. I need to get back to the bar.'

But when she was back in the bar, there were no new customers. Only three remained: the two journalists, and one local man, old Reg, who had once been a fisherman, and now spent his days beachcombing. He sat in a corner mumbling incoherently into his beer, while the two younger men laughed and joked, considerably the worse for six pints each. It was a relief when all three finally stumbled from the doorway and Amy could close up.

She took the money from the till and cashed up, grateful as ever that she'd persuaded Fitz to replace the ancient device with an electronic one. She took all the cash upstairs to the Bridge in the red bank bag. Thrusting it into the safe, she swung the door closed and spun the dial before glancing at the desk. Once again she saw the file. Quickly, she snatched it up, curled it into a cylinder, and strode from the room. Down in the hallway, she shoved it into the sleeve of her Barbour, and then called out to Meriel as she left. Meriel could lock up.

Back at the cottage, she opened the file and read the pamphlet written a hundred years ago by a vicar just before the outbreak of the First World War.

It told of a knight who was noted for his savagery, his intolerable greed, and his bloodthirsty career.

He had not lasted long. The vicar wrote that, like many other knights of his period, he felt snubbed by those who, so he believed, should have honoured him, and as a result he took to the life of a felon and murderer.

Yet there was something odd about his story. Although he had apparently robbed the Templars at Dunwich, he kept to his life of crime, attacking travellers and home-owners. He would turn his nose up at no one, from the stories told, taking money from the rich and poor alike. An equal opportunities thief, she smiled to herself.

But if he had stolen the Templars' gold, why did he have to continue on his murderous crime spree? Surely he could have easily hung up his sword and retired?

There was a clue later in the pamphlet.

Although he had stolen the Templar gold, Sir Gilbert FitzSimon had never benefitted from it. He had been denounced by the outlaw who had been the sole survivor of his attack on the temple at Dunwich, and soon his manor was besieged by the posse of the county. The little place was fired, and the knight made good his escape in the smoke, but he could not take his hoard of gold with him. It was thought that it must have remained in the smoking ruins of his manor, but there was nothing ever found. Rumours abounded of a small chamber underground, into which it had been placed and sealed, while others maintained that there was a large system of caves in the rocks nearby, and the gold was hidden deep within them. Some said the Devil had come back to take his payment. And from that moment on, Gilbert had not a moment's rest. He had lost all for a treasure, and then lost that too.

Amy replaced the papers into the file. Well, perhaps it was true. But if so, the man probably came back later, uncovered his ill-gotten gains, and then fled. Somewhere she had read that the Templars had discovered America. Maybe it was all over there, then. He had put it on a ship to send it abroad for safety!

No, there was nothing much of any use in this lot, she decided. Gold, Knights Templar, outlaws, the whole lot was less credible than *The Da Vinci Code* itself. And worse written (if that were possible). But it did leave an interesting thought: who could have profited from all this twaddle? Ianthe seemed to think that it was an important piece of work. Well, perhaps it was for her. Amy supposed that an editor who succeeded in publishing something like this would earn her monthly crust. But it was such nonsense, Amy would have expected Ianthe to lose her job – for offences committed against English, if nothing else.

Ianthe was definitely keen to see the book published. Perhaps she thought there really was gold down here some-where. The Admiral could have teased her about it – he always enjoyed winding up people he thought were too pompous for their own good. Or maybe he had wound her up some other way?

Amy thought about Ianthe, and how she had been so keen to speak about the MP who had been there at the pub. When it came to the subject of Fitz's death, she had been enormously keen to talk about anyone, really, rather than herself, hadn't she?

CHAPTER FOURTEEN

Willie Sayers wasn't happy about this ingratiating young man's request, but though he wanted to tell him to get lost, he knew all too well from grim experience that it was wise to avoid alienating the media unless you just had to. Bastards at the best of times, if they took against you, they turned into flesh-eating vultures.

He moved the phone to his better ear. 'I don't understand why you want to see me? I'm aware that it's in my constituency, but I've hardly ever been to the Admiral Byng.'

'Since tragically we didn't have the chance to interview Mr Fitzsimmons properly, we're asking some of his close friends to help us paint a picture of him.'

'What makes you think we were close friends?'

Ben lied unblushingly. 'I recognised you in a photograph in his office when I visited him a month or two ago and asked if you were friends. "The best of friends, old boy," he said. "The best. Ever since schooldays."'

Sayers was both flattered and uneasy. He couldn't

remember seeing any photograph displayed on any of his visits to Fitz in the Admiral Byng or anywhere else he'd ever lived. And even though Fitz was a double-dyed hypocrite, would he really have been so two-faced? He tried a self-deprecating laugh and a change of subject. 'I'm honoured that a TV presenter recognises a humble MP.'

'You're very well known in the constituency, Mr Sayers. And I'd done my homework in advance.'

As he tried to work this out, Sayers regretted that he'd had so much to drink the night before at the pump manufacturers' shindig. He wasn't thinking as clearly as he'd like to. 'Fair enough. And well done. But why would you want to interview me about Fitz for a programme that's supposed to be about pubs?' Then he recollected that he was an MP in a party suffering from accusations of being out of touch. 'I mean I like pubs as much as the next man, but isn't it a bit ghoulish to go featuring this one now poor old Fitz is dead? Can't you find somewhere else?'

Ben adopted his most obsequious tone. 'I can quite see why you feel that, Mr Sayers, but I feel that we owe it to Mr Fitzsimmons to finish the programme he cared about so deeply. Rural society depends on its pubs, he told me, and he prayed the sad decline of the Admiral Byng would show the catastrophic social consequences of meddling by uncaring governments.'

'Steady on, Mr Milne. We're not an uncaring government. I myself am a tireless spokesman for preserving our institutions and our enduring English values of fairness and—'

Ben cut in. 'Of course, Mr Sayers. We aren't making

political points. But people have been rather critical. And serendipitously, this would afford you the chance to make a positive case on camera. About the threat to a pub in your own constituency.'

You're a lying toad, thought Sayers. Undoubtedly a Tory-hating metropolitan-elite kind of toad who'll be trying to trip me up and make a fool of me. But if I get it right, it could play well. Surely even the dimmest voters would be impressed by me appearing in a popular TV series and making an emotional plea to save their disappearing way of life and their right to get sozzled close to home?

Besides, Willie Sayers was as keen as anyone to find out what the consensus was on the cause of Fitz's death. Possibly keener than some.

Should he have insisted on being interviewed in his office rather than in the constituency, he wondered, as he sat glumly on the back benches trying not to fall asleep as that boring adolescent twerp with the expensive floppy hair droned on about the need to legislate on aircraft noise. How dare the chief whip have insisted he start turning up on Mondays and Fridays for doughnutting and applauding duties!

Yes, it was true that his voting record was a bit dodgy, but damn it – apart from that night he was out for the count after a few too many and missed the tight budget vote – he wasn't usually missed. Didn't these pursed-lipped puritans understand that a fellow certainly had better things to do on a Friday than crowd around some droning git of a minister, trying to look interested and intermittently shouting 'Hear, hear'?

He felt himself nodding off and forced his eyes open. My God, what a bad day it had been when TV cameras were allowed into the chamber to dominate members' lives! Empty benches made attendance a matter of importance, besides which a chap couldn't absent-mindedly scratch his balls or nod off without fear of being publicly held up to ridicule.

It wasn't as if the public had ever cared if they never saw a parliamentary debate, he reminisced resentfully. Bloody Labour had pushed it for populist reasons, and even the Blessed Maggie hadn't been able to block it.

Had the media had an ounce of decency, they'd explain that if benches were empty it was because members were busy elsewhere in committees or slaving for their constituents, but oh, no, that wouldn't suit the reptiles, who just loved showing acres of unoccupied green leather and implying that MPs were off somewhere else living the high life at taxpayers' expense.

Sayers stopped gazing loyally at the back of the environment minister's head and looked across to a group of middle-aged women in bright jackets on the opposition benches. Blimey, the hysterical way they were clustering and emoting would have seemed OTT in 1940 when Churchill was thundering about fighting the enemy on the beaches. What a gaggle of schoolmarmy prigs! They'd wrecked the Commons with their so-called 'family-friendly' reforms: Friday sittings and hardly any late nights had knocked the heart out of the place. The boozy camaraderie of yore seemed to be as distant a memory as those happy days when MPs were looked up to by the man in the Clapham omnibus. It was only a matter of time before the ban-everything-that-makes-life-bearable brigade imposed limits on how many drinks a fellow could be served in one session.

A cry of 'shame' woke Sayers from his reverie. He'd no idea what had aroused the ire of that harpy in purple – Henrietta thingummy – who seemed today to be the leader of the pack, but she was being copied by the rest of her hen party. Bloody crew of little Dame Echoes, he harrumphed to himself. He caught the eye of Jimmy Wade, who was sitting glumly behind a yelling bird in red, and raised an interrogative eyebrow. Good old Jimmy nodded impercep-tibly, they both looked at their watches, and, each trying to look as if he had to leave because of an urgent appoint-ment, they headed purposefully to the Strangers' Bar.

'Do you ever wonder what you might have been doing if you hadn't become an MP, Jimmy?' asked Sayers, as they settled comfortably into their second pint.

'Frequently. Why didn't I stay in the bloody union? I could have been the boss by now, with a vast expense account that no one in the media would have bothered harassing me about. It was my delusions of grandeur that did for me. Genuinely thought I'd be able to do more for the working man from parliament. Thought being an MP meant something. Didn't realise we were destined to be whipping boys.'

Sayers sighed heavily. 'It meant something before we were demonised and turned into enemies of the people. Corrupt? Us? Because some of us stretched the rules a bit on expenses? Have these sods any idea what political corruption is like when it's at home? Haven't they read about France and Italy and secret bank accounts and massive bribes?'

'Not to mention sexual shenanigans at private parties.'

'And as for being ticked off for our excesses by journalists!' Sayers sat bolt upright with indignation. 'Dear, God, Jimmy. Do you remember the days when those buggers thought nothing of taking one of us to lunch and claiming for a dozen?'

'Yes. Whereas now they just sit over their laptops in Wapping or some such anaemic hellhole, digging up any dirt on us that they can find. Searching through the internet, trying to get fellow politicians to do the dirty on their colleagues.'

Willie Sayers was instantly alert. 'Have you had any experience of that?'

'What – of people trying to dig up dirt on me? Of course I have. These days it goes with the territory.'

'No, I meant more... journalists trying to get you to dish the dirt on your friends and colleagues in the House?'

'They may have tried, but they haven't succeeded.'

'Ah.' But Willie didn't feel completely reassured. He swilled the beer around in his glass before asking tentatively, 'And have any of them ever asked you about me?'

'About you? What, like asking if you have a secret alcohol

habit?' Jimmy roared with laughter. 'No, I'd tell them you had a bloody public alcohol problem!'

Willie Sayers laughed along, but then persisted. 'I didn't mean about that. I meant journalists probing about my life back in the constituency... or, you know, things that happened a long time ago.'

His friend looked puzzled. 'No, no one's asked me about anything like that. Why, is there some terrible secret you're hiding from us all?'

Again Willie laughed off the idea. Again, though, he didn't feel fully reassured. Jimmy Wade might not divulge any secrets he knew about his friend. But there were plenty of other people in the House who would. If, of course, they knew any secrets about him...

He got their conversation back on track by swilling down a large mouthful of beer and saying, 'Bloody journalists!'

'God rot them! But of course now they've been forced to pull in their own horns, they've shafted us just for the hell of it.' They shared a morose moment of disgruntlement. 'It's the sanctimoniousness that kills me, Willie. All these striplings accusing us of being lazy and unprincipled. Us! You and I, we got to parliament the hard way, not by going to bloody Oxbridge and getting a pass straight into the bloody metropolitan elite. We understand the ordinary bloke.'

'Too right, Jimmy.'

Wade looked misty-eyed. 'I did love parliament in the early days. And being a minister was worth getting up for.'

'Having civil servants jumping to your commands...'

'As long as you didn't ask them to do anything that broke their unwritten bloody code.'

'How long were you one, Jimmy? Mid-noughties, wasn't it?'

'Appointed in 2005, but then after eighteen months Tony Blair decided I was too old. And you? You lasted about as long, didn't you?'

'That's right. I'd given up my pharmacy and put up with years and years of boredom on the back benches to stand at the despatch box and feel important and maybe do a bit of good, and then in 2012 David Cameron gave me the chop for not being a woman.'

'You missed a trick, there, Willie. If you'd said you were transgendering he wouldn't have dared fire you.'

In companionable anecdote-swapping and the cursing of political correctness, they passed away the hour until the House rose and the barman announced he was shutting up shop. 'What do you reckon, Willie? Get out of this morgue and pop across the road to St Stephen's?'

'You read my mind, Jimmy. You read my mind.'

At midday on the Sunday, Sayers finished leafing through the newspapers and left his tiny house in Shrimpton. He didn't need a map to find his way to Crabwell. He'd lived and had his early education there, before he'd moved on to grammar school (back in the days when there *were* grammar schools).

He had decided against taking his car. That Ben bloke had said something about lunch, which Sayers hoped would involve plenty of red wine, and even for such a short journey, it would be mad to take the risk of losing his licence. There were some precautions a person in his position just had to take. He'd walk there and get a taxi back. He was feeling rather low, and hoped the four-mile walk to Crabwell might lift his spirits a bit. Betty would have approved.

As he walked towards the beach, he thought once more how much he missed her and how diminished he was now he was alone. He went back in time to that conversation they'd had that evening all those years ago when he'd said how bored he was making up prescriptions. 'I want to make a difference, Betty. Not be a pill-pusher all my life. You make a difference every day delivering babies. I don't.'

'So why not run for the council?' she'd said. 'See if you can make local people's lives better.' And gradually she'd given him the confidence to join the party and speak up at meetings, and within three years he was Councillor Willie Sayers, who went on to be a much-respected leader of the council and easily won the nomination for parliamentary candidate. 'You deserve it,' Betty had said. 'You get things done and make life better for everyone.'

How happy they'd been when she came down to join him in London and work at St Thomas's. There were frustrations at work for both of them, of course, but they both loved most of what they did, and didn't mind the irony that she was a midwife who couldn't get pregnant. Most weekends they'd go back to Suffolk, where Willie found satisfaction in solving problems for constituents in trouble. Betty gardened, and together they thoroughly enjoyed opening fetes and geeing up the party faithful at constituency functions. They were a cheery and popular team.

'We'll be happy anyway,' she'd said when he was fired from the government. 'Now I'm retired, we'll do a lot more travelling.' They were animatedly discussing options when Betty was diagnosed with galloping pancreatic cancer and died within weeks. Sayers chided himself for having disintegrated as he had done, but two years on, life still seemed grey except when he was having a drink or three with good mates. Who didn't include that swine Fitz, he thought, as he remembered why he was striding his way along the beach on a Sunday morning en route to be interviewed on camera in that depressing pub.

He shivered, more because of the biting wind than because of his memories of Fitz. Should they have fallen out all those years ago? After all, at grammar school they'd been inseparable. As usual, he tried to forget how inseparable. Damn it, in those days, with no girls available, lots of chaps indulged in adolescent fumbles. Didn't mean they were wooftahs. He'd often smiled to himself about famous politicians who'd been boarders at public school, and wondered if, as they sat around the Cabinet table, they ever remembered what they'd once done behind the bike sheds.

It had been that silly Jilly who'd messed things up with Fitz that London summer after they left school. What did they see in her? Sayers managed a wintry smile. Well, yes. Jilly's attractions were very obvious indeed. Those boobs were spectacular, and those legs were made for the era of the mini skirt. To sex-starved teenagers who had just realised the joys of heterosexuality, Jilly was irresistible. And did she know it! What a manipulative little bitch she had been, though she didn't deserve what happened to her.

He leaned into a gust of biting wind that made him hunch into his coat and tuck his scarf in more tightly. He thought uncomfortably about that drunken fight. Which of them was more responsible? Probably him. Jilly hadn't been his girlfriend, so he shouldn't have accused Fitz of stealing her from him, not least because she was obviously public property. What was inexcusable, though, was what Fitz did after her murder when he suggested to the cops that his best friend might have pushed her into the canal because of jealousy. 'Get your retaliation in first' was a great Fitz saying. Well, the sod had certainly done that. And he'd never apologised for it either. Always claimed the cops had got the wrong end of the stick.

Sayers was still lost in disturbing memories of the agonies and ecstasies of the sixties when he realised that the Admiral Byng was now in view.

Ben had suggested that owing to the unusually large number of customers – for the combination of TV cameras, unexplained death, and Sunday lunch was packing the place out – the interview would be better conducted in what Amy said Fitz had called the 'Mess' – a small shabby snug with a table and wooden benches that could fit six people at the maximum. Sitting in its best-lit corner and waiting for the camera to roll, Sayers made sure that though his posture was relaxed, he didn't succumb to the temptation to slump. He had combed his hair in the gents, and had noted with pleasure that the walk in the piercing cold had given him a healthy glow. As Betty had so often pointed out, he looked good for his age. Rather to his surprise, his newfound dependence on alcohol didn't yet show in his face, unlike that of Fitz, who had looked like the old soak he was.

Willie was dressed in appropriate style for a pillar of the community in the local pub on a Sunday: check open-necked shirt, chinos, brogues, and one of the sweaters Betty said complemented his once striking blue eyes. Having lowered his first pint of local bitter gratefully, and with his second sitting in front of him, Sayers saw the signal from Ben and went on auto-pilot. Phrases flowed from him about the historic role of the public house in English society, its civilising force, its importance for community cohesion, the damage done to the quality of rural life by punitive drink-driving laws combined with poor local transport (all of which he blamed on the last Labour government), not to speak of supermarkets cynically encouraging young people to get tanked up with loss-leading alcopops. Since the young didn't vote, and no one loved the supermarkets they favoured over the local shops they pretended to care about, this was safe enough.

For good measure he threw in a few kicks at the nanny state, over-zealous Health and Safety officers, and pointless EU rules and regulations, and ended with an eloquent lament that because of these myriad disasters, the young would never know the happy pub culture of darts and dominoes that in the past had introduced them to sensible drinking and wonderful locally-brewed beers, and had along the way cemented families and communities.

Sensing – like the old pro he was – that it was time to say something specific rather than general, he segued smoothly into a regretful complaint that a wonderful pub like the Admiral Byng should have fallen on hard times, on the awful tragedy of Fitz's death, and on a friendship unbroken since boyhood. At grammar school they'd shared a love of cricket. 'I'm afraid Fitz was an awful lot better than me,' he said with a laugh. 'I was a bit of a duffer.' Later on, they'd spent many a happy Saturday afternoon at matches, after which they'd shared many an equally happy pint. 'Were you a frequent visitor here?' asked Ben, and Sayers burbled about the first duty of an MP being to his constituents, and how, alas, although of course he'd been thrilled when he'd heard that Fitz had taken over the Admiral Byng, between his surgeries and his other duties he had only rarely had the chance to see his old friend.

Fed up with the interview and nervous lest Ben press him more about recent history with Fitz, Sayers reached for his pint, said 'Here's to Fitz. He'll be sorely missed,' took a modest sip, smacked his lips appreciatively, and returned to extolling local breweries. Seeing Ben about to ask another question, he smiled, got to his feet and offered to buy him a drink. 'OK,' said Ben, taking the hint and getting Stan to switch off the camera. 'But I insist it's on me. As, of course, is lunch.'

After some negotiations with Amy at the bar, Ben returned carrying a bottle of the Malbec and some cutlery, and reported that though the staff were still under pressure, it was easing, and Meriel Dane had promised that roast beef would appear within twenty minutes.

'Meriel Dane! Do you know I'd forgotten she was still here!'

'A friend of yours?' asked Ben.

'Great girl.' Sayers had another mouthful of wine and sniggered. 'Bit of a goer I understand, but why not?' Then, realising he had said too much to a member of the untrustworthy classes, he abruptly shut up. Ben's best efforts could get nothing more out of him except pious recollections of his old friend Fitz.

It would take another shared bottle of the Malbec, a comforting encounter with Meriel's beef, the emptying of the pub, a whisky chaser, and Amy's post-lunch presence at their table to make Sayers let down his reserve. Amy had found the key by mentioning how much she had liked Betty that time they'd met at the charity event for the Guides. This precipitated Sayers's brief collapse into tears, which Amy had dealt with by unthreatening shoulder-patting. 'Was Betty fond of the Admiral?' she asked, when he had recovered his somewhat drunken composure.

'Fond? Fond? Of Fitz? No, she bloody was not. She thought he was a treacherous bastard who shafted anyone who had done better than him.'

Ben opened his mouth and shut it again when Amy kicked him under the table. She took Sayers's hand. 'Did he try to damage you?'

'Did he just! And not only me! Anything he ever said about anyone we knew was poison. He was like one of Agatha Christie's poisoned-pen people, except he didn't do it on paper. There was that business with Gregory Jepson. Greedy bastard, but I've no reason to suppose his fingers were in the till. And I really didn't believe that lady vicar was dealing in crystal meth!'

'It was kind of you to stay friends with him, Willie. Ben, bring a bottle of scotch from the bar, will you?'

By the time Ben came back, Willie had told Amy about Jilly, and about his suspicions that Fitz had spread that slander about him.

'So why didn't you cut him off, stop seeing him?' the bar manager asked.

'Because I'm a politician. You don't alienate dangerous people more than you have to.'

'You were with him the day he died, weren't you?'

'I was indeed. He summoned me. And for the usual reason, I came.'

'And you went up to the Bridge with him… what, about nine fifteen that evening?'

Willie Sayers looked a little surprised that Amy knew the timing of his meeting with such accuracy, but he didn't comment. He had a quick nip of his whisky. 'Strange meeting we had. Not really the Fitz I'd come to hate. Full of apologies and regrets for having been scurrilous about me in the past. He was a reborn Fitz, he explained. Turning over a new leaf and all that sort of thing.'

He reached again for his glass. 'I found it hard to take

in, to tell you the truth. Wondered if he was up to something even more underhand than usual.'

'Did he give a reason for his change of heart?'

'Well, he claimed that he'd been granted a solution to his financial problems. Strange expression to use, I thought – "been granted".'

Amy and Ben exchanged a look. Neither was about to reveal to the MP the source of Fitz's 'grant'. If Willie Sayers didn't know about Greg Jepson's largesse – and he appeared not to – then they were both happy to let that situation continue.

But Amy wanted to find out more while the booze was making their guest so garrulous. 'Did Fitz say anything else?' she asked. 'To explain his new-found serenity?'

'He did say that a lot of things were becoming clear to him, and that some secrets were about to be revealed.'

'Secrets about him – or about other people?'

'He didn't say which.'

'But did he imply that any of these secrets might involve you?'

'Good Lord no!' Willie Sayers laughed rather too heartily. 'Never any secrets between Fitz and me.'

Amy decided it wasn't the moment to mention the story Ianthe Berkeley had told her about a girl called Jilly who had ended up in Regent's Canal. 'But did he name any names?'

'No. But he did imply that he was about to reveal a secret about someone who had shafted him at some point.'

'Shafted him in his personal or professional life?' asked Ben.

'The implication was that it was professional. Something to do with his will.'

'Was that all he said?' she asked.

'It was, except for a rather odd thing he said as I was leaving. "Sorry again about my misdemeanours, Willie old bean. Good luck. And remember, where there's a will, there's a way of finding out most things…"'

Amy and Ben exchanged another look. In both of their minds the image of Griffiths Bentley bulked large.

CHAPTER FIFTEEN

Meriel Dane finished arranging pieces of roast chicken left over from Sunday lunch on a bed of watercress. She added half slices of orange, cut without pith, scattered over toasted almonds, then anointed the dish with a dressing made with olive oil, a grainy mustard, and sherry wine vinegar combined with seasonings and a smidgen of honey.

She stood for a moment admiring the completed salad, then was unable to resist dabbing a finger onto a dressing-laden piece of chicken, and licking it. She closed her eyes as a flavour of chicken flesh combined with the sour-sweet vinaigrette exercised her taste buds. Heavenly! Would that divine Constable Chesterton appreciate the lunch she was sending up to the CID 'Incident Room', as the Admiral's Bridge was now known? Immediately after Fitz's death there had been a bit of a battle with the police over keeping the pub open, won when Amy had insisted that as no crime had actually been committed on the premises, there was no reason to label the Admiral Byng a crime scene and close it down. She had had to concede that the large first-floor room, Fitz's Bridge, could be given over to their computers and screens for displaying the photos, and those funny scribbles on whiteboard that appeared on so many of the fictional crime series the television found so popular. But DI Cole avoided the place, and DC Chesterton seemed to be the only one who was ever up there, so she and Amy had had no problems getting in and out of the place.

Meriel sighed as she thought of the constable's soulful eyes and his broad figure; surely his poorly-tailored suit concealed a powerful set of toned muscles just waiting to be flexed in someone's bed? She gave a snort of derision at her wayward imagination, but ran a fresh coat of lip gloss on to her mouth before securing cling film over the chicken dish and placing it in the fridge. Then she turned her attention to possible changes to the bar menu.

She had never been kept so busy in this kitchen. First the excitement of the television filming, then the death of poor old Fitz, and even on the following Monday it seemed Crabwell's inhabitants could not keep away from the pub they had ignored for so many years. She had had to make two quiches for lunches instead of the usual one, taking the opportunity to use up the remains of Sunday's roasted vegetables that had accompanied the loin of pork escalopes. The other tart had been the usual cheese and onion, which provided the vegetarian option.

Meriel tapped her biro on her teeth as she mentally trawled her cache of recipes for something that would prove irresistible to Ben Milne, that would make him realise here was someone not only oozing sexual attraction, but a cook who could produce food the television audience was waiting for. This had to be her big chance. The small screen would lap up her combination of culinary expertise and raw sex. Cooking programmes were as much about the personalities as the food.

Meriel reckoned her physical attributes matched what she considered her exceptional ability at the kitchen stove. Her curves were, well, curvy; her lips were fantastically kissable; her eyes a wonderful green. They had had poetry written to them. All right, it wasn't going to match a laureate's efforts, but she would never forget: 'Oh, goddess, I could drown in the emerald pools that see this humble suitor kneeling in worship before you.' She knew exactly how to flutter her eyelashes (enhanced by the best false ones the market had to offer) at an attractive male. There was no shortage of prime pecs for regular sessions in her king-sized bed.

What TV producer, she held, could resist engaging a chef whose food was to die for *and* who matched any Hollywood siren in the looks department?

The natural move for her to make this evening would be on Ben Milne. But the cook could assess a man's willingness to join in the seduction game as easily as she picked out fresh fish from those that had been more than a day on the slab. And Ben's body language seemed to express an inexplicable resistance to her charms.

Apart from that, she liked men who took charge in bed, and Ben didn't ooze that sort of appeal. 'Rough stuff, that's your taste, isn't it?' the burly gardener who'd been hired to sort her shrubs and roses had said on his second visit. She'd lavished chocolate brownies on him for his afternoon tea, together with flirtatious giggles as she'd asked how he was getting on with her beds. There'd been no suggestive moves on his part, he'd pulled her towards him in one delightfully powerful movement, and there'd just been time to take him upstairs to prove she could give as good as she got before she'd had to return to the pub for the kitchen's evening session. The scars on his neck and biceps had taken several days to disappear. Pity he'd decided to move to Spain shortly afterwards.

Reluctantly, Meriel put the matter of who was to share her bed that evening to one side, and returned to the matter of the bar menu.

Dare she introduce *Jansson's Temptation*? Just bringing to mind how potatoes, onions, anchovies, and cream could combine into a dish that married tantalising flavour with an unctuous quality that caressed your every taste bud made Meriel feel randy. Her husband had been Swedish and a chef. He had served this dish to her the night he proposed. She'd been nineteen years old. Even now, twenty-seven years later, Meriel got goosebumps remembering that evening. He'd been tall, powerful, charismatic, and fun. Life together had veered between heaven and hell, but ever since that night, physical passion and food for her went together. One appetite fuelled the other. After sex, raid the fridge!

Sven had taught her so much. Meriel had absorbed all his culinary skills, and had helped to run the small restaurant he'd opened in Northumberland. He'd go off chasing down local suppliers, leaving her to man the kitchen. Oh, it had been so cold up there! Meriel was convinced it had been the cold that had made her miscarry, not once, not twice, but three times. It was after the third occasion that she'd discovered his other women. Local suppliers they certainly had been! To add to her misery, bankruptcy loomed. Faced with her fury, he had laughed!

Meriel forced away her memories of that time. She'd been on her own since, and much the better for it. After all, who wanted the same dish every day? Back to the bar menu. However, she had not done more than note down Duck Fingers with Chilli Dip before the swing door opened to admit Amy Walpole.

What was coming now? That bar manager title was a joke. She didn't just do that. Amy managed – or tried to manage – every department of the pub, particularly now the Admiral was no more.

Meriel had arrived at the pub the Tuesday morning after Amy's discovery to find police everywhere and the television crew in disorder. No one had bothered to witness her reaction to the news, she had been able to retire to the kitchen and compose herself.

She and Fitz had originally met in Northumberland, some fifteen years ago. He'd come into their restaurant, *The Midnight Sun*, a dapper chap heading for what Meriel in those days thought of as the twilight zones, those years after the sunshine days of fifty, but looking still up for it, with an endearing twinkle in his eyes. He'd been accompanied by a pouty blonde teenager. She'd displayed all the signs of wanting to be anywhere else with anyone else. Over dessert, the heavenly *Katrinplommon soufflé*, the girl had erupted, shouted at him, then walked out.

Instead of chasing after her, the old boy had ordered a brandy. There were no other customers, Sven had left on one of his 'supply hunting' excursions, and Meriel had come and sat with the abandoned client. The blonde teenager had not been mentioned. Instead, they'd talked about the Admiral Byng, Fitz's pub on the Suffolk coast. She'd loved the way his eyes had lit up as he described its medieval origins, the view over the North Sea from his 'Bridge', the first-floor room he used as an office. 'Should be used for private functions, but there isn't the demand.' When he'd finally left, he'd pressed a card into Meriel's hand and told her that if she was ever in that part of the world, she should look him up.

She hadn't thought much about it at the time, but three years later, as the fall-out from Sven's shenanigans was settling, the sale of the restaurant had gone through and she was looking for a job. Lo and behold, the classified columns of the *Hotel & Caterer* contained a 'cook wanted' ad for the Admiral Byng in Crabwell.

Meriel hadn't written, she'd gone straight to Suffolk, exchanging one windy seaside location for another, but one that was much warmer, in every sense. Fitz had remembered her the moment she'd walked into the bar. 'My Northern delight,' he'd called her. 'The one high spot in my tour of Roman Britain. The Romans should have kept it, I said afterwards and swore never to leave this place again. I will die right here in Crabwell. Now, what did you say your name was?' It seemed either she hadn't told him, or he'd forgotten. He definitely hadn't connected her with any sordid newspaper story.

There'd been no need for references or a kitchen trial. The job was hers.

It had been the saving of her. Slowly, slowly, her finances had been sorted out. Fitz had offered to lend her money, but she'd refused. Frying pans and fires, she'd said. He'd supported her in every other way, though. There'd been hints that he'd 'look after her' when he'd departed for the Great Bridge in the sky. Which was very nice of him, but what Meriel needed now was the finance to open her own place. The Admiral Byng was never going to provide the clientele that would appreciate the food she wanted to cook. She'd hinted to Fitz that a backer for a chic little eating place could find it a rewarding investment, but had got nowhere.

'Meriel, how are things going?' The cook stiffened. Since Amy had discovered the Admiral's corpse, she seemed to think she had carte blanche to question anybody about anything. Did she think she was Miss Marple?

'"Things going"? What, Amy, would you be meaning by, "things going"?' Meriel was rather pleased with her non-confrontational tone. Ever since Amy had arrived at the Admiral Byng, Meriel had had to fight a long-drawn-out battle for control of the kitchen. Amy seemed to think that as bar manager she could dictate what food Meriel cooked.

Only a few weeks ago she had climbed the stairs to the Bridge. Fitz had been writing at his desk, papers all over the place. The moment she appeared, he'd pushed the sheets together and slipped them underneath a file. Not that she would have tried to see what he'd been working on, she'd been too het up after her last confrontation with Amy.

'She wants me to stick to steak and chips and fish and chips. Says anything else takes too long to produce.'

The Admiral rose. 'Ah, Meriel, my dear,' he'd said with a jovial laugh, 'I wouldn't dare to interfere with the way Amy runs the bar. Equally I wouldn't dare to interfere with the way you run the kitchen.' Then he'd twinkled at her: 'With all your charms, I'm sure you can twist her around the little finger that's so good at sticking into those delicious pies you produce.'

Had he been getting at her? Meriel never knew with Fitz. On the surface he was the perfect gent yet, there were these little glimpses of a quite different man underneath. She was really intrigued to know what his attitude to sex now was. What had been his relationship with the young blonde who'd walked out on him in the Northumberland restaurant? Since their early encounters when she'd first come to the Admiral Byng, she was almost affronted that he'd never made any further advance on her, never even patted her on the bottom. Nor had he ever mentioned the few afternoons of passion they had shared. As Meriel had looked at him that afternoon in the Bridge, she'd had a sudden urge to run her fingers through his hair, draw that really very handsome if slightly wrinkled face down to hers, and give him

227

the longest, most lingering kiss he had ever had. Just to see how he reacted.

The Admiral might have had an inkling of this, for he gave a quick harrumph, fingered his cravat as though to check its arrangement, and added, 'You know, m'dear, we couldn't do without you in the kitchen. And I know you enjoy the way it seems to be your little kingdom. But if I decide to sell, then I'm afraid there would be no guarantees over staffing by the new management.'

She'd been rooted to the spot. What was all this 'I'll look after you'? And was he planning to sell? Before she could stutter out a plea to let her know what he had in mind, he'd looked at his watch, muttered something about a man he had to see, and waved her off his Bridge.

Something seemed to have changed in their relationship. It was a long time since they'd been really close, but she'd thought they were friends. And friends didn't hide monumental changes such as selling the Admiral Byng.

However, he must have said something to Amy, because the bar manager hadn't repeated her demands for culinary changes since. No one knew better than Meriel the place steak and chips and fish and chips had on the bar menu. Together with her famous steak and kidney pies, they meant a cosy arrangement with both the butcher and the fishmonger. But there were other favourites, mostly involving chicken, scallops, and lamb shanks. These were popular with diners in the formal saloon on the other side of the bar, where tables were laid with white damask and proper napkins.

Did Amy's appearance in the kitchen that Monday mean another demand to cut down the dishes on offer? Meriel prepared herself for battle. Surely Fitz's death meant the pub would definitely be put up for sale? Her job, her little kingdom, would depend on the success the food side could be seen to have. With so many people cutting back on the booze these days, food receipts were vital to the balance sheet's bottom line, and with the current popularity of the pub, these must be excellent.

Amy leaned against Meriel's little paperwork shelf in a slightly awkward stance. She didn't look comfortable. 'With us being so busy at present, I wondered how you were coping.'

Meriel's eyes narrowed. The woman had never worried about her being overworked before. 'It's a joy to have so many customers. I hope everyone is well satisfied?'

'We haven't had any complaints.'

If anybody wasn't satisfied, they were quick enough to complain. Compliments, though, were rarer – but not unknown. Meriel knew she was a good cook, but it was always pleasant to have her skills acknowledged. As things stood currently, it was more than pleasant, it was vital.

'And the police? I hope they're happy with what I've been able to send up to… now, what is it they call the Bridge?' She pretended to think for a moment. 'The Incident Room, isn't that it?'

Amy nodded. 'I've had no complaints from them either.'

'I should hope not!' The police should have said they'd never been better fed, or that the Admiral Byng was fortunate to have such a good cook. The sea-green-eyed Constable Chesterton suddenly lost some of his dishiness.

'How much *longer* are they going to be here?'

'Difficult to say. Their investigation doesn't seem to be getting very far.'

'Wasn't suicide mentioned?' Meriel started chopping onions, she didn't have time to stand around nattering without getting on with her prep.

'I hope I've managed to kill that one.' Amy sounded oddly satisfied.

Meriel's knife slipped and she narrowly missed cutting a finger. That hadn't happened since her disastrous parting with Sven. For months afterwards she'd hardly dared cut butter.

She recovered her equilibrium sufficiently to say, 'I got the impression when I last spoke to the revolting Cole specimen that he was still thinking in terms of suicide.'

'Fitz would never have committed suicide,' Amy protested. 'He wasn't that sort of man.' She fiddled with some papers on Meriel's desk shelf. 'After all...' she started to say, and then suddenly stopped.

Meriel paused her chopping. 'What do you mean?' she asked suspiciously; her eyes narrowed. 'There's something you're not telling me. What is it? Have you told the police?'

'Of course.' A couple of menus floated off the shelf and Amy bent to pick them up. That was probably why she looked a little red and flustered as she straightened and replaced them. 'I expect it will all come out in one of their press conferences.'

What sort of man would kill himself? Meriel wondered. Someone who had nothing left to live for? Someone who thought the world would be better off without them? The Admiral certainly didn't fit either of those criteria, not in her estimation. No, Fitz, was a man who had an appetite for life. Who knew where he was going and wouldn't allow anyone to deflect him. She should know!

'Apart from anything else, who in their right minds would commit suicide by drowning themselves in the bottom of a boat?' Amy sounded genuinely distressed. Unsurprising really, after all, it had been she who had discovered the dead body.

Surely, though, suicides couldn't be 'in their right mind'?

'And if Fitz had been wanting to commit suicide...'

Which you had already ruled out, thought Meriel, wishing Amy would get to the point and leave her alone. Amy, on the other hand, was trying to extend their conversation. There was information she wanted to elicit from Meriel.

'... he would definitely have chosen a more comfortable way to go,' she continued.

Now that Meriel could agree with. The Admiral wasn't one of your rough and ready types.

'But the police seem to be getting nowhere,' Amy continued, fiddling with a loose thread at her waist. She was, as usual, wearing a knitted top and nicely fitted jeans, an outfit that didn't get in the way when serving at the bar and showed off her credentials (as Meriel liked to call a woman's shape) whilst not being overly suggestive. No flies on Amy Walpole!

'Ben and I...'

Oh ho! So that was the way the wind was blowing, was it? Well, Meriel wished her good luck with the TV presenter.

'We're looking at the options.'

Meriel looked up from dumping her onions in a pan with arachide oil – so much more nuanced than sunflower – together with cumin seed, suddenly alert. 'What do you mean, options?'

'Well,' Amy shuffled her weight from one leg to the other a little uneasily. 'Who was where at the time he was... that is, when Fitz lost his life?'

Meriel didn't like the sound of this. 'You mean the pair of you are turning *amateur detective*?'

A slight flush coloured Amy's face. Meriel ignored how it suited her, softening her more usual severity.

'I wouldn't say that.'

Which means that you are! Meriel moved on to prepping salad. 'I don't know why you think I could have anything to tell you. Last week I was as surprised as everybody else to hear of your *awful* discovery.' She gave a neat little shudder.

For a moment she seemed to have deflected Amy. All the flattering colour vanished from her face. 'Yes, it was awful. I couldn't believe what I was seeing.' Then she collected herself. 'But that's it, don't you see? If we're to make any sense of what happened, we have to have a proper timeline.'

Meriel couldn't help snorting. 'Honestly, Amy, listen to yourself. "Timeline"? What does it mean, for heaven's sake?'

Strangely, this seemed to focus Amy. 'As I said, we're

sorting out where everyone was that night after ten thirty p.m., which is the last time any of the staff saw Fitz.' It wasn't the right moment to mention that Ianthe Berkeley had gone up to the Bridge with the old boy. She took a deep breath. 'I mean, you'd already gone, Meriel, leaving the kitchen, I have to say, in a terrible mess.'

'Yes, well, I would have cleaned it up the next morning… you know, if it hadn't been for all the police and…' Meriel threw the last of the salad ingredients into a bowl and placed it in the fridge. A jar of dressing was already there, waiting for service. 'It wasn't as though I'd asked you to do it.'

'No, but there was no one to help clear up the bar after it closed. You know we usually do that together.'

Meriel was silent. This was another of her little peeves. Why on earth should she be expected to help with that task? She was a cook, not a waitress or washer-upper. If only her job at the Admiral Byng didn't mean so much to her. She had started to help Amy just after the girl had arrived at the pub. Meriel could remember clearly the bedraggled and wretched piece of humanity that had turned up one rainy night three years earlier. They hadn't met till the following morning, when Fitz had introduced them, but Meriel could see what a bad state Amy was in. She'd often wondered what traumatising life event had brought the young woman to Crabwell, but it was a subject on which Amy would never be drawn. So both women had their secrets.

But Meriel couldn't forget the warmth with which the Admiral had taken Amy in. Nor the way the newcomer had slotted easily into the role shortly afterwards when the regular barmaid had disappeared one afternoon with a brewery rep, neither to be seen ever again in the Admiral Byng. When, at the end of Amy's first evening, Meriel – having finished clearing up the kitchen and sorting out the ordering that needed to be done the next day – saw how exhausted the girl looked as she took in the state of the bar, she had helped collect and wash the glasses and show her how the chairs went up on the tables so the floor could be brushed and washed.

Amy had been so grateful and so sweet that Meriel had continued to help. After all, the additional hour was paid out at double rate. But there were times when it didn't suit her to stay, and the previous Monday night had been one of them.

'So where were you?'

Meriel stirred the onions, just beginning to colour, and didn't look at Amy.

'Come on, what can it matter telling me why you had to leave so early?'

Time to add the balsamic vinegar and brown sugar to the onions. She concentrated on careful stirring, trying to work out whether to tell Amy or not that she had seen Fitz leaving the pub and had snatched up her coat and hurried after him. Just because she had been working in the kitchen didn't mean that she hadn't been aware of the various rounds of drinks he had commanded, or the way he kept on referring to his 'Last Hurrah'. Ever since their little talk up in the Bridge, Meriel had been worried. She couldn't blame him for wanting to sell the pub, if that was what he had in mind. It couldn't be making much money, there were nights when not more than two or three steak and chips were sent out of the kitchen. But what would happen to her if the pub passed into other hands?

If you could cook, it was held that you could always get a job. These days, however, you needed bits of paper to prove you understood Health and Safety, weren't going to poison any diners. And the wretched worldwide web lay waiting to spew out all the sordid details of anyone's name you entered. Meriel had changed hers by deed poll after Sven had disappeared from her life, but that was no guarantee that some busybody wouldn't somehow link Meriel Dane with the Merle Johansson who had so nearly murdered her husband.

After it was all over, she'd been sent on an anger management course, and these days had much more control over the temper that had boiled over far too often, finally with disastrous results as Sven's misdeeds had come to light.

It must have been the effect of that last miscarriage. After discovering the text messages left on his mobile, for once abandoned in the restaurant kitchen when he'd been called out to discuss an outside catering job – at least, that is what he'd told her it was – she had then, with outrage simmering through every vein in her body, gone through the unbelievably untidy kitchen drawer where the bills were kept, and had found final demands and far worse.

It had been the silly smile on his face as he walked back into the kitchen that had detonated the powder keg inside her. Meriel had snatched up the first thing to hand, which turned out to be the steel he used to sharpen his knives. She'd had no idea of the strength in her arms, developed by kneading dough and carrying heavy trays. She swung at his legs with all her might. He came crashing down onto the tiled floor, smashing his head against the stove. Blood poured onto the white tiles as, lying on his back, he bellowed in pain and bewilderment. With anger still raging through her, Meriel had raised the steel again and brought it down on his crotch. Twelve years later she could still hear his scream of agony. Then she had raised the steel again, this time going for his skull.

It had been the fish delivery man who had caught her uplifted arm and wrestled the weapon from her. She had resisted for several minutes, then, suddenly, the rage had left her, as completely as a tide going out, leaving a clean beach.

The fish man had rung the ambulance; the paramedics had called the police, and for the next few days Meriel had gone around not knowing what was happening, only that Sven's most serious injury was the one that meant it was unlikely he would ever satisfy a woman again. The stove had fractured his skull, but his brain, such as it was, did not appear to have suffered.

The case had received blanket coverage in all the gutter press: 'THE CHEF, THE WIFE AND THE LOVERS', ran the most popular headline. 'COOKING THE BOOKS FOR MAXIMUM SATISFACTION', was another. The Receivers had been called in, and the restaurant had been put on the market.

Meriel had expected to be charged with assault if not attempted manslaughter, but Sven had not pressed charges, instead he'd decamped to Sweden the moment the hospital released him, chased by furious husbands and betrayed lovers.

The aftermath had been terrible. The red-top press had chased her. Creditors had demanded satisfaction. Promises had meant that bankruptcy was narrowly avoided. Job hunting quickly revealed that no one wanted to employ a cook who could run amok in the kitchen, even if it wasn't with knives. She had changed her name and finally there had been that advertisement in the *Hotel and Caterer*. Only after she had started work at the Admiral Byng and Fitz had been so caring, had the nightmare of the end of her marriage begun to fade, and she had gradually cleared her debts. But only just. If her job vanished, Meriel did not know how she would manage.

That was why on the Monday evening before he died, only a week before, she had had to run after the Admiral and find out exactly what the position with the pub was.

'Fitz,' she had managed, out of breath after stumbling along the pebbled beach in her kitchen clogs, sea water from the outgoing tide squelching inside them. 'I must speak to you.'

He had turned, and she had recoiled at his contorted expression. He seemed to be in the grip of some passion.

'Fitz?'

'Yes, Mrs Johansson? What do you want?'
She had gasped at his use of her former name.

Back in the kitchen more than a week later, 'It's a simple enough question,' Amy said insistently. 'Where did you go after you left the kitchen that Monday? I know you weren't here after 10.30.'

'That's my business!'

'It won't be when the police start questioning you. And they will. I'm surprised they haven't already.'

Meriel visualised the green-eyed Constable. Would she mind being questioned by him? She thought rapidly.

Skilfully preparing slices of mango she said, 'I have an alibi.'

'An alibi?' It was obvious that was something Amy had not considered. 'What sort of alibi?'

'I was in bed.'

'In bed? Alone?'

'Of course not, but I don't see why I should bring someone else into this. He's got nothing to do with the Admiral.'

'If he's perfectly innocent, then it can't hurt to have his name.'

Meriel sighed. Would giving Amy a name save her from further interrogation? She reached over and stirred the onion marmalade, which, on the side of a slice of her special boiled ham, was little short of perfection. However, for once the idea of blissful food failed to excite her.

'He's a fisherman,' she said, her voice quavering slightly. 'His name's Jed Rhode...'

Amy frowned. 'Jed Rhode… I don't think I know him.'

Meriel summoned up reserves of strength. 'He doesn't live in Crabwell. He fishes out of Lowestoft. I went down to his place that night. He's *divine*, just *divine*, darling,' she managed to burble. 'Hair the colour of old rose gold and shoulders like an ox.'

Amy recognised the description. The fisherman was often hanging around Crabwell, and it shouldn't be too difficult to establish whether the cook was telling the truth or not.

'But,' Meriel continued with something like satisfaction, 'you won't be able to check with him because he's off fishing now and won't be back for days.'

Ben Milne had drunk more than he'd intended during the Sunday lunch with Willie Sayers, and after the MP left he'd continued drinking. Old habits died hard, and his mind was full of thoughts he didn't want to think. Alcohol had always guaranteed oblivion for him. He'd even bought himself a litre of Teacher's from Crabwell's only convenience store (which, with delusions of grandeur, had entitled itself a 'supermarket').

He was a functioning alcoholic who could restrain himself when he was working, and had once gone four months without a drop when he'd been filming in Saudi Arabia. But when idle he was still susceptible to hitting the bottle hard. And he was idle now in Crabwell. He'd finished any filming that could be done; Stan had returned to London. And Ben wasn't anticipating any developments on the murder investigation until Fitz's funeral, now fixed for the Wednesday. The events of the last few days had left him tired and restless.

As usual, nobody would have known how much he was drinking. He just returned to his room continually for little sips from the whisky bottle – and frequent teeth-cleaning to deal with the smell. He was determined not to drink on the Wednesday itself – he'd need all his wits about him at the funeral. He had a feeling something might happen at the event that could be invaluable for his programme, and he was pleased he'd persuaded Victoria Whitechurch to allow Stan the cameraman to return to film the proceedings.

It was late on the Monday evening when he was drinking red wine openly in the almost empty bar of the Admiral Byng that he had the call on his mobile.

'Ben?' The voice was slightly Welsh and vaguely familiar.

'Yes, that's me.'

'It's Griffiths Bentley... you know, the solicitor?'

'I know.'

'And I was just wondering... are you still in Crabwell?'

'Yes.'

'Will you be at the funeral on Wednesday?'

'I will.'

'Good. There's something I want to tell you about.' There was suppressed excitement in Griffiths Bentley's voice. 'Something that might explain the circumstances of Fitz's death.'

'Can't you tell me about it on the phone?' demanded

Ben, his journalistic instincts aroused. 'Or I could come to your office in the morning?'

'No, there are a couple of details I've got to check with other people. We'll talk after the funeral on Wednesday.'

And with that the solicitor rang off. Leaving a very frustrated Ben Milne sitting in the bar of the Admiral Byng.

Soon after, he went upstairs to his bed, and the dwindling contents of his bottle of Teacher's.

CHAPTER SIXTEEN

There was no way around it, Amy said to herself. She would have to confront that little pseud Bob Christie again and try to get out of him some explanation as to why he'd lied to her at their last meeting.

She recalled his demand that he be believed because he was a journalist, and almost laughed out loud. When had anyone ever believed a journalist? Weren't they jostling with estate agents and politicians for last place on that 'who-do-you-trust?' list she'd seen in the paper the other day? He didn't even seem to be a proper journalist, just a pretend one. All that nonsense with the green eyeshade… She had a momentary temptation to adopt a persona that would match his fantasy about himself – some kind of sultry ace-reporter with a slit skirt and a husky voice – and shook her head. She was becoming as mad as everyone else.

It was another grey, windy, depressing day, but Amy was in a dogged mood as she tramped steadily along the beach and into the village, wondering what Bob Christie's office would be like. It was hardly likely to be full of the ringing telephones and reporters banging away on manual type-writers that she remembered from that old Walter Matthau and Jack Lemmon movie. No, that was then and this was now: she guessed the place would be quiet, sad, and shabby.

It turned out to be a small house next to a fish-and-chip shop, the door and window frames needed painting, and even the brass plate outside saying *The Crabwell Clarion* looked tarnished and neglected. Presumably Bob couldn't afford a cleaning woman to polish it, but was too important to deign to do it himself.

She rang the bell and was buzzed inside. The interior smelled of fish. She wondered if the shop provided Bob with food in exchange for old newspapers.

On her left was a door with EDITOR engraved in big black letters on the frosted glass that formed the top half. She knocked, and a harsh voice shouted 'Enter', from which she deduced that Bob was in macho mode.

The room dejected her. The front pages tacked to the walls were yellowed, the piles of newspapers on the floor were dusty, and Bob's desk was covered in unenticing junk, creased bits of paper and an aged desktop computer in much-fingered cream plastic. The editor was wearing an open-necked shirt, a cardigan with holes at the elbows, carpet slippers, and the inevitable green eyeshade, which he certainly didn't need in that gloomy room. And yes, he was still wearing mauve socks, though she hoped he had washed them since Friday. The whole effect was as depressing as it was obviously contrived. She was surprised he hadn't completed the ensemble with a fedora, though a woolly cap with ear muffs would have been more in keeping and much more practical, since the room was freezing despite the best efforts of the one-bar electric fire.

Unasked, she sat in the wooden chair opposite him. 'The kettle isn't working,' he said. 'You could have whisky, I suppose.'

Amy was so cold she was tempted, but she shook her head. 'I don't want anything except to know why you were lying to me last Friday.'

'What business is it of yours?' he asked, in what was intended to be an intimidating bark, but came out as more of a yelp.

'Let's not go through that again, Bob. The funeral is tomorrow, and it's time you cut the crap and told the truth.'

He sagged in his seat and gazed at her wearily. 'I had my reasons.'

'Just tell me what happened with Fitz on Monday, Bob, and then I'll get out of your hair. I'm sure you're busy.'

There was no evidence of busyness anywhere, but the compliment seemed to cheer him up a bit.

'I was doing a profile of him for the *Clarion*. Local character and all that. It's an occasional series. You know the kind of thing.'

'I've seen a few of them.' He looked at her hopefully. 'I enjoyed that one you did of the vicar.'

He brightened up.

'So why were you seeing Fitz?'

'Just to clarify a few details.'

She raised her right eyebrow. 'Anything interesting?'

He shook his head.

'Come on, Bob. You're a seasoned newspaperman. You must have dug up some stuff on Fitz. He was a bit of a mystery man, but you'd have known where to look.'

'I had found a few interesting facts, since you ask. But now he's dead I don't want to betray any secrets.'

Amy did her best to get him to say more, but the more she pressed him, the more he clammed up. Her frustration was giving way to anger, when the doorbell sounded. Bob frowned. 'I'm not expecting anyone,' but he pressed the buzzer, and a pinstripe suit containing Willie Sayers came through the door.

'What an unexpected pleasure,' he said, bowing his head in Amy's direction. 'You must forgive my interrupting you.'

She contemplated offering to vacate the chair and leave them together, but then thought better of it. Maybe Bob Christie's research into Fitz's past had unearthed something about the Admiral's shared history with Willie Sayers. About the young woman who had drowned in the Regent's Canal perhaps…?

Bob adopted his challenging look. 'Amy won't be staying much longer. What's up with you?'

'I'd rather wait.'

Bob sat up straight and managed a bark. 'Come on, spit it out.'

Willie sighed. 'Very well then. Actually, come to think of it, Amy might be able to help.' He turned towards her. 'Do you know anything about the Templar gold that the Crabwell rumour factory claims was buried near your pub?'

She shook her head. 'Sorry. No. Obviously I've heard the rumours, but I think they're complete rubbish.'

He turned back to Bob. 'And you?'

'You want to know because…?' asked Bob.

'Because I like to know what's going on in my constituency,' said Willie rather stiffly.

'I've heard something about it, but I don't know details.'

'Anything more than the rumours?'

'No. I reckon it's just fanciful village gossip.'

There was a pause, which Amy broke. 'I'm here because Bob was doing work on a profile of Fitz and I was wondering if he'd consulted any of the locals about it.'

Bob sat up straight. 'My sources are sacrosanct.'

'Oh, come off it, Bob. I'm not asking you to betray any Cabinet secrets, just to help me find out a bit more about his past, his family history and all that. I was fond of him, you know. As I'm sure you two were.'

They both nodded rather unconvincingly.

'You must surely have talked to Griffiths Bentley,' she said. 'A pro like you.'

'Oh, all right.' Once again Bob Christie responded to flattery. 'Yes, I talked to him, but nothing important was said.'

There was another pause.

'I heard something about an illegitimate child,' proffered

Willie. 'But I don't know who it was supposed to be or who were supposed to be its parents.'

'Fitz's child?' asked Amy.

'I just don't know.'

She turned to Bob, who shook his head and tried to look mysterious. Amy valiantly threw in a few follow-up questions, but knowing when she was defeated, she left them to it, speculating fruitlessly on whether there was some deep connection between the two of them.

After the front door had shut behind her, Bob took a bottle of whisky out of his desk drawer and looked enquiringly at Willie. 'Quick snifter?'

'Thanks, Bob. Just the job on a day like this.'

But the MP wasn't as relaxed as he was trying to appear. There was barely masked anxiety in his tone as he asked, 'What did you actually find out from Griffiths Bentley?'

The editor hesitated only for a moment, and then he spilled the beans.

Amy strode off towards the beach, her mind straying into the familiar territory of wondering which of the old bores would be worst to be stuck with on a desert island. From there her mind drifted towards Ben, and how agreeable it might be to be on the sands with him... in rather more clement weather. And in fact in a rather more congenial environment. Barbados, perhaps...?

She shook herself out of the fantasy and went back to thinking about Fitz. Maybe Griffiths Bentley was the man to give her a lead...?

She rang him on her way back to the Admiral Byng, but there was no reply. Nor was there the other dozen times she tried throughout the rest of the day. Oh, well, she thought, I'll just have to have a word with him after the funeral. He's bound to be there.

CHAPTER SEVENTEEN

'Hypocrites,' Amy muttered to herself under her breath.

Though the regular Sunday congregation rarely achieved double figures, the church was packed for the Wednesday afternoon funeral. Of course Fitz had been a popular resident of the village – no doubt about that. And even more popular for his recent distribution of free drinks at the 'Last Hurrah'. Amy should have been pleased to witness so many friends assembled to see him off. But she strongly suspected that people had heard the rumour that the service would be televised. And indeed, now she looked towards the pulpit, she noticed Ben's cameraman Stan stationed discreetly beside a pillar, his lens sweeping the beaming mourners.

Meriel Dane must have arrived early. She was sitting, or perhaps posing was the correct word, in the front pew, occasionally turning to her neighbour to make some observation and, in the process, allowing the camera to catch her profile. Every now and then she dabbed one eye with a handkerchief, using the other to check whether Stan was filming her or not. Willie Sayers had also opted for an early arrival, and gained a front row seat where the camera could not fail to notice him. He was dressed in a very smart black overcoat and seemed ready to adopt the role of chief mourner, or chief anything, if requested to do so. Bob Christie had conversely positioned himself at the rear of the congregation, as if to observe the various comings and goings. She saw him scribble something on a notebook, then pause and lick his pencil. Did pencils really need to be licked, or was it just something he'd heard that journalists did? The latter probably. He pulled a face, but whether because he'd spotted something or whether he just didn't like the taste of pencil was unclear.

A few rows back from the altar sat DI Cole and DC Chesterton. There was an expression of complacency on the older officer's face. He had used his influence to ensure that the coroner was finally happy and speeded up the process that had led to a suicide verdict being recorded. So far as he was concerned, another case had been neatly wrapped up with a bow on top. And his recurrent fear – that his slowness in reaching solutions to crimes might lead to Scotland Yard being brought in – had once again not been realised. Back at the Admiral Byng, all the police impedimenta had been removed from the Bridge, and life at the pub could continue as normal. And here he was, DI Cole with his subservient sidekick DC Chesterton, attending the victim's funeral 'out of respect'. One of the most satisfactory conclusions to a case that he could remember.

Greta Knox entered hurriedly, as most people had, and

deposited a dripping umbrella at the back of the church. The rain must have got even worse, Amy thought. The church was beginning to smell of damp raincoats and damp wool. Greta looked around for a space where she could sit, started towards it, then frowned, reined back and looked again.

As well she might. Amy's first impression had been that the church was packed, but now she saw that the packing was both partial and selective. Though most pews contained as many damp parishioners as they could reasonably bear, one or two were almost empty – a fact explained by the geographical distribution of leaks from the roof. Water dripped from a great height, splashing onto the oak pews. Latecomers had, it would seem, a choice between standing at the back and getting wet. Well, everyone would get wet enough when they had to go outside for the burial itself, even those who had bagged themselves a dry seat now. Amy smiled briefly, then realised her predicament was precisely the same as Greta's. Where would she sit? Or stand? She was relieved to see Ben wave at her and point to the spot beside him. As she edged, apologetically, along the pew towards Ben, she heard him say: 'I saved a seat for you. I thought you might be a bit late, having to get rid of the drinkers and close up the pub.'

'Thank you,' she said with genuine gratitude. Ben had positioned himself in the middle of things, and had been early enough to lay claim to a yard or so of hard but dry seating. Then she added: 'You look like shit warmed up.'

'I feel like shit warmed up,' he said, not about to mention

the part that Teacher's had played in his condition. 'I couldn't sleep last night.'

Guilty conscience? Amy wondered briefly. Of course, he was playing things fairly straight now – all the indications were that Fitz's death had put on hold whatever hatchet job he had had planned for a failing pub. The programme, if it ever made it to the screen, would now have to be something more far more sympathetic. It would become, Ben had promised her, a eulogy to a popular landlord and pillar of the community. A diamond geezer. Still, Ben must have plenty on his conscience from previous projects. And the fact that he was on the side of the angels one minute didn't mean that he still would be the next. Potential viewing figures were everything. Amy wondered idly how far he'd go to increase his viewing figures. As far as murder…?

But she didn't voice such thoughts as she said, 'Really? A bit restless? Like Lady Macbeth?'

Ben frowned as if distantly remembering a warm after-noon in the Lower Sixth. 'Lady Macbeth…?'

'"Out, damned spot!"'

Ben nodded. 'Of course. It was the dog that kept her awake all night, wasn't it? Sorry. It's just…' He looked briefly over his shoulder and then continued in a very low whisper indeed: 'I can't get it out of my head that Fitz's murderer is here, in this church, now.'

'It could have been suicide…' Amy said teasingly.

Ben shook his head. 'We both know that's not true. Anyway, that's certainly not the line we're planning to take in the…'

'What line you're planning to take?' demanded Amy. 'You mean the documentary is now about the murder? You promised…'

'Sorry – bad choice of words. There's no line. Nothing about amateur detective work. I promise you, that's right out. It's just about good old Fitz. Loved by all. Missed by all. A diamond geezer.'

'So you said.'

'Well, it's true. The diamond geezer. It will be a eulogy. Straight up.'

'Why don't I believe you?'

'Because you are cynical and world weary. Whereas I still have the idealism of youth. On the other hand – wouldn't it be amazing if the killer gave himself away at the funeral? I mean, can you imagine the ratings? They'd be through the roof.'

Amy's gaze was glacial.

'OK. OK. Sorry. Forget I said that too. We're here to honour Fitz. Nothing else. It's not about ratings or even winning a BAFTA, though wouldn't that be great…? Great for Fitz, I mean. Very fitting and a lasting memorial to somebody I'd describe as a diamond geezer… Amy, stop looking at me as if I'm something you've found sticking to the sole of your shoe. It's the lack of sleep. I mean well, but it's all coming out wrong. I realise I'm just blathering.'

'Yes,' said Amy. 'You are blathering all right. But you sort of have a point all the same. I don't want a friend's death turned into fifty-five minutes of entertainment – but we do want to see Fitz's killer caught, and the police are honestly getting nowhere. Maybe Stan will pick something up on film. You really think that the murderer might reveal himself somehow?'

'Or herself. We have to be politically correct.'

'You think that conceding women can kill makes you some sort of feminist?'

Ben hesitated.

Amy shook her head. 'For your information, you're still blathering.'

'I told you: it's the lack of sleep.' It was true. All he wanted to do was to curl back into his bed and sleep off the excesses of the last two days. The hangover seemed to have split his brain down the middle and was now grinding the two parts together. 'But I've just got to stay awake this afternoon and watch everyone. People are a bit conscious of the camera… It's more likely they'll let their guard slip when they think Stan's filming elsewhere. Can you help me watch them? And elbow me hard in the ribs if I do drop off.'

'Elbow you hard? It would be my pleasure, Ben.'

'Did you see Meriel, by the way?'

'Auditioning for her new cookery series in the front row?'

'Yup. And Willie Sayers?'

'Three to the right, looking sincere and compassionate. The caring constituency MP.'

'You caught his expression?'

'Didn't need to. Bob Christie's at the back, making notes. And someone who from your description must be Greg Jepson's there too, working on his tablet, no doubt making a few more millions. I'm not sure what the protocol is about bringing tablets into church – unless you're Moses, of course. Oh, and there's that schoolgirl.'

'Schoolgirl?'

'The one you pointed out to me. I told you, she kept trying to order drinks at the Admiral Byng although she was underage.'

'Oh, Tracy Crofts.'

Why on earth would she be at Fitz's funeral, Amy wondered. She doubted whether the girl had even met him.

'Anyway,' Ben went on, 'who else should be here?'

Amy considered for a moment. 'Where's whatshername, your buddy from uni?'

'Who?' asked Ben.

'You know,' said Amy, ignoring Ben's studied innocence. 'That bitch-mutton-dressed-as-lamb Ianthe.'

A cough from the other side of Ben answered that question.

'Hi, Ianthe,' said Amy, sinking back into the pew.

She heard Ben suppress a juvenile snigger. He'd dropped her right in that one. Well, if he fell asleep, it would now be down to Ianthe to elbow him hard in the ribs, because, after that cheap trick, Amy wouldn't be doing him any more favours. Not in this life.

For a while they both sat there not speaking, the expectant hum of conversation all around them. Amy flicked through the prayer book. Ben, staring, cranium aching as though it had been scoured with wire wool, was reading the Decalogue, written in very faded gold lettering on a board behind the pulpit. 'Thou shalt not kill,' he mouthed silently. Why was that only number six? Making graven images was a relatively minor offence, surely? Who on earth rated that as number two? He wondered whether there was any scope for a reality show based on the Ten Commandments, one commandment getting voted off by the public every week until The Nation's Favourite Commandment could be revealed...? The problem was that the only prohibition most people remembered was the one about not coveting your neighbour's ass.

Ben felt, rather than heard, a gentle swish as Ianthe shifted in her seat, nyloned leg rubbing against nyloned leg in a way that he had always found vaguely erotic – even at a funeral. Maybe especially at a funeral, when eroticism was in short supply. While Ianthe's charms were clearly invisible to Amy, in Ben's book she was still a very attractive woman. Especially in a short black dress and black stockings. He was increasingly coming around to the idea that they had gone to bed together at university, though he couldn't remember any of the details. Maybe it was worth chatting her up a bit, seeing if something could be rekindled...? You never knew. He turned to her and said: 'Ianthe, I've been thinking...' and then, annoyingly, his sleep-deprived mind went blank again.

'Yes?' she said.

'Erm...' He really needed to do better than this. She was looking at him with mild interest, turning rapidly to bemused pity. Oh, God! What should he say to amuse and impress a publisher that he might want to sleep with if all else failed? 'It's funny,' he heard himself announce, 'if we were in a crime novel, now would be about the time we'd discover the Second Body.'

Wrong thing to say. Ianthe scowled at him. 'If I were ever in a novel, I assure you that it would not be a crime novel.'

'Why not?'

'Because all the crime novels that come across my desk are totally unrealistic. Still influenced by the so-called Golden Age, following fatuous rules formulated by some idiot called Ronald Knox.'

'Oh yes, I made a programme about those once,' said Ben. 'His Decalogue. Crime novels weren't allowed any identical twins, no Chinamen either.'

'All bloody nonsense!' Ianthe snorted. 'All crime fiction is bloody nonsense.'

Fair enough, he thought. You're talking to me like I'm an idiot. And I am an idiot. A sleep-deprived and hungover idiot, but an idiot for all that. He sighed, yawned, and studied the gold leaf Decalogue again. 'Thou shalt not steal' was at number eight, he noticed, just after adultery. Maybe that was it? They could get the viewing public to vote, and each week they'd rearrange the order? 'This week's big faller, down from number five, "Honour Thy Father and Thy Mother". And a new entry at number nine, "Eat Five a Day"...'

'Crime writers!' Ianthe exploded. It was one of those sauce bottle moments. At first she had refused to be drawn. Now it all flooded out onto Ben's plate. 'Formulaic tosh!

Six or seven suspects all of whom have a chapter devoted to them so that, by the end of each, the reader is manipulated into thinking that this is the killer. Then, when he's finished the first draft, the writer reads it all through again, decides which was the least likely suspect, and then pins the blame on that one, regardless of the actual evidence presented. And, my God, the number of fictional serial killers that there are out there! I mean, in real life, how many do you get? One or two a year? If that? And yet crime fiction is stuffed with them. Every bloody crime is committed by a serial killer – preferably one who mocks the police by leaving elaborate clues – clues that it is clear will eventually convict him. Does he realise that? Of course he does, but he still leaves the stupid clues. Because he's stupid.'

'I don't read a lot of detective fiction,' said Ben. He yawned again.

'As for thriller writers,' Ianthe continued, 'who do they direct all of the violence against? Which characters – or should I say which sex – will be beaten black and blue for the titillation of the reading public?'

Ben rubbed his eyes. Of course, what Ianthe was saying was true. There was a lot of very violent stuff out there these days. Didn't somebody recently say that she wouldn't review any more crime fiction with extreme violence against women? Quite right too. But Ianthe's voice was fading into the general hum of conversation. Ben nodded to show that he was still listening.

'What's worst of all,' Ianthe was saying, 'is the way crime

writers include in their books all sorts of obscure references to the genre – Chandler and his Mean Streets, say – and expect everyone to pick them up.'

Ben nodded again. They did that.

Then, suddenly and without any warning, it was all kicking off. A panel in the wainscoting, just below the Decalogue, moved slightly, then fell into the aisle with a crash. A Chinese gentleman emerged and smiled benignly at the congregation.

'Good grief! A secret passage!' Ben exclaimed aloud.

Then, a little further down the same wall, another panel broke into two and fell away. An identical Chinese gentleman appeared from a second passage.

'Bloody hell – twins!' said Ben. 'I certainly wasn't prepared for that.'

The second twin smiled. 'We came,' he said, 'because we had a strange and unaccountable premonition that something was afoot.' With a flourish, he took a small bottle out of his pocket.

I know what that is, thought Ben. It's a lethal but previously unknown poison. And I know exactly why he's done that, because of the thing his brother has just shown me – a vital clue that I'll keep to myself for the moment. Still, my intuition tells me...

Greta Knox was however already on her feet.

'Enough!' Knox said. 'There are rules that have to be followed in cases like this. This is not playing fair with anyone. You two have absolutely no business here. Out, both of you!'

'It was the policeman who did it!' one the twins shouted at the congregation. 'But it's a policeman you haven't encountered yet!'

'Yeah, right,' said Knox.

Taking the two gentlemen by the arm she hustled them to the back of the church. There was a loud creaking sound as the door opened, and some footsteps, then Victoria Whitechurch said something in a loud voice.

'Ouch!' exclaimed Ben. 'What the...'

'Sorry,' whispered Amy. 'You said to prod you hard in the ribs if you fell asleep. You were actually snoring.'

'Was I?' His headache was worse than ever.

'Yes,' she hissed. Then stopped and looked over her shoulder.

'And the very worst thing,' Ianthe continued, on the other side of Ben, 'is when something weird happens in the book and the writer passes it off as a dream or something stupid like...'

Then she too fell silent.

'I am the resurrection and the life sayeth the Lord,' Victoria intoned from the back of the church. 'He that believeth in me, though he were dead, yet shall he live: and whosoever liveth and believeth in me shall never die.'

The organ was playing some tune that Ben found vaguely familiar. Handel? Bach? No, it was 'I Do Like to Be Beside the Seaside', at a deadly slow tempo. Fitz's choice, no doubt, stipulated in that will of his. If he was looking down on them, he would have had a smile on his face.

'Did I miss anything?' whispered Ben. 'When I was…
not paying attention for a moment.'

'You were dead to the world,' said Amy. 'Head slumped
forward, eyes shut. Another couple of minutes and they'd
have buried you too. And you did miss something interesting.
Greta Knox left…'

'Yes, with the Chinese twins…'

'Sorry? We're back to blathering again,' said Amy.

'No twins?'

'No twins that I saw.'

'Deadly but unknown poison?'

'Oh yes, masses of that.'

'Really?'

'Don't be an idiot, Ben. Greta simply ran out of the
church just when the vicar came in…'

Amy stopped speaking, even in a whisper. Victoria
Whitechurch and the pall-bearers, in their slow march
down the aisle, had drawn level with their pew. As she
walked slowly past them, Victoria frowned her disapproval.
Both Amy and Ben assumed an undeserved look of
innocence.

'Ran out?' hissed Ben, as soon as the coffin had passed
them. 'Why?'

'How on earth am I supposed to know that? She didn't
stop and explain it all to me.'

'Too emotional for her?'

'Too something or other. You don't leave a funeral just
before the coffin arrives unless you are pretty desperate.'

'Needed a pee?'

'A pee? You do know how to raise the tone of a funeral, don't you?'

'Do I? Look, you could go after her and I'll stay here to watch the congregation.'

'You could go after her just as the service is starting, if it will make any difference to your ratings. I'll stay here and pay my respects to Fitz, if you don't mind.'

'Yes, sorry, I...'

Ben looked up. Victoria was now staring directly at him from her vantage point of the pulpit. He picked up his prayer book and studied it carefully.

'We have come here today,' said Victoria, 'to remember before God our dear brother Geoffrey, and to give thanks for his life.'

'Unless you've got other plans, Ben,' Amy muttered.

In the address that followed shortly after, Victoria did not actually say that Fitz was the dimwit who tried to screw up the phone mast deal to save the church. She was far too professional for that. Nor did she say that if death hadn't intervened, the roof would continue to leak until the church was demolished, or turned into chic flats for weekenders. But somehow she managed to get the message across. It was, in a sense, a class act, but most of the mourners would have failed to notice, their attention being almost entirely on Stan and his camera as it roved around the church. Ben hoped that Stan had caught something earlier – perhaps including Greta's flight. Once or twice, when he managed to scan the congregation himself, he noticed that Bob Christie was casting his own glances towards the door, as if expecting Greta to return. Nobody else had budged from their seats, but Ben had a strange feeling that somebody was missing from the church. Who should have been there but was not?

'Somebody's gone AWOL,' he said to Amy. 'There's somebody who hasn't shown up.'

Another cough from the pulpit suggested that he had again been too loud. He hoped Stan hadn't picked it up too – well, they could always edit that out. 'Psalm 39,' Victoria announced. '"I said, I will take heed to my ways: that I offend not in my tongue."' She looked at Ben as if the Psalmist might have had him in mind when he wrote those words.

'Don't take it personally,' Amy whispered. 'It's standard. And you may like to turn your prayer book the right way up.'

'"I will keep my mouth as it were with a bridle,"' Victoria continued, still looking at Ben, '"while the ungodly is in my sight. I held my tongue, and spake nothing: I kept silence, yea, even from good words; but it was pain and grief to me."'

'Do you think that's some sort of clue?' hissed Ben. 'She's saying she knows who the killer is, but can't reveal it.'

'In that case it was King David who knew who killed Fitz,' said Amy.

'King David?'

'He wrote most of the psalms. You don't go to church much, do you?'

'I was baptised once. Not recently though.'

'I don't think it's one of the psalms they use for baptism.'

There was another look of disapproval from on high.

'"For I am a stranger with thee: and a sojourner, as all my fathers were,"' continued Victoria. '"O spare me a little, that I may recover my strength: before I go hence, and be no more seen."'

Ben gave Amy a significant look, but Amy shook her head. There was no coded message there. Still, some of those words rang true. How many of them were strangers and sojourners in the village? How many had come, one way or another, to gather their strength from this bleak stretch of coast?

'Did you see which bit they're going to bury him in?' asked Ben.

They were now trooping out of the church into the damp air of the churchyard. The rain had mercifully ceased, but the grass squelched underfoot. Amy zipped up her Barbour. 'If you think I went for a wander around just before the service, you're in for a disappointment, Ben. It was pouring. Like everyone else I just made a run for the door. I think we're going over to the far side – by the sea. It's a nice spot. I wouldn't mind being buried there myself when my time comes.'

Ben pulled a face. He had no plans to be buried anywhere. 'Where exactly?'

'You can't see it yet. It's a bit hidden away behind those bushes.'

'I've just thought who wasn't there,' said Ben. 'It was Griffiths Bentley. You don't think he's done a runner? I always thought he was the most likely murderer. I mean, that's what Willie Sayers was implying on Sunday, wasn't he? Anyway, Bentley was doing all that fiddling around, helping Fitz change his will. I bet he's on a healthy tickle from that.'

'But why should that make him want to murder the old boy?' asked Amy.

'My instinct tells me that he drowned Fitz,' said Ben. 'I've never trusted solicitors – all they have to do is pass some fairly easy exams when they're in their twenties, and for the rest of their lives charge people exorbitant fees for services they wouldn't require if solicitors hadn't invented them. Mark my words – Griffiths Bentley killed Fitz. That's what happened. You heard it from me first.'

Amy shrugged. Stan was ahead of them, walking backwards, camera focussed on the coffin as it covered the last few yards it would ever travel. Ropes were positioned by the grave, ready to lower it. The sexton pulled back the tarpaulin that had protected his recent digging from the rain. As the coffin reached the graveside, Stan panned left to take in the sea and its choppy grey waves, then downwards into the grave itself. Then he swore and almost dropped the camera.

Ben, his hangover forgotten and sensing excellent footage, rushed to his side, closely followed by a frowning Amy. Victoria too stepped quickly across from the coffin, her surplice billowing in the wind. All four stared down together into the muddy depths. There were two or three inches of water at the bottom of the hole, but that was not what had caused Stan to cease filming so abruptly. The words 'parts of this programme may be disturbing for some viewers' flashed into Ben's mind.

Looking back up at them, his eyes wide open but unseeing, was the grey and indisputably dead face of Griffiths Bentley.

CHAPTER EIGHTEEN

'Are you all right now?' asked Alice.

Greta gave a final determined wipe to her eyes and nose and said she was. She had rushed back to the house from St Mary's and was still crying when Alice returned from her afternoon Mother and Baby Clinic.

'I should have been in the church with you, Greta.'

'You were needed in the surgery.'

'Yes, but someone could have covered for me. I should have realised what a strain it would have been for you. I was insensitive.'

'No one could ever call you that,' Greta said. 'You're the nearest thing to a mindreader I've ever met, and much too kind for your own good.'

'I should have been there,' Alice insisted.

Greta looked at her partner, and, as so often happened, gratitude flooded through her. To have found someone so caring, so understanding, was more than she had ever dared hope for. Someone with whom she could share everything.

Almost everything. Not for the first time, Greta felt a tug of guilt about the one secret that she had never felt strong enough to share with Alice.

'No, I was just stupid,' she said. 'I should have known that at some point the reality of Fitz's death would get to me. And when I saw his coffin being brought down the aisle...'

Once again tears threatened.

'You'll get over it.' Alice's tone was as dry as ever, but her hand on Greta's shoulder expressed all the support that had never failed in their life together.

Steadied, Greta turned to face her, adding: 'What I don't understand – if this stuff about the will and the money is true – is how he found out.'

Alice nodded, looking even more like a wise owl than usual. Her brown eyes were sharp with intelligence, but her mouth was soft. The dark, heavy rims of her glasses gave her a wholly misleading air of severity.

'Who did know?'

'At the time? My mother, our GP – your predecessor but two – and the nun who ran the mother-and-baby home.'

'Was it awful?' Alice asked, taking off her glasses to clean the lenses on her scarf. Without their protection, her wit and vulnerability were both as clear as neat vodka. 'The home, I mean.'

'Absolutely not. Nothing like those Magdalen laundries in Ireland. Very nice and discreet, attached to a convent in Hertfordshire. My nuns were Anglicans, and intelligent, and they looked after their old girls.' Greta laughed at her memories. 'They had a home for drug-addicts, too: mainly amphetamine-dependent from too many slimming pills, they always said. But I expect it was worse. Anyway, that was never my problem. But they told me on the day I left school that old girls always had priority at both homes, so I knew where to go when...'

She didn't need to say any more. Alice said, 'Yes, of course.' Then paused before continuing. 'Listen: I know we never talk about the tricky past, but I have to ask, just this once. Do you regret what you did?'

Greta stood up so that she could put both hands on Alice's arms. 'Never. Absolutely never. Of course I think about him sometimes. Who wouldn't? And when I see a particularly fine specimen of a man in his early thirties, I wonder. But no. If I hadn't done what I did, I'd never have been able to go to college and get my A levels, get into Oxford, achieve my first in maths, or meet you. Because of that decision, I... well, I found myself and my life. No, darling, I've never regretted it.'

'Good.' Alice looked at her watch. 'Come on, we'd better get to the pub for the funeral baked meats. If we don't, my patients and your pupils are going to think there really is something nefarious behind his intention to leave you his fortune.'

'As if there could be a fortune! Poor old Fitz never had any spare cash. But I still wish I knew who'd told him.'

'The child himself?'

'How could he know? When I agreed to have him

269

adopted, I decided to have "father unknown" on the birth certificate. It didn't seem fair to Fitz not to tell him about the baby, but then to name him as the father.'

'And your mother wouldn't have told anyone?'

'Neither she nor the doctor – if he was anything like you.' Greta had never minded that Alice told her nothing about any of her patients. They were both safer that way because, in spite of being a rational mathematician, Greta's own instincts had always been to tell. She'd never liked secrets, and had had to fight herself ferociously to keep her own from everyone except Alice. Only she had ever seemed trustworthy enough to be told about the baby Greta had had when she'd been two weeks short of her seventeenth birthday – or about the identity of his father.

'So, someone in the house, then. It must have been. I know your mother never had what used to be called servants, but did anyone clean for her?'

Greta felt a surge of anger as she made the connection. 'Bloody Tracy's grandmother! I never thought. God knows why not. Perhaps it runs in the family.'

'What does?'

Close to the window a seagull shrieked with all the coarse violence of a bullying thug.

'Blackmail.'

They set out for the Admiral Byng. Ancient trees hung over the footpath, their branches now whipped this way and that by the usual icy wind from the Urals. The pub was less than half a mile away, and they let their heads droop and set their shoulders as they walked into the wind in silence, both thinking of Tracy.

What a good thing the police had come to the funeral to pay their respects. In the chaos in the churchyard following the macabre discovery in the freshly dug grave, DI Cole knew at once that the crowning moment of his detective career had arrived. He stepped forward and the man known as The Lump was transformed into King Cole, authoritative, assertive, impossible to challenge. For years he had been assigned to the dullest and most dispiriting cases that came the way of Suffolk CID, most of them suicides. All the juicy murder enquiries were handed to other detectives. And during the last investigation he'd been delegated to do on his own, he'd suffered the indignity of having had Scotland Yard brought in to find the solution. Cole would never understand why his talents weren't recognised by the high-ups. It had reached the point when he was programmed to think every dead body he investigated must be another suicide.

This one had to be a murder.

Cometh the hour, cometh the man.

'Stand aside, all of you.'

Heads turned. Even the heads of the pall-bearers tried to turn, and the coffin lurched dangerously to one side.

'You, too, Vicar. This is no longer a burial service, it's a crime scene.' With a flourish, Cole pulled back the hood of his black plastic mac, rather like Robin Hood at the moment he revealed he was the Earl of Huntingdon. To the undertaker, he said, 'You'll have to return the deceased – the one in the coffin, I mean – to your premises for the time being. The funeral will be resumed at a later date.'

There wasn't any other option. The pall-bearers were under strain, and they were only too pleased to return their burden to the hearse.

'As for the rest of you,' Cole said, 'I shall require statements, so kindly repair to the Admiral Byng, where comestibles are being served, and my assistant, Constable Chesterton, will make a list of all present and begin the process of interviewing you. But let's be clear: no one is to leave without permission. You are all, in effect, under arrest.' The latter statement was sweeping, but it needed to be said.

The people of Crabwell knew the voice of authority when they heard it. In fact, some of them broke into a run in their keenness to get to the pub, though it isn't certain whether they were scared of the inspector or eager to be first at the bar.

'Shall I go with them, guv?' Chesterton asked.

'Herd them in, Constable. Don't let a single one escape.'

'What will you be doing?'

'Sealing the scene, summoning the police surgeon and forensics.'

'Do you want me to phone for reinforcements?'

'Leave that to me.' Cole didn't want any of the so-called murder experts muscling in on his big opportunity. He would phone one of the private crime-scene investigation firms.

Someone cleared his throat nearby – a nice touch of deference. It was the sexton, holding a spade. 'Would you like me to cover him up, sir?'

'No, no, no, no. I'm arranging for a forensic tent. You dug the grave, I take it? When did you finish?'

'Yesterday evening, sir. Six o'clock. It was getting dark by then. It's no fun being in a graveyard after dark.'

'And did you cover the grave with the tarpaulin then?'

'Yes, sir. I could feel in my bones it was going to rain. And I didn't want the walls of the grave to cave in. There's a lot of sand in the earth here, you know, being so near the sea.'

But Cole wasn't interested in the composition of Crabwell's soil. 'So the unintended corpse must have been put there some time in the last twenty and a bit hours.' He stepped closer to the grave and took another look. 'Strictly between you and me, sexton, do you have any idea who this is?'

'That be Mr Bentley, sir. Griffiths Bentley, the solicitor.'

'I don't believe I've met him.'

'A bit late now.'

'Is he local?'

'He isn't any more, sir. He's gone to another place. But he used to have a little office over a Chinese takeaway in the village.'

'I see.' Cole enjoyed his food. He thought it might be necessary to visit Bentley's premises before the day was out.

But first he intended to solve the murder. It was safe to assume that this one *was* a murder and not a suicide. And it was ideally set up, with all the worried suspects gathered in the library... well, the public bar of the Admiral Byng. He would be at least the equal of one of the great fictional detectives, dominating the final chapter of the book and startling everyone with his brilliance before naming the killer.

Already the crowd in the pub sounded like party-goers. People always got more cheerful after a funeral than a wedding. Perhaps it was a way of fending off thoughts of their own inevitable demise that made them determined to enjoy themselves while they could. Or perhaps it was because the dead were safe from everything the fates or their enemies could do to them, whereas the newly married had years of difficulty and angst to come. Greta bit her lip hard and told herself not to be such a cynic.

Amy greeted them near the door, as if taking on the role of Fitz's daughter, or perhaps widow. For the first time in ages, Greta wondered just a little about Fitz's private life in recent years.

'Have a drink,' Amy said, waving towards a metal tray bearing glasses of something red, something white, and something fizzy.

You could make up a ditty for funerals, like the wedding one about old, new, borrowed and blue, Greta thought, apparently unable to stop her subconscious throwing up unsuitable ideas.

Something fizzy
Makes you dizzy
Something red
Mourn the dead
Something white
Life is sh...

What would her girls think, if they could ever get a glimpse of her unspoken thoughts?

'You do look windblown: *both* of you.' Meriel Dane could make the most innocent comment sound loaded with sexual innuendo, exactly the kind of thing to make Alice pucker up in disapproval. 'Have a canapé. Devils-on-horseback. Fitz always said eating one of *them* made him think of oral—'

'Thank you, Ms Dane,' Greta said repressively, glancing at Alice with concealed anxiety. Luckily there was a gleam of naughtiness behind the forbidding spectacles.

Alice took a devil-on-horseback and touched it gently to her lips in case it was too hot. 'Mmm: delicious. That lovely mixture of salty fat and sweetness. May I take another?'

Meriel's disappointment nearly made Greta laugh. Instead she, too, took a prune wrapped in crisp bacon and swallowed it down.

All desire to laugh disappeared as Amy skittered across the floor towards them, twisting her carroty hair in the way she did only when she thought she was about to cause trouble.

Greta turned her back, but she wasn't quick enough to get away before Amy's thin white hand gripped her wrist.

'Well, we've got two murders to solve now, haven't we?'

'What on earth do you mean?'

'Oh, of course you wouldn't know. You left the church before he was found, didn't you?'

'Before who was found?'

With great relish Amy proceeded to tell them about the discovery of Griffiths Bentley's body. Alice looked more surprised by the news than Greta did.

'Presumably the police have been called?'

'Of course. They said they'd be coming here to take some statements. I asked if we should actually go ahead with Fitz's wake... you know, given the circumstances. They said it was fine. I think, although they didn't put it in words, they were pleased at the thought of having all of the suspects gathered together in one place.'

'Do you reckon we're all suspects?' asked Greta.

'Of course we are.'

Amy restrained herself from continuing, 'Particularly those who rushed out of the church before the funeral had started.' Instead she said, 'Greta, I need your help. At least, not just me: Ben and me.'

'Amy, I cannot imagine what you think I can do for you. But if you're still playing amateur detective, I can tell you now that I know nothing about either of the murders that could possibly help either of you.'

'It's just your Girl Guides, Greta.' Amy's voice was full

of synthetic sweetness, like fake maple syrup. 'I can't believe that none of them saw anything. I mean…'

'How many more times? Everyone left together. If you'd heard them all complaining all day you wouldn't bother to ask so often. Modern girls aren't used to being cold and wet in the way we were in my day. There was never any chance that they were going to spend the night in those tents. They legged it off that beach as soon as I said they could go.'

'But, Greta, I'm sure…'

'Sorry, Amy,' she said in the tone that had never failed to control a recalcitrant pupil, 'but I see Victoria Whitechurch on her own in the corner. I have things to say to her. I'll talk to you later.' If I have to, she added to herself in silence.

The vicar saw her coming through the crowd and smiled in gratitude at the thought of rescue. Greta had never understood quite why Victoria was so unpopular. She always seemed pleasant enough and, as far as Greta knew, had never done anyone any harm.

'Hello, Victoria.' She made herself forget Amy and put plenty of warmth into her voice. 'I'm so sorry I had to rush out of the church.' Greta gestured vaguely towards her abdomen as she lied, 'Bit of a tummy bug, I'm afraid. But everyone says it was a good service… in spite of the way it ended… you know, in the graveyard. I'm sure Fitz would have been pleased.'

'D'you think so?' Victoria's face was thin, but had somehow avoided the kind of lines a woman of her age ought to have. 'Though he fulfilled his duties as a church-warden, I know he wasn't exactly a believer.'

'Not in the holy mysteries, perhaps, but he was a great believer in old England and her traditions. The church would have been part of that for him.'

'Couldn't agree more.' They had been joined by Bob Christie, his maintenance dose of alcohol well topped up. 'Very good service, Vicar. I'm glad you stuck with the 1664 prayer book. Fitz'd definitely have appreciated that. And he'd have sung the hymns with great gusto. Who chose them, by the way?'

Victoria inserted her right forefinger between her neck and the starched dog collar, and she flushed a little. 'Well, me. I hope you don't think I...'

'Somebody had to. And I do think Fitz would have enjoyed "When a Knight Won his Spurs in the Stories of Old". I don't think I've ever heard that at a funeral before.'

'It was just all this talk of Templar gold and that sort of thing. I had a vision of knights and lances and fluttering pennants.'

'As I say, he'd have liked it.'

'Greta.' Alice's voice was full of anxiety, and Greta turned at once to see that she was staring at Tracy Crofts. The girl sat huddled beside the fire, staring down at the flames. 'Look at her face. There's something very wrong.'

Greta moved a little so that she could see more than the back of Tracy's head. The expression on the girl's narrow little face looked as though she was facing the flames of hell rather than a comforting pub's blazing fire. And, in spite of its heat, her skin was very pale.

'D'you think she's ill, Alice?' Greta whispered. 'Or pregnant?'

'Not possible,' Alice said in the voice of one who knew.

Morning-after pill? A coil? Greta had often wondered how Alice dealt with the contradictions inherent in being a good GP.

'She resents me,' Alice went on, 'since our last encounter in the surgery, so I think this might be one for her vicar.' She interrupted Bob Christie's pontifications to say, 'Victoria, can you tackle Tracy? She looks terrified.'

'I don't think ghostly counsel is what that young woman needs. I did once try to talk to her about the unhappiness that was likely to follow a life of sin, but she...' Victoria produced a ghastly smile. 'She showed me in no uncertain terms that she would not listen to anything I might say and, indeed, would do her best to cause trouble if I continued.'

I wonder what she used to threaten you, Greta thought, imagining financial malfeasance, or possibly heresy. Except that Tracy's world was not likely to encompass anything as esoteric as heresy, even if she knew what it meant. Embezzling the collection was a much more likely accusation.

'Do you mean she threatened to blackmail you?' she asked.

Amy, passing with a tray of drinks, heard the word and lingered, waiting for the vicar's response.

Victoria Whitechurch coloured and said unconvincingly, 'There's nothing anyone could blackmail me with.'

'No?' Greta looked straight at Victoria, who avoided eye contact. 'Most of us have done things in our past that we wouldn't want to be common knowledge… and Tracy Crofts seems to have a knack for finding those things out.'

'Well, there's nothing she could find out about me.' Trying to be assertive, the vicar just sounded flustered.

'Are you going to talk to the girl? She's in a bad way.'

'No. One of you'd do it far better than I would,' Victoria said, aiming her voice between the two of them.

Greta took it on, preferring to spare Alice. They had always been very protective of each other.

'Tracy,' she said quite gently.

'What now?' The girl's voice was not encouraging, but Greta pulled forward a cushioned stool and perched on it. Amy, realising that it'd be too obvious if she tried to eavesdrop on their conversation, moved on.

'Tracy, you look…' Greta hesitated over the most useful and least threatening word, and eventually decided on '… worried. What's the problem?'

'Why do you think there should be a problem? Not everyone lives a pathetic life, worrying about what everyone else thinks about them.'

'Certainly not.' Greta remembered the wine glass in her hand and took a healthy swig of Shiraz. 'But you're not yourself. It can't be sadness over Fitz's death because you hardly knew the man.'

'No. But you did, didn't you?'

'Every adult in the village knew him.' Greta was keeping her temper, not rising to the girl's insinuation. 'What is it, Tracy?'

'Lots of people hated him.' For the first time this evening, the nasal voice sounded real. 'I mean, really hated him. Like Jack the Ripper hated his victims.'

'What on earth do you mean? Did you see something?'

'Ms Knox?' A pleasantly deep male voice sounded from behind Greta.

'Yes?' she said, turning to see Gregory Jepson, the chubby hedge-fund manager, offering to refill her glass. He was about the only man in the room not wearing a suit; his worn jeans, T-shirt, and hoodie demonstrated his lack of interest in traditional funeral protocol.

Greta put her hand over her glass. 'I think I've got enough, thank you.'

'OK.' He put the bottle on the table and focussed his dark eyes on her. 'I rather wanted to talk to you – if you're not too busy.'

'Tracy and I were just…'

'Oh, for goodness sake!' Tracy shouted. 'Leave me alone. I don't want to talk to you, you dreadful old witch. I've told you what I need from you – if you want to avoid trouble!'

'And I've told you that I won't—'

'Shut up! Why won't everyone just leave me alone?' And with that the girl stomped out of the pub.

Greta blinked and allowed herself to be helped up from the stool as though she was eighty rather than fifty.

'What can I do for you, Mr Jepson?'

'Nothing at all.' He smiled again, showing off the most beautifully straight, white teeth, which were somehow at odds with his general scruffiness. 'But poor Fitz told me the last time I saw him that I ought to get to know you better.'

With a hand on her throat, Greta tried to control her imagination and failed.

'Why?' she whispered, telling herself that this successful, rich, scruffily-dressed young man could not possibly be the result of her brief embarrassing fling with Fitz. She scanned the shape of his face and the cut of his lips and longed to believe it could be true. The dark, almost black eyes were the giveaway. It was like looking into a mirror.

'I think you know why,' Greg replied. 'But on the day the poor old boy is buried, I thought I ought to do as he asked.'

'You lived here in Crabwell once, didn't you?' Greta said, trying to sound lightly social. 'Why did you move away?'

'The commute was a nightmare and I got an amazing offer for the Old Manor,' he said, then flushed a little. 'Actually, that's not true. A relationship broke down, and I needed to make a new start. I think you and your partner had just arrived here, hadn't you?'

'That's right. My mother had died and left me her house, and we were trying to decide what to do with it when Alice discovered that the local GP practice was looking for a new partner. It made sense to sell up in London and move down here.'

'Brave though to come back after...' His voice faltered.

'What do you mean?'

'Well, Fitz told me you ran away from here years and years ago after he proposed to you.' Gregory smiled a little ruefully. 'He wasn't very sophisticated, was he? I think he found it hard to imagine that someone he had... well, loved, could prefer a woman to him.'

'Not a lot of self-knowledge, you mean.' Greta saw Alice watching them and waved. 'I think most people would understand why anyone would choose someone like Alice over someone like Fitz. Poor Fitz.'

'Special, is she?'

Greta felt as though all her joints were softening out of their habitual ache. 'Oh, yes.'

'Then I think I need to get to know her better, too.'

'Mr Jepson, I...'

'Couldn't you call me Greg? Or even Gregory. I mean...' He looked around to make sure there was no one in earshot. 'After Fitz made such a business of telling me to get to know you, I made some enquiries. Bob Christie, the editor of *The Crabwell Clarion*, was very useful to me. He'd done a lot of research into... I don't know the right name to call him...'

'Fitz.'

'Fitz, OK. And in the end, I had sight of my real birth certificate.'

'You? No. I mean, I...'

'I think you'd better sit down again.' He steered her towards a chair. 'You look very pale. Is the idea so terrible?'

She shook her head, dumb, and feeling the hot wetness

of tears in her eyes. 'I never... I mean, I... We can't do this here, Gregory.' She breathed carefully, and then said his name again. 'Gregory.'

'Perhaps I shouldn't have tried in public. It's just that I... I knew it would be hard, and somehow I thought we might both find it easier if we were in a place where we couldn't give way to everything we felt, where there were other people around. You see, I...'

Now that he was finding words hard, Greta regained some of her own confidence. She smiled up into his face.

'Are you horrified?'

'Absolutely not. And I want to get to know you. You and Alice.'

Greta tensed up. 'Don't for heaven's sake, say anything to Alice about this. Not yet. She'll be very shocked. Let me prepare the ground.'

'Fine,' said Greg. 'I'm all in favour of taking things gently. Our lives have been so very different, and we'll have a lot of ground to cover.'

'Gently all the way. I couldn't agree more. So long as you're not appalled.'

'I'm very far from appalled,' said Gregory Jepson, with a smile the memory of which Greta would always treasure.

'The champagne is real,' Amy said, interrupting their tête-à-tête. 'Fitz hated cava and Prosecco alike, and when I asked Griffiths Bentley – the *late* Griffiths Bentley, that is – about paying for the funeral, he said there was plenty in the will, and testamentary expenses are always allowed

– and before tax too, so you shouldn't be too worried at the cost, Greta.'

Feeling Alice's hand on her back, Greta controlled herself and her galloping emotions. It wasn't easy, but this was neither the time nor the place to tell Amy to stop being so patronising or so intrusive.

'I think that is something for the executors, not for me, Amy.'

Amy's flush and scowl were reward enough for Greta's self-control, and helped her smile sweetly before moving towards the tray and picking up another glass of red wine. She hoped it was a New World one. The pub's stock of French wine had always struck her as being dire, but Fitz had been old-fashioned about that. He believed only the French knew how to make wine properly. But he kept the best stuff for his own private supply. Otherwise he would occasionally take himself off on a day-trip to Calais in a hired van and stock up on the cheapest, thinnest, sourest stuff he could buy for a euro or two.

Greta sipped and relaxed. This was more of the perfectly decent fruity Australian Shiraz. She gave Alice an approving nod.

'But, Greta, before you go and talk to anyone,' Amy said, pushing between them to grab another glass of champagne for herself, 'I have to ask you again whether any of your Guides stayed on the beach after the rest of you left.'

Greta put down her glass so sharply that wine slopped over the edge. She had to lick the back of her hand to clean it.

'I've told you – they all left at the same time.'

'All, are you sure?'

'Well, that is, Tracy Crofts stayed to do a bit of tidying up inside the tents.'

Greta could not believe the speed with which Amy rushed out of the pub.

CHAPTER NINETEEN

It was still raining, but Amy hardly noticed. In the distance she could see Tracy Crofts walking fast, almost stumbling, along the beach. The tide was coming in, wavelets sucking at the pebbles and threatening the girl's spangled trainers. Her head down, she seemed unware of the weather.

Amy caught up with her. 'Tracy,' she put her hand on the teenager's arm, 'I need to talk to you,' she said, trying to sound conciliatory.

The arm was pulled away. 'I got nothing to say to you.'

Amy skipped out of the way of a sudden surge from the tide. 'Look, we can't talk here. I live just over there.' She pointed in the direction of her cottage, now a mere moment's walk away. 'Why don't you come with me and dry off?' She saw Tracy's look of sulky disdain and added, 'I've got a bottle of wine open.' The girl was under age, but this was an emergency, and the weather could almost mean alcohol was a medical necessity.

Tracy halted, looked towards the cottage, then at Amy, finally gave a defeated shrug and said, 'OK, then.'

Amy hadn't left any heat on but, after the dismal weather outside, the cottage seemed warm as she opened the door and led Tracy inside.

'Where's this wine, then?' The girl flung herself into Amy's favourite chair and drew her thin jacket with its badly sewn-on badges, none of which appeared to have anything to do with the Guides, closely around her.

Amy lit the log-burner, found two glasses and a bottle of the pub's Merlot; Fitz had given her a case only the other day. 'You can think of me when you drink it,' he'd said with one of his endearing twinkles.

Tracy knocked back half the glass in one gulp.

Amy found some cheese and biscuits. She hadn't seen the girl eat anything at the pub, and she needed her to keep sober. On the other hand, this being Tracy Croft, she could probably drink anyone under the table. Even so...

'Now,' she said, sitting down opposite the girl. 'Why were you tidying up inside the tents the night Fitz was killed? I don't have you down as someone born to housework.'

The glass, now empty, was held out for a refill. Amy obliged.

'You don't know nothin',' Tracy sneered. 'My nan said I was a dab hand at washing up, better'n what she was.' For an instant she forgot to be sulky, then her face crumpled. 'My nan and me, we got on really great.' Tears started to roll down her cheeks.

'Oh, Tracy,' Amy leaned forward and took her hand, the girl seemed really upset. 'Is it something I've said?'

Tracy gulped, pulled her hand out of Amy's grasp, and scrubbed at her eyes. 'Today wasn't my first funeral.'

'You mean your grandmother died recently?'

The girl nodded and more tears flowed. 'The other week. She lived with us, and she used to tell me all sorts of things. Been in Crabwell for ever she had. When she heard I'd joined the Guides and it was run by Miss Knox, she didn't half have a laugh.' Tracy sat up and dashed away the last of the tears. She was scornful now. 'Said she was no better than she ought to be and I should watch myself, Nan said. She used to do for old Mrs Knox; years ago that was. She worked in lots of Crabwell houses, she did. D'yer see that Gregory Jepson at the funeral? Well, she worked for Mrs Jepson, too, was there when he arrived as a baby.' She paused for a moment. 'They say he's a success, but 'e can't be, I mean, look at him!'

Amy wasn't interested in this, in her experience Tracy rubbished everybody. Now that the girl had lost some of her sulkiness it was time to get to the important matter. She topped up the empty glass. 'You may well have a Duke of Edinburgh Award for housekeeping, but you can't fool me that is what you were doing in the tents that night. Come on, who were you waiting for?'

A sly look came into Tracy's eyes. 'Wouldn't you like to know? Maybe you had an eye on him yourself!'

'On whom?'

'Jed Rhode,' Tracy said proudly. 'He told me I was cute and all.'

'Jed Rhode? That hunk…' Amy caught herself. 'I mean that strapping fisherman with the red hair?'

Tracy nodded vigorously. 'He said he'd come by that evening, and if I was there and no one else was, well, we might have some fun. Only, I was tired, see; Miss Knox had kept us all hard at it, and then we'd had the bonfire and sausages and, well, I fell asleep in one of the tents. Thought he'd come and wake me, call me a sleeping beauty!' Only, Amy thought, if Meriel Dane was to be believed, her mature charms had trumped Tracy's youth.

Amy looked at the bedraggled hair that was just beginning to dry out, the pointed little face, the three nasty spots on the chin, the stubby eyelashes and indeterminate grey of the eyes, and gave an inward sigh. How soul-destroying your teenage years could be! 'And did he? Wake you up?'

Tracy shook her head. 'I woke up freezing. Then I heard voices, so I put my head out of the tent.'

Amy knew, she just knew, that now, at last, she was going to find out what had happened to the Admiral.

'What did you see?'

'It wasn't Jed; it was the Admiral who was talking.'

'Who to?'

'To that television chap, Ben what's-his-name. I knew Jed wasn't going to turn up, so I sort of melted away.'

'And that's all you saw, Ben Milne and the Admiral talking? Nothing else?'

'I had to get home, see; get in the back way without my mum seeing me or she'd give me a right thrashing.' Tracy's mouth pinched up and she shivered.

Mrs Crofts was an Amazon of a woman whose arms featured a whole gallery of tattoos. For the first time Amy began to see why the girl behaved the way she did.

She took the wine glass out of Tracy's hand. 'You get home now. And better not let your mum know you've been drinking.'

'Reckon it's illegal what you've done, giving me wine.' Tracy's truculence was back.

'In the bar it would be, yes. Not on private premises, so don't get any ideas.' Amy didn't know whether this was in fact true, but she had to get rid of the girl.

Amongst the swirling thoughts in Amy's head one predominated. And inevitably it had to do with Ben Milne. There was no romance in the thought, only suspicion.

When he'd been so insistent that they should share all the information they found out on the case, she'd thought he was just keen to find out the truth. Now his actions offered another explanation. For reasons of his own he wanted to know exactly where her suspicions were focussing.

She knew she had to confront him, but now didn't feel like the right moment. He was still in the pub, and her duty as bar manager should have taken her straight back there. She needed time to compose her thoughts, though. Even more than that she needed more evidence. Evidence that would confirm her darkening suspicions.

And there was no question in her mind as to where she should search for that evidence.

*　　*　　*

The reason why Rosalie Jepson was not seen much on the streets of Crabwell became apparent when Amy knocked on the door of her seafront cottage. It was at the far end of the village, separated from the other houses by a small footbridge over a narrow stream that had over many years marked its passage through the shingle to the sea.

Though not yet six o'clock, to Amy it felt much later. Walking into St Mary's for Fitz's funeral seemed an age away as she waited on Rosalie Jepson's doorstep. She was about to knock again when the hall light came on. Sounds of effort preceded the homeowner's reaching and unlocking her front door.

It opened to reveal an old woman supporting herself on a three-wheeled blue walker. The size of the ankles beneath a long skirt explained her lack of mobility. The straps on her huge shoes had nearly reached the limit of their Velcro. The rest of her body also looked grotesquely swollen. In spite of her disabilities, Rosalie Jepson's face was truly beautiful. Framed by white hair gathered in a bun at the back, there was a calmness about it, a serenity.

'You'll have come from the pub, I dare say. You're Amy, aren't you?' she said. 'Do come in. It's perishing out there, isn't it? Go straight through into the sitting room.' She gestured the way. 'I'll come at my own pace – a pace that makes tortoises think they're Formula One drivers.'

Amy did as instructed, wondering how Rosalie Jepson knew her name, but at the same time feeling excitedly certain that the old lady knew a lot more about things that went on in Crabwell.

The room into which she had been directed was a shrine to china figurines. On every surface porcelain ladies swirled their skirts. It wasn't a world of collectibles that Amy knew much about, but she got the impression that she was not looking at top-of-the-market products. These weren't Meissen or Royal Doulton. But the care with which they were displayed told how much they were valued by their owner.

The other striking thing in the room, in the bay window that looked out towards the sea, was a large telescope on a stand, which was pointing to the right along the Crabwell sea front. Amy reckoned its range went at least as far as the bit of beach on which Fitz's body had been found in his dinghy.

'I'd offer you a cup of tea or something,' said the voice behind her, 'but you'd have to wait for it. Getting back to the kitchen would take approximately twice as long as it has taken me to get here from the front door.'

'No, I've just had a drink, thank you,' said Amy.

'At the wake for the dear old Admiral, I dare say.'

'Yes.'

With practised ease Rosalie Jepson swung her huge bulk into a large armchair beside a fireplace where electric logs burned eternally without ever making any ash. 'And,' she continued once she was settled and had folded her walker behind the chair, 'I gather it's become a wake for more than one now.'

'I'm sorry?' asked Amy, puzzled as she moved to the armchair towards which Rosalie had gestured.

'I hear Griffiths Bentley's dead too.'

'How on earth did you know that? His body's only just been discovered. Have the police been in touch with you?'

'No,' she replied, mystified by the question.

'Were they in touch with you about Fitz – the Admiral's death?'

A firm shake of the head. Amy wasn't that surprised. She had yet to be impressed by the efficiency – or even competence – of Cole and Chesterton.

'So, Rosalie, how did you hear about Griffiths Bentley's death?'

The old woman's smile would have been complacent had it not been for the twinkle in her eye. 'Crabwell's a small place. Even though I can't get around now like I used to, I still hear the jungle drums.'

Amy pointed towards the telescope. 'And watch what goes on?'

'Not very often. That was Ritchie's pride and joy. He loved monitoring the shipping.' She gestured towards a bookshelf packed with spiral-bound notebooks. 'Wrote down all the details of what he saw through the telescope. I hadn't the heart to move it after he passed.'

'And how long ago...?'

'Six years now.'

'I'm sorry.'

'Yes, so am I. Still, I mustn't be maudlin. Ritchie and me were very happy while it lasted. Many people don't even have that much. And of course I've got Gregory.'

'Yes.' Amy had been wondering how to bring up the

name, and now Rosalie had done the job for her. 'You adopted him?'

'Yes. Having our own children didn't work for us. I'm sure now there are all kinds of medical things we could have done about it, but back then... Anyway, Ritchie wouldn't have liked going through tests and... As I say, we couldn't have children of our own, so... I'd always wanted a little boy called Gregory, and when we first saw him in the orphanage... those dark, dark eyes... I loved him from that moment on.'

'Where was the orphanage? Somewhere local? '

'Oh, good heavens no. It was miles away in Hertfordshire. Ritchie and I had a very anxious time after we'd first seen Gregory... you know, wondering whether the adoption would go through. Because Ritchie was a good few years older than me, on the edge of the age that they then thought would be unsuitable as an adoptive parent. But God – or someone similar, I don't care who – was on our side. It all went through without a hitch...' her old eyes glistened '... and Gregory has brought more joy into my life than I ever thought possible.'

'And become astonishingly successful.'

'So I believe.' Rosalie Jepson casually dismissed his millions. 'He's always trying to give me money, but I keep telling him I've got everything I need. Ritchie thought that too, he never wanted to take money from anyone else, even his son. He'd worked all his life for his state pension, and that was enough for him. And then I'd got my private pension too.'

'Oh? What did you do, Rosalie?'

'I was the village schoolteacher.'

'Here?'

'Yes, right here in Crabwell. Until the school closed. Not enough pupils, government cutbacks, you know the story. Now the kids have to get buses to Dunwich.'

'So there's now no school in Crabwell?'

'Well, no state school. Only the private one.'

'Is that where Greta Knox teaches?'

'Yes. Anyway, I was into my late fifties when the local primary closed, so I reckoned that was a message I should retire. And the pension I got was surprisingly healthy. So I never needed any extra.

'Of course, I'm delighted for Gregory... you know, the money he's got. I think it really frustrated him that we wouldn't take anything from him. He wanted to spread his largesse.' She smiled nostalgically. 'He was always good with figures... as a boy he was always top of the class when it came to sums.'

A facility inherited from his mother, thought Amy.

'It was sometimes embarrassing, what with me being his teacher. Some of the parents thought I must have been giving him extra coaching. But I didn't. He didn't need it. He just had this natural ability.'

'And Gregory keeps in touch with you, does he?'

'Oh yes, he's very good at that. Doesn't come down to Crabwell as often as he used to, but he rings me at least once a day.'

'Was it from him that you heard about Griffiths Bentley's

death?' Amy asked, and a nod from the old woman confirmed her intuition. 'And he didn't say who he thought might have done the murder?'

'No. He didn't actually use the word "murder". He just said the body had been found in St Mary's churchyard.'

Amy couldn't see much point in telling Rosalie how she knew the solicitor was murdered. Besides, she had a more pressing line of enquiry. 'Was it Greg – Gregory who discovered the identity of his birth parents?'

'No. He never expressed any interest in them. Ritchie and I told him when he was eighteen he'd be able to find out who they were, but he said he didn't want to. He said we'd looked after him and loved him, and we were the only parents he ever wanted.' A shy smile crossed the old lady's beautiful face. 'Which shows at least that we did something right.'

'I think you did a lot of things right. But did you and Ritchie know about Gregory's birth parents?'

'No. Maybe we could have found out, but we didn't want to. Gregory was ours, that's all that mattered.'

'So, if you didn't know, and he didn't search out the information himself, how did he find out who his birth parents were?'

'It was kind of a coincidence. But as soon as he discovered his birth father was Fitz... and knowing how badly the Admiral Byng was doing... well, it gave him great pleasure to bail the old boy out.'

'With the two million he transferred to Fitz's account?'

'Exactly.'

'Why did he make over so much?'

The old woman's huge shoulders shrugged. 'For someone who's so good at making it, Gregory doesn't really have much sense of the value of money. Two million just felt the right amount to him.'

Which was fair enough. And certainly explained the glee and generosity of the Admiral's 'Last Hurrah'. Though it didn't bring Amy any closer to the reason why someone would want to murder him.

'Going back to how Gregory found out about his birth parents, you said it was "kind of a coincidence". What exactly did you mean by that?'

'Well, it all concerns that young man Ben.'

'Ben Milne? The one who's making the television documentary?'

'Yes, him.'

Amy felt an inward shudder. Too many details were coming together, and all pointing in the same direction. 'So how was Ben involved?' she asked in a resigned voice.

'He contacted me about some research he was doing.'

'Recently? Research about the Admiral Byng?'

'Ooh no, this was a long time back. Last May it was. I remember because the day he rang me was the sixth anniversary of Ritchie's death.'

'So what was he ringing you about?'

'Another programme he was working on. Something to do with people's family history.'

'*Skeletons in the Cupboard*?'

'Yes, I think that was it. Finding out about what

celebrities' ancestors got up to. I tried watching it once. Didn't like it, all seemed very… what's the word? "Snide"? Yes. Keen on digging up the dirt, if you know what I mean.'

'I know exactly what you mean. And was Ben researching a programme on Gregory?'

'Oh, good Lord, no. Gregory's not a celebrity. No, Ben was researching the background to one of my much earlier pupils, one of the first intake I taught. Cheeky little boy called William Sayers.'

'Willie Sayers, the MP?'

'Yes, that's who he is now.'

'So Ben came down to Crabwell to interview you about him?'

'Not in person, no. He sent a girl to talk to me. She called herself a researcher.'

'That would figure. And were you able to tell her much about Willie Sayers?'

The old woman chuckled. 'Not really. I just remembered him as rather naughty. I met his parents when they came to the school, but I didn't *know* them. And I certainly didn't know anything shameful about his ancestors. I don't think I was much help to the poor girl.'

'Did she ask you about anything else? Like Gregory's birth parents?'

'No, Gregory's name wasn't mentioned. I don't think she knew I had a son.'

Amy looked puzzled. 'But you said it was through Ben that Gregory found out about his birth parents.'

'Yes, but not directly from me. This researcher girl asked

me if there was anyone else who knew Willie Sayers well, who might have some information on his family background. And I mentioned Fitz at the Admiral Byng, because I'd heard the two of them had been friends at some point. So maybe she went and talked to him.'

'Did you suggest she contacted anyone else?'

'I mentioned Griffiths Bentley, the solicitor.'

'Why?'

'Because he knew everything about the inhabitants of Crabwell.'

'Oh?'

'He'd acted for most of them in some capacity or other. House purchase, conveyancing, wills, that kind of stuff.'

'But surely all that would have been confidential, between solicitor and client?'

Rosalie Jepson smiled wryly. 'I gather you don't know Griffiths very well. He'd spill the beans about anything if the money was right.'

'Really?'

'Oh yes. Not a great credit to the British legal system, that one. He also had an unhealthy interest in people's family histories, was always keen to dig up the dirt.'

'With a view to blackmailing them?'

The huge shoulders shrugged. 'I have no proof of that, but why else would he be interested?'

'So you put the researcher in touch with him?'

'Yes.'

'And do you reckon she would have paid him for information of the kind she was after?'

'I'm sure she would have done. She offered me money.'

'Did you take it?'

Rosalie Jepson looked affronted. 'Of course I didn't. I hadn't got any information of the kind she wanted about Willie Sayers. And even if I had, I wouldn't have taken her money for it.'

'When you say "her" money, you mean Ben Milne's money?'

'I assume so, yes. Or money from the television company he works for.'

'Yes.' What Amy had just heard put a new complexion on things. If Griffiths Bentley was a repository for all of Crabwell's grubby secrets and was prepared to sell the information for hard cash, the list of people who might want to murder him had suddenly been enlarged. 'So, going back to how Gregory found out about his birth parents. Did that happen last year... when's Ben's researcher was making her enquiries in Crabwell?'

'No. It happened very recently. The weekend before last it was, the Saturday.'

'Just a couple of days before Fitz died?'

'That's right. I had a call from Griffiths Bentley.'

'Was that a surprise? Had you had any professional dealings with him before?'

'Oh yes. He'd sorted out a will for Ritchie and me.'

'Which presumably left everything to Gregory?'

'Yes.' A throaty chuckle. 'As if he needed our pathetic inheritance. But Ritchie and I weren't the kind to leave stuff to a cats' home.'

301

'No. So what did Griffiths say?'

'He told me he knew who Gregory's birth father was.'

'And did he ask you for money in exchange for his keeping quiet about it?'

'He tried that, but I pretty soon made it clear he wasn't going to get anything out of me. I told him I already knew who Gregory's father was.'

'Did he believe you?'

'Yes – even to the point of doing something rather stupid.'

'What do you mean?'

'He mentioned Fitz's name. Assuming I already knew it, which needless to say I pretended I did.'

'He didn't say who the birth mother was?'

'Didn't mention that. Which makes me think he probably didn't know her identity.'

'Did he say anything else?'

'He was quite rude to me, annoyed that I wasn't about to play ball with him. He said that he knew other people who would be prepared to pay for the information.'

'I suppose it would be too much to ask whether he mentioned names...'

Rosalie Jepson grinned. 'Far too much. He just told me that Fitz's name was going to come out anyway. Soon it'd be all over the television, and everyone would know. I think he was hoping the threat might make me change my mind and cough up. Which of course I didn't. I told him I didn't give a damn who knew the name of Gregory's birth father. I knew it wouldn't change the relationship I had with my son.'

'Hm.' Amy nodded thoughtfully. She was intrigued by
what Rosalie had said about Fitz's name being 'all over the
television'. She didn't want to raise the suggestion with
the old woman, but she thought it might well mean that
Griffiths Bentley would next try to sell the secret to Ben
Milne. The presenter had a track record of paying for scurrilous information. And maybe he had been planning that
his documentary on the Admiral Byng wouldn't turn out
so differently from the programmes he had made in the
Skeletons in the Cupboard series. He'd intended to expose
the scandal of Fitz's illegitimate child, but then been offered
a much better story when the old boy was murdered.

'And, Rosalie, was it you who told Gregory about Fitz
being his father?'

'Yes. I rang him as soon as I'd put down the phone from
speaking to Griffiths. If the truth was going to come out
anyway, I wanted him to know about it as soon as possible.'

'And how did Gregory react?'

'He seemed to take it quite coolly. But clearly it affected
him, because pretty soon after he made over the two million
to his birth father.'

'Yes. And presumably that was why he went to see Fitz
on the Monday?'

Rosalie nodded. 'And it was then that the Admiral told
him who his birth mother was.'

'Amazing that both of them ended up in Crabwell.'

This did not seem to impress the old woman much. 'I've
seen so much coincidence happening in real life that nothing
surprises me anymore.'

Amy had a lot of new information to digest, but she also felt that she wasn't going to get much more out of Rosalie Jepson. She thanked her hostess for her co-operation and said she'd better be on her way. As she stood up she looked at the telescope in the window bay.

Rosalie Jepson read her thoughts. 'And in answer to your unspoken question,' she said, 'yes, I do sometimes look through it. Not very often, but occasionally at night. I don't sleep so well these days, not since Ritchie passed.'

'And did you by any chance happen—?'

'Yes,' the old woman interrupted her. 'I did happen to be looking out over the beach the night that Fitz died.'

And Rosalie Jepson told Amy exactly what she had seen.

On her way back to the pub, Amy rang the Crabwell Surgery. Among other things, she asked, because she frequently picked them up for him, whether there was an outstanding repeat prescription to be collected in the name of Geoffrey Horatio Fitzsimmons. The answer came back that there wasn't.

The crowd had thinned considerably when she got back to the Admiral Byng. And if DI Cole and DC Chesterton had taken the opportunity to ask questions about Griffiths Bentley's murder, they hadn't spent long on the task. There was no sign of them. Meriel Dane, who was rather resentfully serving free drinks from the bar – she reckoned such drudgery was beneath her – said they had been in briefly. And no, they hadn't gone up to the Bridge.

'Oh, and that woman with the ridiculous name…' Meriel

went on. Amy's brow wrinkled in puzzlement. 'The resident, one with the dyed blonde hair...'

'Ianthe Berkeley?'

'That's the one.'

'Anyway, she's demanding "Room Service".'

'What?'

'She teetered up to her room about twenty minutes ago, saying she wanted Room Service to bring her a bottle of vodka and an ice bucket. I told her you'd sort it out when you got back.'

'Thank you very much,' said Amy with considerable edge. 'She doesn't seem to have taken on board that this is a pub with rooms, not a five-star hotel.'

Meriel shrugged. 'I said you'd sort it,' she repeated as she returned to what she regarded as her proper domain, the kitchen.

Amy knocked on the door of Ianthe Berkeley's room, but a moment or two passed before it was opened. The blurry expression in the publisher's eyes suggested that she had just been woken from a deep – and probably inebriated – sleep.

There was no love lost between the two women, and Amy had no compunction in saying quite forcefully, 'I gather you've been asking for Room Service. We don't do Room Service in the Admiral Byng. If you want a bottle of vodka and an ice bucket, you can order it at the bar and bring it up here yourself!'

'Oh. All right.' Ianthe was still too fuddled to come back with her customary asperity.

And Amy suddenly realised that, given the way her suspicions were now moving, this was the perfect opportunity to pump Ianthe for information.

'The night Fitz died,' she demanded baldly, 'were you with Ben Milne?'

'Was I with...? Are you meaning did I spend the night with him?'

'Yes.'

'Well, I...' Ianthe Berkeley tried to reassemble her fractured memory. And suddenly, for no good reason, the events of that Monday night, up until now so fuzzy, came back to her with dispiriting clarity. 'No, I didn't,' she replied. 'I mean, obviously he came on to me and suggested that I should cross the landing to his room.'

'Of course,' said Amy, not believing a word of it. 'And did you?'

'No. Well, I mean I had known him at uni. I certainly wasn't planning to have sex with him...'

'No,' said Amy, still unconvinced.

'But I thought it might be nice to have a chat over old times, mutual acquaintances, you know...'

'Yes,' said Amy. 'So you did "cross the landing to his room"?'

'I did.' Ianthe sounded defensive now.

'Any idea what time that might have been?'

'Not really. One in the morning perhaps...?'

'And how long did you stay with him?'

'No time at all.'

'What do you mean?'

'I knocked on his door. There was no reply, so I thought he was probably asleep. I pushed the door open, but...' Ianthe raised her hand to her forehead as if to wipe away a persistent headache.

'But what?'

'Ben wasn't there. His bed hadn't been slept in.'

Amy found him in the Mess, ensconced in a corner. He had claimed one of the bottles of Shiraz from the wake and was working his way down it.

'Ben,' she said, 'we need to talk.'

CHAPTER TWENTY

When she had finished talking to Ben, Amy went back to her cottage and sent emails to Ianthe Berkeley, Bob Christie, Victoria Whitechurch, Meriel Dane and DI Cole. Since she didn't have an email address for them, she phoned Greta Knox and Alice Kennedy. She also rang Rosalie Jepson, asking her to pass a message on to Gregory. She would have liked to contact Willie Sayers, but she had neither phone number nor email address for him.

The contents of the message were the same for all of them. They were invited to a meeting in the Bridge at ten the following morning, 'to talk about recent events at the Admiral Byng'.

'Blues and twos,' Detective Inspector Cole told his assistant.

'Too bad,' Chesterton responded, trying to sound sympathetic, thinking he was about to hear about Cole's latest bout of depression. They'd been driving for some time towards Crabwell without a civil word being spoken. The boss had been fiddling with his iPhone as if it were a string of worry beads. Maybe he wanted to stop at a chemist's for some medication.

'I said blues and twos. Don't you watch TV, college boy? Switch on the bloody *alarm*!'

'Sorry.' Chesterton may have heard the phrase at Police College, but it had gone over his head. He activated the flashing lights and ear-splitting siren, and shouted, 'What's the emergency?'

'Only this,' Cole tried to make himself heard. 'A text from the assistant commissioner herself. She's called in the Yard.'

'Shakespeare?' Chesterton yelled, wide-eyed with wonder.

'The Yard, not the Bard. Scotland bloody Yard. She thinks two corpses in Crabwell is more than you and I can handle. They're sending Allingham.'

'Who's he?'

'Give me strength. Detective Superintendent Allingham, their top man, known as the Casecracker. He's a legend in London.'

'Bit insulting, isn't it?' Chesterton shouted back, mainly to rile Cole. 'I thought we'd got it sorted.'

'Can't hear you,' Cole replied. 'Turn the bloody thing off and put your foot down.'

Chesterton was glad to oblige. Little else was on the roads to make way for them. 'I was saying it's unnecessary, sending some super sleuth from London when we've cracked the case already.'

'It's all about reputations,' Cole said. 'He'll march in and reach the same conclusion we have, and take credit for another Scotland Yard success.'

'The suicide of the Admiral and the murder of the solicitor?'

'Two mysteries solved. So it's up to us to get there first and put the case to bed before Allingham shows up.'

'How?'

'By calming everybody down. A word to that interfering coroner will help. He's still doubtful about the Admiral's suicide. Then we collar the killer of Griffiths Bentley and make sure the media know about it before Allingham gets here.'

'Have we worked out who did it?'

'You should know. You questioned all the suspects at the wake.'

'But we don't even know *how* he was murdered, do we?'

'That's a side issue. Doesn't matter at all. The post-mortem this afternoon will answer that. Bullet through the heart, bump on the head, knife in the belly, or strangling. It'll be obvious when he's stretched out on the slab. Who's your murderer?'

Chesterton swallowed hard. 'I'm not sure, sir.'

Cole was silent for some time, deeply disappointed in his young colleague. He'd banked on him coming up with a name. 'I don't think you're cut out for CID.'

'Who is it, then?'

Cole hadn't a clue, but he had more face than the Sphinx, so he hinted at superior knowledge. 'Elementary, my dear

Chesterton. If you can't work it out, I'm not going to tell you.'

'Are we about to make the arrest?'

'Yes, but in a professional fashion. Do you know the words of the official caution?'

'We had to learn it by heart at Police College.'

'Good. You'll need it. We'll do this on our own terms, at a moment of our choosing.'

'When's that?'

'The sooner the better,' Cole said. 'However…'

'Is there a problem?'

'I just found an email sent last night by the bossy broad who runs the pub.'

'Amy Walpole.'

'Her, yes. She's had the gall to invite most of the village – well, all the regulars plus you and me, would you believe? – to "talk about recent events at the Admiral Byng". I could tell she was trouble the minute I set eyes on her. And I wouldn't mind betting the TV man, Ben Milne, is in league with her.'

'What are they up to?'

'Muddying the waters. This is a police investigation, not the last chapter of some old-fashioned detective novel. Their suggestion might make good television, but it's not the real world.'

'Are we going to join them?'

Cole was incensed. 'Are you completely off your trolley?'

'I thought if all the suspects are there, we might hear something we can latch onto. Maybe I could put in an appearance, somewhere at the back of the room, and record it all.'

'You'll do no such thing. You could compromise my whole investigation. You and I are going to the grave to look for the shoeprints of Bentley's killer. The final piece of the jigsaw.'

Amy was surprised to see that Willie Sayers was present at the meeting in the Bridge at ten the following morning. Clearly he had heard something along the Crabwell bush telegraph. Not for the first time she wondered about connections between the various people involved in the case – the people whom she now silently thought of as 'suspects'. Some of those connections she had found out about, but she felt there was a whole substructure of other former relationships and previous encounters of which she knew nothing.

There seemed to be no question that she, as the convener of the meeting, should be the one in charge of proceedings. There weren't enough chairs in the Bridge, so Ted, the odd-job man, was despatched to bring more up from the bar. While he was doing this, there was an uneasy silence. Amy looked around the room.

The only suspect who looked at ease was Ianthe Berkeley, and her insouciance had probably been engendered by the bottle of vodka she had bought (not from Room Service but at the bar) the previous evening.

Willie Sayers, still immaculate in pinstripe, looked distinctly edgy. So did Bob Christie, his impression of the hard-bitten

Fleet Street veteran now distinctly unconvincing. The outward confidence of Meriel Dane, dressed up to the voluptuous nines, was betrayed by her eyes darting nervously around the room. The Rev Victoria Whitechurch's eyes were closed as if she were praying, which perhaps she was. The tension felt by Greta Knox and Alice Kennedy showed in the fact that they were holding hands, a sight not previously seen in public in Crabwell. Greg Jepson's face was visibly twitching, making him look further along the Asperger's scale than usual.

And Ben Milne, sitting a little apart from the others, was distinctly subdued. During their conversation, which had continued long into the previous evening, Amy had at one point asked if he wanted to bring Stan the cameraman along to record proceedings in the Bridge. The fact that a muckraker as avid as Ben had said no spoke volumes.

Finally, everyone had a seat. Ted had left the room and closed the door behind him.

Amy had read enough detective stories to avoid beginning with the words 'You may be wondering why I've brought you here.' Instead, she said, 'We're here to talk about Fitz's death.' Nobody expressed any surprise at that. 'And also the death of Griffiths Bentley, which I am sure is not unconnected.' Again, no surprise. Or argument.

'The reason for the two murders...' No one reacted to her use of the word '... is a secret in Fitz's past, a secret he was unaware of until the Monday before last... which, as it turned out, was his last day on earth. The secret was that he had an illegitimate son.'

Everyone in the room looked towards the son in question. Clearly the Crabwell bush telegraph had been doing its stuff.

'And it was that son, Greg Jepson, who told Fitz the glad news when he came to see him in this room that Monday afternoon. Greg also told him that he'd made over a large amount of money to his new-found birth father, more than enough money to modernise, refurbish, and save the Admiral Byng. So it's no wonder that Fitz was in generous mood as he celebrated his "Last Hurrah" that evening.

'Then of course comes the question of who was Greg's birth mother...'

There was a tense silence. Expressions of puzzlement demonstrated that this piece of information had not made it on to the bush telegraph. Greg Jepson studiously avoided looking at Greta Knox. Alice Kennedy held her hand more tightly.

'That,' Amy continued, 'was the secret for the protection of which someone wanted Fitz dead.' She looked around the room. Still a lot of puzzlement, feigned or real.

To her surprise, Amy found that she was enjoying being centre stage. She liked being able to unroll the narrative at her own pace.

'So we have to ask ourselves,' she resumed, 'who was in a position to find out about Fitz's secret? Yesterday I went to see Rosalie Jepson, Greg's adoptive mother. She heard about her son's birth father from Griffiths Bentley.'

There was a sharp intake of breath from Bob Christie,

who made eye contact with Willie Sayers. The MP turned abruptly away.

'Some of you may know that Griffiths Bentley was a great hoarder of secrets. In the course of his work as a solicitor he became the repository of many details about which his clients might have preferred to keep quiet. And he was not above asking for money to ensure his confidentiality about keeping those secrets.'

'Blackmail?' asked Meriel Dane, looking rather shaky.

Still remembering her reading of crime fiction, Amy restrained herself from the classic response: 'It's such an ugly word – blackmail.' Instead, she said, 'I wonder, though, whether Griffiths Bentley actually found out the details about Fitz's son for himself, or whether he got the information from someone else. Whether he even paid that person for the information.' She turned to face Bob Christie. 'You did quite a lot of research on Fitz, didn't you, for a profile you were thinking of doing on him?'

The editor's face empurpled as he blustered, 'Yes, but he didn't pay me money for what I told him.'

'But you admit you did tell Griffiths about the illegitimate child?'

'I did. I had come across the truth in my research. But, as I say, no money changed hands.'

'So what did change hands?' Amy felt her intuition had never been so finely honed. 'Was the deal an exchange of information?'

Bob Christie's blush now threatened apoplexy. 'Yes, all right, it was.'

'So what did you reveal to Griffiths Bentley?'

Bob Christie looked around the Bridge for support. None of the faces offered any, so he said in a subdued tone, 'I told him that Meriel Dane's real name was Merle Johannsson, and that she had been all over the papers when she very nearly murdered her husband.'

The only colour left in the cook's face came from her make-up. She looked pleadingly around the room, but, like Bob Christie, did not see anyone about to come to her rescue. The expressions of surprise, though, told her that until that moment no one present had known about her lurid past. Unusually, she remained silent. She was hyperventilating so much that she couldn't speak.

Amy didn't look at her. She focussed again on Bob Christie. 'What you didn't know, though, was that Griffiths Bentley hadn't found that information from his own research. He was told about it by someone else.'

'Was he?'

'Oh yes. By someone whose business was trading dirty secrets.' She turned to face the MP. 'Someone who had investigated your past, Mr Sayers, and found out about the unexplained drowning in Regent's Canal of a girl called Jilly.'

Willie Sayers looked suddenly hollow in his pinstriped shell.

'Someone,' Amy continued implacably, 'whose profession is finding *Skeletons in Cupboards*!'

They all turned their gazes on Ben Milne, whose customary laid-back calm deserted him as he said, 'All right, I'm not denying anything Amy has accused me of. Yes, I

316

do trade in dirty secrets. There's an insatiable popular appetite for them. Someone's got to feed that hunger, and that's what I do. I'm bloody good at it too. I don't feel any shame about my profession. If I wasn't doing it, someone else would be. I don't feel the need to have my actions inhibited by some outdated moral code.'

The response to this came from a new voice. Greta Knox hadn't spoken in the meeting before. She asked coolly, 'Would you describe committing murder as an offence against some outdated moral code?'

'No, I wouldn't. Nor,' Ben replied, 'have I ever been near to murdering anyone... unlike someone else in this room. Someone who has committed murder twice.'

This allegation did produce a confused reaction in the Bridge, as all of the suspects started to put forward their defences, the reasons why they could not have had anything to do with the killings of Fitz and Griffiths Bentley. All of the suspects, that is, except for one.

Ben Milne looked across at Amy and gave a curt nod. That was the signal they had agreed between themselves during their long discussions the night before.

Amy Walpole drew a deep breath and then began.

'In spite of the coroner's hastily-reached verdict, I don't think there is anyone in this room who believes that Fitz committed suicide. We all know that he was murdered, though probably only three of us know who killed him.

'I wouldn't know either, but for the fact that there was a witness to the murder.'

This revelation produced a series of assorted gasps.

'There was a kind of fatal logical sequence in what happened. When Greg Jepson found out who his birth father was, he arranged to meet Fitz and tell him. Fitz then said something during his "Last Hurrah" that made the murderer think he was about to spread the news around. So he had to be silenced. When Griffiths Bentley offered the same threat, he was fated to meet the same end.

'The second murder had, so far as we know, no witnesses. But the first did. Through a telescope, the murderer was seen drowning Fitz in his own dinghy.

'There was also, found in the bottom of the boat, a gold-coloured button that had been torn off during the struggle. It hadn't come off the Admiral's blazer.

'Do I need to say more?'

'No, you don't.' Releasing her partner's hand as she spoke, Alice Kennedy stood up.

They sat side by side on Ben's bed as he typed up the dossier on his laptop, but there was no warmth between them. The task was not a difficult one. Even without the confession, witness statements from Rosalie Jepson and the Crabwell Surgery, where Amy had found Alice had not turned up for the Mother and Baby Clinic the previous afternoon, would have provided enough evidence for a prosecution.

When they had both agreed the text, Ben emailed it off to DI Cole. And Amy was so excited that she wondered whether she'd be able to resist texting the officer the name of the person who'd confessed to the two murders.

* * *

'So many bloody footprints,' DC Chesterton said, close to despair.

'Shoeprints, you berk,' Cole said. 'Anyone would think Man Friday had been here, the way you talk.'

For over an hour, the two policemen had been in the churchyard at Crabwell beside the open grave where Griffiths Bentley's corpse had been found. They had several large drums of plaster, buckets of water, and spades, and were diligently making casts of all the impressions they could find. Already they had ruined their clothes, and might have stepped out of a slapstick film. Chesterton had asked if this wasn't really a job for the scene-of-crime team, but Cole insisted the work had to be done before Allingham of the Yard got there.

'This will be the clincher,' Cole said. 'You may not appreciate it right now, but a shoe impression is as good as a fingerprint in modern forensic science. It's not so much the pattern of the tread as the wear pattern, the thousands of little nicks and scratches that show up under the microscope. Do you understand what this means?'

'We can match the killer's prints to the shoes worn by one of the suspects,' Chesterton said in a bored voice. 'But there are so many, including yours and mine and the grave-digger's and the vicar's and the people who lifted the body out, not to mention the world and his wife who came to have a gawp.'

'We can eliminate all those.'

'But it's going to take an age.' He gave the inspector a penetrating look. 'If you really know who the murderer is, as you say you do, wouldn't we be better employed in the interview room?'

Cole wiped some plaster away from his face. 'No, this is the answer. Statements under questioning are no substitute for the proof a shoeprint provides. It's visual, too. It will look good in the papers and on television news.'

'Are you willing to state what sort of shoes your suspect was wearing?' Chesterton asked. 'Trainers, wellies, or even high heels?' His superior had stubbornly declined to reveal who the killer was. Maybe he would reveal the gender. Chesterton doubted this. He secretly suspected Cole had been bluffing all along, and that this farce in the graveyard was desperation.

'I'll check my phone again,' Cole said. He had a man posted at the station to notify him when Allingham of the Yard stepped off the London train. After some scrolling, he said, 'It's not good news. He's at Ipswich already, and a driver was sent to meet him. Jesus, Joseph and Mary, what can we do?'

Chesterton treated this as a rhetorical question.

'How many casts have we made?' Cole asked, starting to panic.

Chesterton leaned on his spade and looked at the tarpaulin where their products were arrayed like a catch of white fish.

'Over fifty, but most of them haven't dried yet.'

'Call the station, see if they can stall him, take him out for a meal or something.'

'Wouldn't it be better coming from you, sir?'

But Cole seemed to be hyperventilating. He handed his mobile to Chesterton, and it pinged.

'There's a text just in from Amy Walpole. Do you want me to read it?'

Cole had his arms around the legs of a stone angel and was gazing upwards as if he needed a miracle. He managed to give a nod.

Chesterton read the message rapidly. 'Well, here's a turn-up. She says they had their meeting and Alice Kennedy has confessed to murdering Fitzsimmons and Bentley.'

'Confessed?' Cole asked, starting to get control of himself again.

'That's what she says.'

'Alice who?'

'Kennedy. Isn't she the partner of the Girl Guide leader, Greta Knox?'

'You're right.' He straightened up and draped a companionable arm over the angel's wing. 'I knew all along. Her shoeprint will be here somewhere.'

'She murdered the Admiral as well?' Chesterton queried.

'Oh, yes,' Cole said, 'and we must go to Knox's cottage right now and make the arrest.'

'In this state?' Chesterton said. 'Have you seen yourself, sir?'

'Doesn't matter, man. No time to lose. This will go down as my biggest triumph. Bloody Allingham can skulk back to Scotland Yard and tell them Suffolk Police had it under control all along. Sod Allingham of the Yard. Let the world know Cole of Crabwell solved this one. With some help,' he added, looking up at the angel and crossing himself.

'But we thought the Admiral committed suicide, fell into his boat and died after a lethal cocktail of drink and drugs.'

'Not so,' Cole said, back to his assertive best. 'I never believed that. There was definite evidence of a struggle.' He dipped his plaster-white hand into a pocket and took out the evidence bag containing the blazer button Chesterton had found in the Admiral's boat. 'The vital clue. I didn't want everyone panicking over a murder, so I played a canny hand and put it about that Fitz committed suicide. It was always obvious there had been a struggle and this little item was ripped off the old man's blazer.'

'But you said it caught on something as he fell.'

'So unlikely I scarcely dared suggest it, but you swallowed it, and so did the rest of them. One of the rowlocks.'

'Rollocks,' said Chesterton.

They hurried off to make the arrest.

Greta Knox unlocked the front door and led the way into the living room. As it always did, the painting above the fireplace caught her eye. The spare Pyrenean landscape had only one human touch: an abandoned jacket lying beside a wine flask; it was as though something had happened to call away their owner just before the artist came along. The air of mystery had captivated her when she first saw the picture. Now, though, there was no time for contemplating art. She turned to her partner.

'Dearest Alice, we shan't have long before the wretched

police arrive. Should we try and do a moonlight flit in the middle of the day?' She'd tried to speak lightly, but her voice failed as she saw Alice was trembling. She put her arms around the person who meant the most to her in the whole world and held her close. 'It's all right,' she murmured. 'Everything will be all right.' Inside, though, she wondered whether anything would be all right ever again.

After a moment Alice drew back. 'Perhaps a glass of brandy?' She sat down in her usual chair.

'Of course.' Greta hurried to the drinks table and poured them each a substantial glass of Courvoisier. 'I'm sure you can't really have murdered Fitz, or that wretched solicitor. Why did you say you had? Did you think I was going to be accused?' She gave Alice her brandy and watched while a generous quantity disappeared, and colour came back into the GP's face. Then she went to her chair and sat, trying to grasp a sense of normality. There had been an air of unreality about the whole session in the pub after the funeral; surely it belonged in an Agatha Christie novel?

Alice took a deep breath. Her trembling had stopped and she looked very, very tired. An attempt at smiling failed miserably. 'Darling Greta, there's nothing you can do. I have confessed. It wasn't that I was afraid you would be accused, I knew you hadn't killed either Fitz or Griffiths Bentley because I murdered both.'

Greta felt shock run through her with the force of electricity. It seemed that something, some deep belief that this couldn't be happening, had insulated her until now from the facts. She flung herself at Alice's feet. 'Why?' she cried. 'Why?'

Alice sighed and reached for her hands. 'I couldn't let your life be ruined by that dreadful man.'

'Fitz? But he wasn't dreadful.' This was a nightmare and it was getting worse.

'He'd told Gregory Jepson that you were his mother.'

'But Gregory wasn't going to tell anyone else, nor was Fitz.'

'Wasn't he? He'd been banging the drum in the bar that evening. You were involved with your Guides and didn't hear him, but he announced again and again that it was his "Last Hurrah". And that slimy TV presenter, Ben Milne, was trying to get him to confess sordid details of his life for his wretched programme. The more I thought about it, the more I was afraid for your secret. So I set off back to the pub along the beach and found him by his dinghy. He was het up, a couple of local lads had borrowed the boat and left it a long way from its usual mooring. Safe enough, the anchor was well sunk in the shingle, but he was always a fusspot about the wretched craft; it had to be in its particular place. I tried to get him to promise he wouldn't tell Milne about you and him, but he became almost incoherent. Of course he'd had far too much to drink and he kept on telling me it was all good news and he'd tell everyone the next day. It sounded as though he was going to announce he was Jepson's father and you were his mother. I could just see the TV programme relating all the facts of Fitz's scandalous life. I got all wound up and went at him in a fury.'

'What scandals?'

'There've always been rumours about him: drug smuggling, illegal opening hours, and someone the other day was suggesting he could be bringing in illegal immigrants in that boat of his.'

'Oh, for heaven's sake, Alice. None of that is true.' Greta felt a terrible chill take hold of her.

'But what is true is that he fathered an illegitimate child whose mother now is a pillar of the community, a brilliant maths teacher who runs a Girl Guide troop. If that was broadcast on national television, you – and I – wouldn't have a hope. The parents would have demanded your resignation, and so would the Guide Association. The scandal would have crucified us.'

Greta dropped her head onto Alice's knees. A huge sob wracked her frame.

'I don't think I meant to kill him, but I certainly felt I could. Our precious, precious life together, in the dust, all the fault of this ridiculous man. So I pushed him as hard as I could, screaming out that he mustn't do this. We were standing in the stupid boat; it rocked, he staggered back and fell. And that was that.' Another long sigh from Alice. Greta tried to take in the enormity of what she was saying.

'I looked at him lying there. Could I make it look like suicide? Maybe if I supplied a farewell letter, the police would think he'd intended to take the boat out and throw himself off it, and that was the "Last Hurrah", but that he had had an accident before he could launch the boat.'

Greta looked up. 'So you actually wrote a note?'

'I thought it had to be tied to the pub, so I went there. Nobody was about. I found the computer, printed out a brief note, found an envelope, and then got back to the dinghy without anyone seeing me. At least, I thought I had. That dreadful man Bentley, however, apparently was walking his dog late at night and saw me returning to the boat. He rang me the day before the funeral and offered to keep quiet if I paid him some ridiculous sum, far more than I could raise and, anyway, you can't trust blackmailers to keep their word.'

'So what did you do to him?' Greta said numbly.

'He was one of my patients, of course, and already on digitalis for his heart. I told him I'd bring the money to the funeral and give it to him by the grave before the service. Instead, I had prepared a syringe and gave him a massive overdose. He never knew a thing. One grave, two bodies: very suitable, I thought.' Alice's voice was hard and emotionless.

'And you did all that for me?' Greta was awed.

Her partner's expression softened; she put her hands on either side of Greta's head and looked deep into her eyes. 'There's nothing I would not do for you, dearest.'

Greta gazed back at her, her heart so full she could hardly speak. 'We haven't got much time,' she said breathlessly. 'I'm sure the police will be here any minute. Alice, darling, will you marry me? I believe one can have the ceremony performed in prison these days.'

Somehow they were then both on their feet and in each

other's arms. 'I will wait for you, my darling, however long it takes,' Greta said passionately.

The doorbell rang.

It was lunchtime at the Admiral Byng. Amy, in her customary position behind the bar, could hardly believe it was still the same day. Thursday, less than twenty-four hours after the beginning of Fitz's funeral. So much seemed to have happened since then.

But she felt good. Taking control in the Bridge that morning had restored her confidence to a level that she hadn't felt since long before she had left London for Crabwell. Since before she had started her affair with the married man. Since she'd made that stupid suicide attempt. Now she felt confident to live life on her own terms. And if that life did involve a male partner... or if it didn't... Amy Walpole knew she'd be able to cope either way.

Anyway, the only partner she was thinking about that morning was a business partner. Greg Jepson had been so firm in his decision that he was going to buy the Admiral Byng and refurbish it. And so determined that Amy was going to manage the place for him. Her mind was already full of plans for the future.

The lunchtime trade in the pub was fairly brisk. News of Griffiths Bentley's death had spread around the village, and the curious of Crabwell thought they might find out more about it in the Admiral Byng. But the crowd wasn't as big as it would have been if a television camera had been there.

Most of the people who'd been in the Bridge that morning had melted away. Greg Jepson had been told by Greta not to make contact until she rang him. After making his business proposal to Amy, he had gone to his mother's to give Rosalie support during the inevitable police interviews that were to come.

Meriel Dane, who had found from the reactions at the meeting that the revelation of her lurid past had only added to her allure as a femme fatale, was cheerily cooking away in her kitchen. She comforted herself further with the thought of ringing to see whether Jed Rhode was back from his fishing trip. And since she didn't yet know that Amy was going to be her new boss, there wasn't even the smallest cloud on her hedonistic horizon.

The Rev Victoria Whitechurch had gone back to the vicarage to ring that helpful young man about the phone mast.

Willie Sayers had caught the first train back to London and the House of Commons.

Ianthe Berkeley, though still marinated in the previous night's vodka, had started off in her battered VW to face the complications of husband and boss.

And Bob Christie had returned to the unreproachful bottle of gin in his office.

'Hi.'

At the sound of the voice, Amy looked up from pouring a pint of Guinness to see Ben Milne. He wore an expensive waterproof, and had his bag slung over his shoulder. 'I'm off,' he said. 'Ordered a cab.'

'Would you like a drink? On the house.'

'No, I don't think so, thanks.'

Amy passed the Guinness over and took the customer's money. There was an awkward silence. 'I suppose we're both likely to be contacted by the police.'

'Probably,' he agreed.

Another silence was broken by the sound of a car approaching. Ben looked through the glass of the pub's front door. 'My cab.'

'Yes.' Amy reached her hand across the bar and they shook formally.

'Probably won't meet again,' said Ben.

'Probably not.'

'Cheerio then.'

'Cheerio.'

Amy was pleased to be distracted by another order as Ben Milne left the Admiral Byng. When she looked back, his cab had gone.

Just as well, she thought. He always had been a bit of a prick. Attractive, yes, but still a prick.

ABOUT THE CONTRIBUTORS

Simon Brett is the author of over ninety-five books, including the Charles Paris, Mrs Pargeter, Fethering, and Blotto and Twinks series of crime novels. He wrote a best-selling book about a baby's first year called *How To Be A Little Sod*. His writing for radio and television includes *After Henry, No Commitments* and *Smelling of Roses*. He has been Chair of the Crime Writers' Association and The Society of Authors, and was President of the Detection Club from 2001 to 2015. In 2014 he was awarded the CWA Diamond Dagger 'for Excellence', and in the 2016 New Year's Honours he was made an O.B.E. 'for services to literature'. You can find him online at: www.simonbrett.com.

Kate Charles, a past Chairman of the Crime Writers' Association and the Barbara Pym Society, is American by birth but has lived in England for thirty years. A former parish administrator, she sets her books against the colourful backdrop of the Church of England. She has been co-organiser of the annual St Hilda's Crime and Mystery Conference in Oxford since its beginnings in 1994 and was awarded the George N. Dove Award for her 'outstanding contribution to the serious study of mystery and crime fiction'. Kate has a vast collection of 'clerical mysteries', and lectures on that subject. Kate's latest book, *False Tongues*, is the fourth in a series featuring newly ordained curate Callie Anson. Her first series, the Book of Psalms mysteries, remains popular and has recently been republished. She lives on the English side of the Welsh borders with her husband and their Border Terrier.

Natasha Cooper was a historical novelist before she turned to crime. She has written three crime series: the first featuring part-time civil servant Willow King, who moonlights as a romantic novelist; a second led by barrister Trish Maguire; and most recently the Isle of Wight sequence about forensic psychologist Dr Karen Taylor. The latest of those, *Vengeance in Mind*, was shortlisted for the 2012 Gold Dagger. Natasha's particular interests lie in the psychology of offenders, the plasticity of the brain, and the way emotion can change its physical structures. When not writing novels and short stories, she reviews other people's work for, among others, the *TLS* and the *Catholic Herald*. She also writes a monthly crime column for www.bookoxygen.com.

Stella Duffy has written thirteen novels, over fifty short stories, and ten plays. She has twice won Stonewall Writer of the Year and twice won the CWA Short Story Dagger.

HBO have optioned her Theodora novels for a TV mini-series. Her story collection, *Everything is Moving, Everything is Joined*, and her Doctor Who novella, *Anti-Hero,* were published in 2014. Stella is also a theatre-maker, Associate Artist with Improbable, Artistic Director of Shaky Isles Theatre, and founder of The Chaosbaby Project. She is the Co-Director of Fun Palaces, the campaign for greater engagement for all – in ALL culture.

Martin Edwards is the author of eighteen novels, including the Lake District Mysteries, the most recent of which is *The Dungeon House*. His other publications include *The Golden Age of Murder*, a study of detective fiction between the world wars with a focus on the early years of the Detection Club. He has edited twenty-six anthologies of crime fiction and fact, has won the CWA Short Story Dagger and the CWA Margery Allingham Prize, and is series consultant for the British Library's Crime Classics. He is archivist of the Crime Writers' Association and the Detection Club, and succeeded Simon Brett as President of the Detection Club in November 2015.

Ruth Dudley Edwards is a historian and journalist. The targets of her satirical crime novels include the civil service, Cambridge University, gentlemen's clubs, the House of Lords, the Church of England, and literary prizes. She won the 2010 CWA Gold Dagger for non-fiction for *Aftermath: The Omagh Bombings and the Families' Pursuit of Justice*, the 2008 CrimeFest Last Laugh Award for

Murdering Americans, which was set in an Indiana university, and the 2013 Goldsboro Last Laugh Award for her twelfth novel, *Killing the Emperors*, a black comedy about the preposterous world of conceptual art. You can find her online at: www.ruthdudleyedwards.com.

Tim Heald was educated at Sherborne School and Balliol College, Oxford. He started his professional life as a journalist and has continued to write extensively for the *Sunday Times*, *The Times*, *The Daily Telegraph*, *The Daily Express*, *The Spectator* and many other publications. He has travelled all over the world on journalistic assignments (including playing elephant polo in Nepal with Ringo Starr and Billy Connolly). Tim has written biographies of Prince Philip and Princess Margaret and, demonstrating his strong interest in cricket, of Denis Compton and Brian Johnston. His crime writing has included a series about the Board of Trade investigator Simon Bognor (televised starring David Horovitch) and another featuring the academic Reader in Criminal Studies Dr Tudor Cornwall.

Michael Jecks is best known for his popular Knights Templar medieval crime series, but he also writes modern spy novels (*Act of Vengeance*), short story collections, a series set during the reign of Bloody Mary, and the acclaimed Vintener trilogy about archers in the Hundred Years War. He is working on a new series set during the Crusades. The founder of Medieval Murderers, Michael has been Chairman of the Crime Writers' Association (2004/5) and is a keen supporter of new writing. He organised the CWA's Debut Dagger competition for two years, and works with the Royal Literary Fund to help students, charities and businesses with writing skills. He is a popular guest speaker all over the world, but his greatest claim to fame is that he was once Grand Marshal of the first parade at the New Orleans Mardi Gras. Michael lives in Devon and plots murder at all times.

Janet Laurence is the author of three series of crime novels: a contemporary one of ten novels featuring the cook, Darina Lisle; and one around the Italian painter, Canaletto, set in the mid-eighteenth century during his time in London. Her latest series is set at the start of the twentieth century and features Ursula Grandison, an American girl in her late twenties experiencing England and murder, aided by an English detective, Thomas Jackman. An ex-Chairman of the UK Crime Writers' Association, and member of the Detection Club, Janet lives in Somerset, and has recently been elected to the Management Committee of the Society of Authors. She is also the author of *Writing Crime Fiction*: *Making Crime Pay*, and several cookery books. Under the pen name of Julia Lisle she has published women's contemporary fiction.

Peter Lovesey was once told that with a name like his he should be writing romantic fiction. Instead he took up crime writing and found himself in the company of authors with names like Slaughter and Gash. Slightly hard of hearing, in 1974 he joined what he thought was a friendship group known as the Affection Club and found himself being asked to place his hand on a human skull and promise to observe a seemly moderation in the use of gangs, conspiracies, death rays, ghosts, hypnotism, trapdoors, Chinamen, super-criminals and mysterious poisons unknown to science. He has been trying to leave ever since, but is too polite to mention it. Amongst many awards, Peter has received the CWA Diamond Dagger. He would like it to be known that his contributions to *The Sinking Admiral* are the few bits you could safely read to the vicar.

Michael Ridpath, before becoming a writer, used to work as a bond trader in the City of London. He has written eight financial thrillers, a couple of spy novels, and the Fire and Ice series, featuring the Icelandic detective Magnus Jonson.

David Roberts was a publisher for thirty years before turning to crime. He is the author of a ten-book series published by Constable & Robinson set in the 1930s featuring Lord Edward Corinth and Verity Browne. Peter James described *Sweet Sorrow*, the final book in the series, as 'A gripping, richly satisfying whodunit, with finely observed characters, sparkling with insouciance and stinging menace'.

L.C. Tyler was born in Essex and was educated there and at Oxford University and City University Business School.

His comic crime series featuring author-and-agent duo Ethelred Tressider and Elsie Thirkettle has been twice nominated for Edgar Allan Poe awards in the US and he won the Goldsboro Last Laugh Award (best comic crime novel of the year) with *Herring in the Library* and *Crooked Herring*. His new historical crime series (the latest of which is *A Masterpiece of Corruption*) features seventeenth-century lawyer, John Grey. He has lived and worked all over the world but more recently has been based in London and West Sussex. He can be found online at: www.lctyler.com.

Laura Wilson's acclaimed and award-winning crime novels have won her many fans. Her novel *Stratton's War* won the Ellis Peters Award, while *The Lover* and *A Thousand Lies* were both shortlisted for the CWA Gold Dagger. Laura is the *Guardian's* crime fiction reviewer. She lives in London.